CRITICAL ACCLAIM FOR

THE FAULT IN OUR STARS

"Green writes with empathy about some of the biggest questions there are—Why me? Why now? Why bother with love?—producing a story about two incandescent kids who will live a long time in the minds of the readers who come to know them." —*People*

"Funny . . . Poignant . . . Luminous." —*Entertainment Weekly*

"The love between Hazel and Gus—the courage and humor with which they manage their grief for each other and for themselves—is as real and intense as any I've seen in recent fiction."

—*TIME* magazine

"Remarkable . . . A pitch-perfect, elegiac comedy." —*USA Today*

"Because we all need to feel first love again. . . . Sixteen-year-old Hazel faces terminal cancer with humor and pluck. But it isn't until she meets Augustus in a support group that she understands how to love or live fully."

—Oprah.com, a Best Book selection and one of the "5 Books Every Woman Needs to Read Before Her Next Birthday"

"[Green's] voice is so compulsively readable that it defies categorization. You will be thankful for the little infinity you spend inside this book." —NPR.org

"Hilarious and heartbreaking . . . reminds you that sometimes when life feels like it's ending, it's actually just beginning."

—*Parenting* magazine

"A smarter, edgier *Love Story* for the Net Generation."

—*Family Circle*

"John Green deftly mixes the profound and the quotidian in this tough, touching valentine to the human spirit."

—*The Washington Post*

"You know, even as you begin the tale of their young romance, that the end will be 100 kinds of awful, not so much a vale as a brutal canyon of tears. . . . Green's story of lovers who aren't so much star-crossed as star-cursed leans on literature's most durable assets: finely wrought language, beautifully drawn characters and a distinctive voice."

—Frank Bruni, ***The New York Times***

"A novel of life and death and the people caught in between, *The Fault in Our Stars* is John Green at his best. You laugh, you cry, and then you come back for more."

—Markus Zusak, **bestselling and Printz Honor–winning author of *The Book Thief***

"*The Fault in Our Stars* takes a spin on universal themes—Will I be loved? Will I be remembered? Will I leave a mark on this world?—by dramatically raising the stakes for the characters who are asking."

—Jodi Picoult, **bestselling author of *My Sister's Keeper* and *Sing You Home***

"John Green is one of the best writers alive."

—E. Lockhart, **National Book Award Finalist and Printz Honor–winning author of *The Disreputable History of Frankie Landau-Banks* and *We Were Liars***

"Perfect in every way." —***The Sacramento Bee***

"*The Fault in Our Stars* is [not] just another good book. It's an important book." —***The Kansas City Star***

"A tour de force." —***Montreal Gazette***

"I wish this book had lasted forever." —***Vancouver Sun***

"A bittersweet story of life, death, and love in between."
—***Deseret News***

"Green proves through his characters that lasting love requires the risk of losing it. This is not a morbid book. Hazel and Gus invite us to laugh and live life to the fullest for as long as we can."
—***Shelf Awareness***

"Hilarious, joyous, outrageous, and utterly sad."
—***Scripps Howard News Service***

★ "In its every aspect, this novel is a triumph."—***Booklist,*** **starred review**

★ "Acerbic comedy, sexy romance, and a lightly played, extended meditation on the big questions about life and death."
—***The Horn Book,*** **starred review**

★ "An achingly beautiful story about life and loss." —***SLJ,*** **starred review**

★ "A smartly crafted intellectual explosion of a romance . . . Readers will swoon on nearly every page. [Green's] carefully structured dialogue and razor-sharp characters brim with genuine intellect, humor and desire." —***Kirkus Reviews,*** **starred review**

★ "Smart, witty, profoundly sad, and full of questions worth asking."
—***Publishers Weekly,*** **starred review**

ALSO BY JOHN GREEN

Looking for Alaska

An Abundance of Katherines

Paper Towns

Turtles All the Way Down

Will Grayson, Will Grayson
WITH DAVID LEVITHAN

THE FAULT IN OUR STARS

THE FAULT IN OUR STARS

JOHN GREEN

PENGUIN BOOKS

PENGUIN BOOKS
An imprint of Penguin Random House LLC
375 Hudson Street
New York, New York 10014
penguin.com

First published in the United States of America by Dutton Books,
a member of Penguin Group (USA) Inc., 2012
Published by Penguin Books, an imprint of Penguin Group (USA) LLC, 2014

THE LIBRARY OF CONGRESS HAS CATALOGED THE DUTTON BOOKS EDITION AS FOLLOWS:
Green, John, date.
The fault in our stars / John Green.—1st ed.
p. cm.
Summary: Sixteen-year-old Hazel, a stage IV thyroid cancer patient, has accepted her terminal diagnosis until a chance meeting with a boy at cancer support group forces her to reexamine her perspective on love, loss, and life.
ISBN 978-0-525-47881-2 (hardcover)
[1. Cancer—Fiction. 2. Terminally ill—Fiction. 3. Love—Fiction.] I. Title.
PZ7.G8233Fau 2012
[Fic]—dc23 2011045783

This edition ISBN 9780142424179

Printed in the United States of America

27th Printing

TO ESTHER EARL

As the tide washed in, the Dutch Tulip Man faced the ocean: "Conjoiner rejoinder poisoner concealer revelator. Look at it, rising up and rising down, taking everything with it."

"What's that?" I asked.

"Water," the Dutchman said. "Well, and time."

—PETER VAN HOUTEN, *An Imperial Affliction*

AUTHOR'S NOTE

This is not so much an author's note as an author's reminder of what was printed in small type a few pages ago: This book is a work of fiction. I made it up.

Neither novels nor their readers benefit from attempts to divine whether any facts hide inside a story. Such efforts attack the very idea that made-up stories can matter, which is sort of the foundational assumption of our species.

I appreciate your cooperation in this matter.

THE FAULT IN OUR STARS

CHAPTER ONE

Late in the winter of my seventeenth year, my mother decided I was depressed, presumably because I rarely left the house, spent quite a lot of time in bed, read the same book over and over, ate infrequently, and devoted quite a bit of my abundant free time to thinking about death.

Whenever you read a cancer booklet or website or whatever, they always list depression among the side effects of cancer. But, in fact, depression is not a side effect of cancer. Depression is a side effect of dying. (Cancer is also a side effect of dying. Almost everything is, really.) But my mom believed I required treatment, so she took me to see my Regular Doctor Jim, who agreed that I was veritably swimming in a paralyzing and totally clinical depression, and that therefore my meds should be adjusted and also I should attend a weekly Support Group.

This Support Group featured a rotating cast of characters in various states of tumor-driven unwellness. Why did the cast rotate? A side effect of dying.

The Support Group, of course, was depressing as hell. It met every Wednesday in the basement of a stone-walled Episcopal church shaped like a cross. We all sat in a circle right in the middle of the cross, where the two boards would have met, where the heart of Jesus would have been.

I noticed this because Patrick, the Support Group Leader and only person over eighteen in the room, talked about the heart of Jesus every freaking meeting, all about how we, as young cancer survivors, were sitting right in Christ's very sacred heart and whatever.

So here's how it went in God's heart: The six or seven or ten of us walked/wheeled in, grazed at a decrepit selection of cookies and lemonade, sat down in the Circle of Trust, and listened to Patrick recount for the thousandth time his depressingly miserable life story—how he had cancer in his balls and they thought he was going to die but he didn't die and now here he is, a full-grown adult in a church basement in the 137th nicest city in America, divorced, addicted to video games, mostly friendless, eking out a meager living by exploiting his cancertastic past, slowly working his way toward a master's degree that will not improve his career prospects, waiting, as we all do, for the sword of Damocles to give him the relief that he escaped lo those many years ago when cancer took both of his nuts but spared what only the most generous soul would call his life.

AND YOU TOO MIGHT BE SO LUCKY!

Then we introduced ourselves: Name. Age. Diagnosis. And how we're doing today. I'm Hazel, I'd say when they'd get to me. Sixteen. Thyroid originally but with an impressive and long-settled satellite colony in my lungs. And I'm doing okay.

Once we got around the circle, Patrick always asked if anyone wanted to share. And then began the circle jerk of support: everyone talking about fighting and battling and winning and shrinking and scanning. To be fair to Patrick, he let us talk about dying, too. But most of them weren't dying. Most would live into adulthood, as Patrick had.

(Which meant there was quite a lot of competitiveness about it, with everybody wanting to beat not only cancer itself, but also the other people in the room. Like, I realize that this is irrational, but when they tell you that you have, say, a 20 percent chance of living five years, the math kicks in and you figure that's one in five . . . so you look around and think, as any healthy person would: I gotta outlast four of these bastards.)

The only redeeming facet of Support Group was this kid named Isaac, a long-faced, skinny guy with straight blond hair swept over one eye.

And his eyes were the problem. He had some fantastically improbable eye cancer. One eye had been cut out when he was a kid, and now he wore the kind of thick glasses that made his eyes (both the real one and the glass one) preternaturally huge, like his whole head was basically just this fake eye and this real eye staring at you. From what I could gather on the rare occasions when Isaac shared with the group, a recurrence had placed his remaining eye in mortal peril.

Isaac and I communicated almost exclusively through sighs. Each time someone discussed anticancer diets or snorting ground-up shark fin or whatever, he'd glance over at me and sigh ever so slightly. I'd shake my head microscopically and exhale in response.

So Support Group blew, and after a few weeks, I grew to be rather kicking-and-screaming about the whole affair. In fact, on the Wednesday I made the acquaintance of Augustus Waters, I tried my level best to get out of Support Group while sitting on the couch with my mom in the third leg of a twelve-hour marathon of the previous season's *America's Next Top Model*, which admittedly I had already seen, but still.

Me: "I refuse to attend Support Group."

Mom: "One of the symptoms of depression is disinterest in activities."

Me: "Please just let me watch *America's Next Top Model.* It's an activity."

Mom: "Television is a passivity."

Me: "Ugh, Mom, please."

Mom: "Hazel, you're a teenager. You're not a little kid anymore. You need to make friends, get out of the house, and live your life."

Me: "If you want me to be a teenager, don't send me to Support Group. Buy me a fake ID so I can go to clubs, drink vodka, and take pot."

Mom: "You don't *take* pot, for starters."

Me: "See, that's the kind of thing I'd know if you got me a fake ID."

Mom: "You're going to Support Group."

Me: "UGGGGGGGGGGGG."

Mom: "Hazel, you deserve a life."

That shut me up, although I failed to see how attendance at Support Group met the definition of *life.* Still, I agreed to go—after negotiating the right to record the 1.5 episodes of *ANTM* I'd be missing.

I went to Support Group for the same reason that I'd once allowed nurses with a mere eighteen months of graduate education to poison me with exotically named chemicals: I wanted to make my parents happy. There is only one thing in this world shittier than biting it from cancer when you're sixteen, and that's having a kid who bites it from cancer.

Mom pulled into the circular driveway behind the church at 4:56. I pretended to fiddle with my oxygen tank for a second just to kill time.

"Do you want me to carry it in for you?"

"No, it's fine," I said. The cylindrical green tank only weighed a few pounds, and I had this little steel cart to wheel it around behind me. It delivered two liters of oxygen to me each minute through a cannula, a transparent tube that split just beneath my neck, wrapped behind my ears, and then reunited in my nostrils. The contraption was necessary because my lungs sucked at being lungs.

"I love you," she said as I got out.

"You too, Mom. See you at six."

"Make friends!" she said through the rolled-down window as I walked away.

I didn't want to take the elevator because taking the elevator is a Last Days kind of activity at Support Group, so I took the stairs. I grabbed a cookie and poured some lemonade into a Dixie cup and then turned around.

A boy was staring at me.

I was quite sure I'd never seen him before. Long and

leanly muscular, he dwarfed the molded plastic elementary school chair he was sitting in. Mahogany hair, straight and short. He looked my age, maybe a year older, and he sat with his tailbone against the edge of the chair, his posture aggressively poor, one hand half in a pocket of dark jeans.

I looked away, suddenly conscious of my myriad insufficiencies. I was wearing old jeans, which had once been tight but now sagged in weird places, and a yellow T-shirt advertising a band I didn't even like anymore. Also my hair: I had this pageboy haircut, and I hadn't even bothered to, like, brush it. Furthermore, I had ridiculously fat chipmunked cheeks, a side effect of treatment. I looked like a normally proportioned person with a balloon for a head. This was not even to mention the cankle situation. And yet—I cut a glance to him, and his eyes were still on me.

It occurred to me why they call it eye *contact.*

I walked into the circle and sat down next to Isaac, two seats away from the boy. I glanced again. He was still watching me.

Look, let me just say it: He was hot. A nonhot boy stares at you relentlessly and it is, at best, awkward and, at worst, a form of assault. But a hot boy . . . well.

I pulled out my phone and clicked it so it would display the time: 4:59. The circle filled in with the unlucky twelve-to-eighteens, and then Patrick started us out with the serenity prayer: *God, grant me the serenity to accept the things*

I cannot change, the courage to change the things I can, and the wisdom to know the difference. The guy was still staring at me. I felt rather blushy.

Finally, I decided that the proper strategy was to stare back. Boys do not have a monopoly on the Staring Business, after all. So I looked him over as Patrick acknowledged for the thousandth time his ball-lessness etc., and soon it was a staring contest. After a while the boy smiled, and then finally his blue eyes glanced away. When he looked back at me, I flicked my eyebrows up to say, *I win.*

He shrugged. Patrick continued and then finally it was time for the introductions. "Isaac, perhaps you'd like to go first today. I know you're facing a challenging time."

"Yeah," Isaac said. "I'm Isaac. I'm seventeen. And it's looking like I have to get surgery in a couple weeks, after which I'll be blind. Not to complain or anything because I know a lot of us have it worse, but yeah, I mean, being blind does sort of suck. My girlfriend helps, though. And friends like Augustus." He nodded toward the boy, who now had a name. "So, yeah," Isaac continued. He was looking at his hands, which he'd folded into each other like the top of a tepee. "There's nothing you can do about it."

"We're here for you, Isaac," Patrick said. "Let Isaac hear it, guys." And then we all, in a monotone, said, "We're here for you, Isaac."

Michael was next. He was twelve. He had leukemia.

He'd always had leukemia. He was okay. (Or so he said. He'd taken the elevator.)

Lida was sixteen, and pretty enough to be the object of the hot boy's eye. She was a regular—in a long remission from appendiceal cancer, which I had not previously known existed. She said—as she had every other time I'd attended Support Group—that she felt *strong*, which felt like bragging to me as the oxygen-drizzling nubs tickled my nostrils.

There were five others before they got to him. He smiled a little when his turn came. His voice was low, smoky, and dead sexy. "My name is Augustus Waters," he said. "I'm seventeen. I had a little touch of osteosarcoma a year and a half ago, but I'm just here today at Isaac's request."

"And how are you feeling?" asked Patrick.

"Oh, I'm grand." Augustus Waters smiled with a corner of his mouth. "I'm on a roller coaster that only goes up, my friend."

When it was my turn, I said, "My name is Hazel. I'm sixteen. Thyroid with mets in my lungs. I'm okay."

The hour proceeded apace: Fights were recounted, battles won amid wars sure to be lost; hope was clung to; families were both celebrated and denounced; it was agreed that friends just didn't get it; tears were shed; comfort proffered. Neither Augustus Waters nor I spoke again until Patrick said, "Augustus, perhaps you'd like to share your fears with the group."

"My fears?"

"Yes."

"I fear oblivion," he said without a moment's pause. "I fear it like the proverbial blind man who's afraid of the dark."

"Too soon," Isaac said, cracking a smile.

"Was that insensitive?" Augustus asked. "I can be pretty blind to other people's feelings."

Isaac was laughing, but Patrick raised a chastening finger and said, "Augustus, please. Let's return to *you* and *your* struggles. You said you fear oblivion?"

"I did," Augustus answered.

Patrick seemed lost. "Would, uh, would anyone like to speak to that?"

I hadn't been in proper school in three years. My parents were my two best friends. My third best friend was an author who did not know I existed. I was a fairly shy person—not the hand-raising type.

And yet, just this once, I decided to speak. I half raised my hand and Patrick, his delight evident, immediately said, "Hazel!" I was, I'm sure he assumed, opening up. Becoming Part Of The Group.

I looked over at Augustus Waters, who looked back at me. You could almost see through his eyes they were so blue. "There will come a time," I said, "when all of us are dead. All of us. There will come a time when there are no human beings remaining to remember that anyone ever existed or that our species ever did anything. There will be no one left to remember Aristotle or Cleopatra, let alone you. Everything that we did and built and wrote and thought and discovered will be forgotten and all of this"—I gestured encompassingly—"will have been for naught. Maybe that time is coming soon and maybe it is millions of years away, but even if we survive the collapse of our sun, we will not survive forever. There was time before organisms experienced consciousness, and there will be time after. And if the inevitability of human oblivion worries you, I encourage you to ignore it. God knows that's what everyone else does."

I'd learned this from my aforementioned third best friend, Peter Van Houten, the reclusive author of *An Imperial Affliction*, the book that was as close a thing as I had to a Bible. Peter Van Houten was the only person I'd ever come across who seemed to (a) understand what it's like to be dying, and (b) not have died.

After I finished, there was quite a long period of silence as I watched a smile spread all the way across Augustus's face—not the little crooked smile of the boy trying to be sexy while he stared at me, but his real smile, too big for his face. "Goddamn," Augustus said quietly. "Aren't you something else."

Neither of us said anything for the rest of Support

Group. At the end, we all had to hold hands, and Patrick led us in a prayer. "Lord Jesus Christ, we are gathered here in Your heart, *literally in Your heart*, as cancer survivors. You and You alone know us as we know ourselves. Guide us to life and the Light through our times of trial. We pray for Isaac's eyes, for Michael's and Jamie's blood, for Augustus's bones, for Hazel's lungs, for James's throat. We pray that You might heal us and that we might feel Your love, and Your peace, which passes all understanding. And we remember in our hearts those whom we knew and loved who have gone home to you: Maria and Kade and Joseph and Haley and Abigail and Angelina and Taylor and Gabriel and . . ."

It was a long list. The world contains a lot of dead people. And while Patrick droned on, reading the list from a sheet of paper because it was too long to memorize, I kept my eyes closed, trying to think prayerfully but mostly imagining the day when my name would find its way onto that list, all the way at the end when everyone had stopped listening.

When Patrick was finished, we said this stupid mantra together—LIVING OUR BEST LIFE TODAY—and it was over. Augustus Waters pushed himself out of his chair and walked over to me. His gait was crooked like his smile. He towered over me, but he kept his distance so I wouldn't have to crane my neck to look him in the eye. "What's your name?" he asked.

"Hazel."

"No, your full name."

"Um, Hazel Grace Lancaster." He was just about to say something else when Isaac walked up. "Hold on," Augustus said, raising a finger, and turned to Isaac. "That was actually worse than you made it out to be."

"I told you it was bleak."

"Why do you bother with it?"

"I don't know. It kind of helps?"

Augustus leaned in so he thought I couldn't hear. "She's a regular?" I couldn't hear Isaac's comment, but Augustus responded, "I'll say." He clasped Isaac by both shoulders and then took a half step away from him. "Tell Hazel about clinic."

Isaac leaned a hand against the snack table and focused his huge eye on me. "Okay, so I went into clinic this morning, and I was telling my surgeon that I'd rather be deaf than blind. And he said, 'It doesn't work that way,' and I was, like, 'Yeah, I realize it doesn't work that way; I'm just saying I'd rather be deaf than blind if I had the choice, which I realize I don't have,' and he said, 'Well, the good news is that you won't be deaf,' and I was like, 'Thank you for explaining that my eye cancer isn't going to make me deaf. I feel so fortunate that an intellectual giant like yourself would deign to operate on me.'"

"He sounds like a winner," I said. "I'm gonna try to get me some eye cancer just so I can make this guy's acquaintance."

"Good luck with that. All right, I should go. Monica's waiting for me. I gotta look at her a lot while I can."

"Counterinsurgence tomorrow?" Augustus asked.

"Definitely." Isaac turned and ran up the stairs, taking them two at a time.

Augustus Waters turned to me. "Literally," he said.

"Literally?" I asked.

"We are literally in the heart of Jesus," he said. "I thought we were in a church basement, but we are literally in the heart of Jesus."

"Someone should tell Jesus," I said. "I mean, it's gotta be dangerous, storing children with cancer in your heart."

"I would tell Him myself," Augustus said, "but unfortunately I am literally stuck inside of His heart, so He won't be able to hear me." I laughed. He shook his head, just looking at me.

"What?" I asked.

"Nothing," he said.

"Why are you looking at me like that?"

Augustus half smiled. "Because you're beautiful. I enjoy looking at beautiful people, and I decided a while ago not to deny myself the simpler pleasures of existence." A brief awkward silence ensued. Augustus plowed through: "I mean, particularly given that, as you so deliciously pointed out, all of this will end in oblivion and everything."

I kind of scoffed or sighed or exhaled in a way that was vaguely coughy and then said, "I'm not beau—"

"You're like a millennial Natalie Portman. Like *V for Vendetta* Natalie Portman."

"Never seen it," I said.

"Really?" he asked. "Pixie-haired gorgeous girl dislikes authority and can't help but fall for a boy she knows is trouble. It's your autobiography, so far as I can tell."

His every syllable flirted. Honestly, he kind of turned me on. I didn't even know that guys *could* turn me on—not, like, in real life.

A younger girl walked past us. "How's it going, Alisa?" he asked. She smiled and mumbled, "Hi, Augustus." "Memorial people," he explained. Memorial was the big research hospital. "Where do you go?"

"Children's," I said, my voice smaller than I expected it to be. He nodded. The conversation seemed over. "Well," I said, nodding vaguely toward the steps that led us out of the Literal Heart of Jesus. I tilted my cart onto its wheels and started walking. He limped beside me. "So, see you next time, maybe?" I asked.

"You should see it," he said. "*V for Vendetta*, I mean."

"Okay," I said. "I'll look it up."

"No. With me. At my house," he said. "Now."

I stopped walking. "I hardly know you, Augustus Waters. You could be an ax murderer."

He nodded. "True enough, Hazel Grace." He walked past me, his shoulders filling out his green knit polo shirt, his back straight, his steps lilting just slightly to the right as he walked steady and confident on what I had determined was a prosthetic leg. Osteosarcoma sometimes takes a limb to check you out. Then, if it likes you, it takes the rest.

I followed him upstairs, losing ground as I made my way up slowly, stairs not being a field of expertise for my lungs.

And then we were out of Jesus's heart and in the parking lot, the spring air just on the cold side of perfect, the late-afternoon light heavenly in its hurtfulness.

Mom wasn't there yet, which was unusual, because Mom was almost always waiting for me. I glanced around and saw that a tall, curvy brunette girl had Isaac pinned against the stone wall of the church, kissing him rather aggressively. They were close enough to me that I could hear the weird noises of their mouths together, and I could hear him saying, "Always," and her saying, "Always," in return.

Suddenly standing next to me, Augustus half whispered, "They're big believers in PDA."

"What's with the 'always'?" The slurping sounds intensified.

"Always is their thing. They'll *always* love each other and whatever. I would conservatively estimate they have texted each other the word *always* four million times in the last year."

A couple more cars drove up, taking Michael and Alisa away. It was just Augustus and me now, watching Isaac and Monica, who proceeded apace as if they were not leaning against a place of worship. His hand reached for her boob over her shirt and pawed at it, his palm still while his fingers moved around. I wondered if that felt good. Didn't seem like it would, but I decided to forgive Isaac on the grounds that he was going blind. The senses must feast while there is yet hunger and whatever.

"Imagine taking that last drive to the hospital," I said quietly. "The last time you'll ever drive a car."

Without looking over at me, Augustus said, "You're killing my vibe here, Hazel Grace. I'm trying to observe young love in its many-splendored awkwardness."

"I think he's hurting her boob," I said.

"Yes, it's difficult to ascertain whether he is trying to arouse her or perform a breast exam." Then Augustus Waters reached into a pocket and pulled out, of all things, a pack of cigarettes. He flipped it open and put a cigarette between his lips.

"Are you *serious*?" I asked. "You think that's cool? Oh, my God, you just ruined *the whole thing*."

"Which whole thing?" he asked, turning to me. The cigarette dangled unlit from the unsmiling corner of his mouth.

"The whole thing where a boy who is not unattractive or unintelligent or seemingly in any way unacceptable stares at me and points out incorrect uses of literality and compares me to actresses and asks me to watch a movie at his house. But of course there is always a *hamartia* and yours is that oh, my God, even though you HAD FREAKING CANCER you give money to a company in exchange for the chance to acquire YET MORE CANCER. Oh, my God. Let me just assure you that not being able to breathe? SUCKS. Totally disappointing. *Totally*."

"A *hamartia*?" he asked, the cigarette still in his mouth. It tightened his jaw. He had a hell of a jawline, unfortunately.

"A fatal flaw," I explained, turning away from him. I stepped toward the curb, leaving Augustus Waters behind me, and then I heard a car start down the street. It was Mom. She'd been waiting for me to, like, make friends or whatever.

I felt this weird mix of disappointment and anger welling up inside of me. I don't even know what the feeling was, really, just that there was a *lot* of it, and I wanted to smack Augustus Waters and also replace my lungs with lungs that didn't suck at being lungs. I was standing with my Chuck Taylors on the very edge of the curb, the oxygen tank ball-and-chaining in the cart by my side, and right as my mom pulled up, I felt a hand grab mine.

I yanked my hand free but turned back to him.

"They don't kill you unless you light them," he said as Mom arrived at the curb. "And I've never lit one. It's a metaphor, see: You put the killing thing right between your teeth, but you don't give it the power to do its killing."

"It's a metaphor," I said, dubious. Mom was just idling.

"It's a metaphor," he said.

"You choose your behaviors based on their metaphorical resonances . . ." I said.

"Oh, yes." He smiled. The big, goofy, real smile. "I'm a big believer in metaphor, Hazel Grace."

I turned to the car. Tapped the window. It rolled down. "I'm going to a movie with Augustus Waters," I said. "Please record the next several episodes of the *ANTM* marathon for me."

CHAPTER TWO

Augustus Waters drove horrifically. Whether stopping or starting, everything happened with a tremendous JOLT. I flew against the seat belt of his Toyota SUV each time he braked, and my neck snapped backward each time he hit the gas. I might have been nervous—what with sitting in the car of a strange boy on the way to his house, keenly aware that my crap lungs complicate efforts to fend off unwanted advances—but his driving was so astonishingly poor that I could think of nothing else.

We'd gone perhaps a mile in jagged silence before Augustus said, "I failed the driving test three times."

"You don't say."

He laughed, nodding. "Well, I can't feel pressure in old Prosty, and I can't get the hang of driving left-footed. My doctors say most amputees can drive with no problem, but . . . yeah. Not me. Anyway, I go in for my fourth driving test, and it goes about like this is going." A half mile in front of us, a light turned red. Augustus slammed on the brakes, tossing me into the triangular embrace of the seat belt. "Sorry. I swear to God I am trying to be gentle. Right, so anyway, at the end of the test, I totally thought I'd failed again, but the instructor was like, 'Your driving is unpleasant, but it isn't technically unsafe.'"

"I'm not sure I agree," I said. "I suspect Cancer Perk." Cancer Perks are the little things cancer kids get that regular kids don't: basketballs signed by sports heroes, free passes on late homework, unearned driver's licenses, etc.

"Yeah," he said. The light turned green. I braced myself. Augustus slammed the gas.

"You know they've got hand controls for people who can't use their legs," I pointed out.

"Yeah," he said. "Maybe someday." He sighed in a way that made me wonder whether he was confident about the existence of *someday*. I knew osteosarcoma was highly curable, but still.

There are a number of ways to establish someone's approximate survival expectations without actually *asking*. I used the classic: "So, are you in school?" Generally, your parents pull you out of school at some point if they expect you to bite it.

"Yeah," he said. "I'm at North Central. A year behind, though: I'm a sophomore. You?"

I considered lying. No one likes a corpse, after all. But in the end I told the truth. "No, my parents withdrew me three years ago."

"Three *years*?" he asked, astonished.

I told Augustus the broad outline of my miracle: diagnosed with Stage IV thyroid cancer when I was thirteen. (I didn't tell him that the diagnosis came three months after I got my first period. Like: Congratulations! You're a woman. Now die.) It was, we were told, incurable.

I had a surgery called *radical neck dissection*, which is about as pleasant as it sounds. Then radiation. Then they tried some chemo for my lung tumors. The tumors shrank, then grew. By then, I was fourteen. My lungs started to fill up with water. I was looking pretty dead—my hands and feet ballooned; my skin cracked; my lips were perpetually blue. They've got this drug that makes you not feel so completely terrified about the fact that you can't breathe, and I had a lot of it flowing into me through a PICC line, and more than a dozen other drugs besides. But even so, there's a certain unpleasantness to drowning, particularly when it occurs over the course of several months. I finally ended up in the ICU with pneumonia, and my mom knelt by the side of my bed and said, "Are you ready, sweetie?" and I told her I was ready, and my dad just kept telling me he loved me in this voice that was not breaking so much as already broken, and I kept telling him that I loved him, too, and everyone was holding hands, and I couldn't catch my breath, and my lungs were acting desperate, gasping, pulling me out of the bed trying to find a position that could get them air, and I was embarrassed by their desperation, disgusted that they wouldn't just *let go*, and I remember my mom telling me it was okay, that I was okay, that I would be okay, and my father was trying so hard not to sob that when he did, which was regularly, it was an earthquake. And I remember wanting not to be awake.

Everyone figured I was finished, but my Cancer Doctor Maria managed to get some of the fluid out of my lungs, and shortly thereafter the antibiotics they'd given me for the pneumonia kicked in.

I woke up and soon got into one of those experimental trials that are famous in the Republic of Cancervania for Not Working. The drug was Phalanxifor, this molecule designed to attach itself to cancer cells and slow their growth. It didn't work in about 70 percent of people. But it worked in me. The tumors shrank.

And they stayed shrunk. Huzzah, Phalanxifor! In the past eighteen months, my mets have hardly grown, leaving me with lungs that suck at being lungs but could, conceivably, struggle along indefinitely with the assistance of drizzled oxygen and daily Phalanxifor.

Admittedly, my Cancer Miracle had only resulted in a bit of purchased time. (I did not yet know the size of the bit.) But when telling Augustus Waters, I painted the rosiest possible picture, embellishing the miraculousness of the miracle.

"So now you gotta go back to school," he said.

"I actually *can't*," I explained, "because I already got my GED. So I'm taking classes at MCC," which was our community college.

"A college girl," he said, nodding. "That explains the aura of sophistication." He smirked at me. I shoved his upper arm playfully. I could feel the muscle right beneath the skin, all tense and amazing.

We made a wheels-screeching turn into a subdivision with eight-foot-high stucco walls. His house was the first one on the left. A two-story colonial. We jerked to a halt in his driveway.

I followed him inside. A wooden plaque in the entryway was engraved in cursive with the words *Home Is Where the Heart Is*, and the entire house turned out to be festooned in such observations. *Good Friends Are Hard to Find and Impossible to Forget* read an illustration above the coatrack. *True Love Is Born from Hard Times* promised a needlepointed pillow in their antique-furnished living room. Augustus saw me reading. "My parents call them Encouragements," he explained. "They're everywhere."

His mom and dad called him Gus. They were making enchiladas in the kitchen (a piece of stained glass by the sink read in bubbly letters *Family Is Forever*). His mom was putting chicken into tortillas, which his dad then rolled up and placed in a glass pan. They didn't seem too surprised by my arrival, which made sense: The fact that Augustus made me *feel* special did not necessarily indicate that I *was* special. Maybe he brought home a different girl every night to show her movies and feel her up.

"This is Hazel Grace," he said, by way of introduction.

"Just Hazel," I said.

"How's it going, Hazel?" asked Gus's dad. He was tall—almost as tall as Gus—and skinny in a way that parentally aged people usually aren't.

"Okay," I said.

"How was Isaac's Support Group?"

"It was incredible," Gus said.

"You're such a Debbie Downer," his mom said. "Hazel, do you enjoy it?"

I paused a second, trying to figure out if my response should be calibrated to please Augustus or his parents. "Most of the people are really nice," I finally said.

"That's exactly what we found with families at

Memorial when we were in the thick of it with Gus's treatment," his dad said. "Everybody was so kind. Strong, too. In the darkest days, the Lord puts the best people into your life."

"Quick, give me a throw pillow and some thread because that needs to be an Encouragement," Augustus said, and his dad looked a little annoyed, but then Gus wrapped his long arm around his dad's neck and said, "I'm just kidding, Dad. I like the freaking Encouragements. I really do. I just can't admit it because I'm a teenager." His dad rolled his eyes.

"You're joining us for dinner, I hope?" asked his mom. She was small and brunette and vaguely mousy.

"I guess?" I said. "I have to be home by ten. Also I don't, um, eat meat?"

"No problem. We'll vegetarianize some," she said.

"Animals are just too cute?" Gus asked.

"I want to minimize the number of deaths I am responsible for," I said.

Gus opened his mouth to respond but then stopped himself.

His mom filled the silence. "Well, I think that's wonderful."

They talked to me for a bit about how the enchiladas were Famous Waters Enchiladas and Not to Be Missed and about how Gus's curfew was also ten, and how they were inherently distrustful of anyone who gave their kids curfews *other* than ten, and was I in school—"she's a college student," Augustus interjected—and how the weather was truly and absolutely extraordinary for March, and how in spring all things are new, and they didn't even once ask me about the oxygen or my diagnosis, which was weird and wonderful, and then Augustus said, "Hazel and I are going to watch *V for Vendetta* so she can see her filmic doppelgänger, mid-two thousands Natalie Portman."

"The living room TV is yours for the watching," his dad said happily.

"I think we're actually gonna watch it in the basement."

His dad laughed. "Good try. Living room."

"But I want to show Hazel Grace the basement," Augustus said.

"Just Hazel," I said.

"So show Just Hazel the basement," said his dad. "And then come upstairs and watch your movie in the living room."

Augustus puffed out his cheeks, balanced on his leg, and twisted his hips, throwing the prosthetic forward. "Fine," he mumbled.

I followed him down carpeted stairs to a huge basement bedroom. A shelf at my eye level reached all the way around the room, and it was stuffed solid with basketball memorabilia: dozens of trophies with gold plastic men mid-jump shot or dribbling or reaching for a layup toward an unseen basket. There were also lots of signed balls and sneakers.

"I used to play basketball," he explained.

"You must've been pretty good."

"I wasn't bad, but all the shoes and balls are Cancer Perks." He walked toward the TV, where a huge pile of DVDs and video games were arranged into a vague pyramid shape. He bent at the waist and snatched up *V for Vendetta*. "I was, like, the prototypical white Hoosier kid," he said. "I was all about resurrecting the lost art of the midrange jumper, but then one day I was shooting free throws–just standing at the foul line at the North Central gym shooting from a rack of balls. All at once, I couldn't figure out why I was methodically tossing a spherical object through a toroidal object. It seemed like the stupidest thing I could possibly be doing.

"I started thinking about little kids putting a cylindrical peg through a circular hole, and how they do it over and over again for months when they figure it out, and how basketball was basically just a slightly more aerobic version of that same exercise. Anyway, for the longest time, I just kept sinking free throws. I hit eighty in a row, my all-time best, but as I kept going, I felt more and more like a two-year-old. And then for some reason I started to think about hurdlers. Are you okay?"

I'd taken a seat on the corner of his unmade bed. I wasn't trying to be suggestive or anything; I just got kind of tired when I had to stand a lot. I'd stood in the living room and then there had been the stairs, and then more standing, which was quite a lot of standing for me, and I didn't want to faint or anything. I was a bit of a Victorian Lady, fainting-wise. "I'm fine," I said. "Just listening. Hurdlers?"

"Yeah, hurdlers. I don't know why. I started thinking about them running their hurdle races, and jumping over these totally arbitrary objects that had been set in their path. And I wondered if hurdlers ever thought, you know, *This would go faster if we just got rid of the hurdles.*"

"This was before your diagnosis?" I asked.

"Right, well, there was that, too." He smiled with half his mouth. "The day of the existentially fraught free throws was coincidentally also my last day of dual leggedness. I had a weekend between when they scheduled the amputation and when it happened. My own little glimpse of what Isaac is going through."

I nodded. I liked Augustus Waters. I really, really, really liked him. I liked the way his story ended with someone else. I liked his voice. I liked that he took *existentially fraught* free throws. I liked that he was a tenured professor in the Department of Slightly Crooked Smiles with a dual appointment in the Department of Having a Voice That Made My Skin Feel More Like Skin. And I liked that he had two names. I've always liked people with two names, because you get to make up your mind what you call them: Gus or Augustus? Me, I was always just Hazel, univalent Hazel.

"Do you have siblings?" I asked.

"Huh?" he answered, seeming a little distracted.

"You said that thing about watching kids play."

"Oh, yeah, no. I have nephews, from my half sisters. But they're older. They're like—DAD, HOW OLD ARE JULIE AND MARTHA?"

"Twenty-eight!"

"They're like twenty-eight. They live in Chicago. They are both married to very fancy lawyer dudes. Or banker dudes. I can't remember. You have siblings?"

I shook my head no. "So what's your story?" he asked, sitting down next to me at a safe distance.

"I already told you my story. I was diagnosed when—"

"No, not your cancer story. *Your* story. Interests, hobbies, passions, weird fetishes, etcetera."

"Um," I said.

"Don't tell me you're one of those people who becomes their disease. I know so many people like that. It's disheartening. Like, cancer is in the growth business, right? The taking-people-over business. But surely you haven't let it succeed prematurely."

It occurred to me that perhaps I had. I struggled with how to pitch myself to Augustus Waters, which enthusiasms to embrace, and in the silence that followed it occurred to me that I wasn't very interesting. "I am pretty unextraordinary."

"I reject that out of hand. Think of something you like. The first thing that comes to mind."

"Um. Reading?"

"What do you read?"

"Everything. From, like, hideous romance to pretentious fiction to poetry. Whatever."

"Do you write poetry, too?"

"No. I don't write."

"There!" Augustus almost shouted. "Hazel Grace, you are the only teenager in America who prefers reading poetry to writing it. This tells me so much. You read a lot of capital-G great books, don't you?"

"I guess?"

"What's your favorite?"

"Um," I said.

My favorite book, by a wide margin, was *An Imperial Affliction*, but I didn't like to tell people about it. Sometimes, you read a book and it fills you with this weird evangelical zeal, and you become convinced that the shattered world will never be put back together unless and until all living humans read the book. And then there are books like *An Imperial Affliction*, which you can't tell people about, books so special and rare and *yours* that advertising your affection feels like a betrayal.

It wasn't even that the book was so good or anything;

it was just that the author, Peter Van Houten, seemed to understand me in weird and impossible ways. *An Imperial Affliction* was *my* book, in the way my body was my body and my thoughts were my thoughts.

Even so, I told Augustus. "My favorite book is probably *An Imperial Affliction*," I said.

"Does it feature zombies?" he asked.

"No," I said.

"Stormtroopers?"

I shook my head. "It's not that kind of book."

He smiled. "I am going to read this terrible book with the boring title that does not contain stormtroopers," he promised, and I immediately felt like I shouldn't have told him about it. Augustus spun around to a stack of books beneath his bedside table. He grabbed a paperback and a pen. As he scribbled an inscription onto the title page, he said, "All I ask in exchange is that you read this brilliant and haunting novelization of my favorite video game." He held up the book, which was called *The Price of Dawn*. I laughed and took it. Our hands kind of got muddled together in the book handoff, and then he was holding my hand. "Cold," he said, pressing a finger to my pale wrist.

"Not cold so much as underoxygenated," I said.

"I love it when you talk medical to me," he said. He stood, and pulled me up with him, and did not let go of my hand until we reached the stairs.

. . .

We watched the movie with several inches of couch between us. I did the totally middle-schooly thing wherein I put my hand on the couch about halfway between us to let him know that it was okay to hold it, but he didn't try. An hour into the movie, Augustus's parents came in and served us the enchiladas, which we ate on the couch, and they were pretty delicious.

The movie was about this heroic guy in a mask who died heroically for Natalie Portman, who's pretty badass and very hot and does not have anything approaching my puffy steroid face.

As the credits rolled, he said, "Pretty great, huh?"

"Pretty great," I agreed, although it wasn't, really. It was kind of a boy movie. I don't know why boys expect us to like boy movies. We don't expect them to like girl movies. "I should get home. Class in the morning," I said.

I sat on the couch for a while as Augustus searched for his keys. His mom sat down next to me and said, "I just love this one, don't you?" I guess I had been looking toward the Encouragement above the TV, a drawing of an angel with the caption *Without Pain, How Could We Know Joy?*

(This is an old argument in the field of Thinking About Suffering, and its stupidity and lack of sophistication could be plumbed for centuries, but suffice it to say that the existence of broccoli does not in any way affect the taste of chocolate.) "Yes," I said. "A lovely thought."

I drove Augustus's car home with Augustus riding

shotgun. He played me a couple songs he liked by a band called The Hectic Glow, and they were good songs, but because I didn't know them already, they weren't as good to me as they were to him. I kept glancing over at his leg, or the place where his leg had been, trying to imagine what the fake leg looked like. I didn't want to care about it, but I did a little. He probably cared about my oxygen. Illness repulses. I'd learned that a long time ago, and I suspected Augustus had, too.

As I pulled up outside of my house, Augustus clicked the radio off. The air thickened. He was probably thinking about kissing me, and I was definitely thinking about kissing him. Wondering if I wanted to. I'd kissed boys, but it had been a while. Pre-Miracle.

I put the car in park and looked over at him. He really was beautiful. I know boys aren't supposed to be, but he was.

"Hazel Grace," he said, my name new and better in his voice. "It has been a real pleasure to make your acquaintance."

"Ditto, Mr. Waters," I said. I felt shy looking at him. I could not match the intensity of his waterblue eyes.

"May I see you again?" he asked. There was an endearing nervousness in his voice.

I smiled. "Sure."

"Tomorrow?" he asked.

"Patience, grasshopper," I counseled. "You don't want to seem overeager."

"Right, that's why I said tomorrow," he said. "I want to see you again tonight. But I'm willing to wait *all night and much of tomorrow*." I rolled my eyes. "I'm *serious*," he said.

"You don't even know me," I said. I grabbed the book from the center console. "How about I call you when I finish this?"

"But you don't even have my phone number," he said.

"I strongly suspect you wrote it in the book."

He broke out into that goofy smile. "And you say we don't know each other."

CHAPTER THREE

I stayed up pretty late that night reading *The Price of Dawn*. (Spoiler alert: The price of dawn is blood.) It wasn't *An Imperial Affliction*, but the protagonist, Staff Sergeant Max Mayhem, was vaguely likable despite killing, by my count, no fewer than 118 individuals in 284 pages.

So I got up late the next morning, a Thursday. Mom's policy was never to wake me up, because one of the job requirements of Professional Sick Person is sleeping a lot, so I was kind of confused at first when I jolted awake with her hands on my shoulders.

"It's almost ten," she said.

"Sleep fights cancer," I said. "I was up late reading."

"It must be some book," she said as she knelt down next to the bed and unscrewed me from my large, rectangular oxygen concentrator, which I called Philip, because it just kind of looked like a Philip.

Mom hooked me up to a portable tank and then reminded me I had class. "Did that boy give it to you?" she asked out of nowhere.

"By *it*, do you mean herpes?"

"You are too much," Mom said. "The book, Hazel. I mean the book."

"Yeah, he gave me the book."

"I can tell you like him," she said, eyebrows raised, as if this observation required some uniquely maternal instinct. I shrugged. "I told you Support Group would be worth your while."

"Did you just wait outside the entire time?"

"Yes. I brought some paperwork. Anyway, time to face the day, young lady."

"Mom. Sleep. Cancer. Fighting."

"I know, love, but there is class to attend. Also, today is . . . " The glee in Mom's voice was evident.

"Thursday?"

"Did you seriously forget?"

"Maybe?"

"It's Thursday, March twenty-ninth!" she basically screamed, a demented smile plastered to her face.

"You are really excited about knowing the date!" I yelled back.

"HAZEL! IT'S YOUR THIRTY-THIRD HALF BIRTHDAY!"

"Ohhhhhh," I said. My mom was really super into celebration maximization. IT'S ARBOR DAY! LET'S HUG TREES AND EAT CAKE! COLUMBUS BROUGHT SMALLPOX TO THE NATIVES; WE SHALL RECALL THE OCCASION WITH A PICNIC!, etc. "Well, Happy thirty-third Half Birthday to me," I said.

"What do you want to do on your very special day?"

"Come home from class and set the world record for number of episodes of *Top Chef* watched consecutively?"

Mom reached up to this shelf above my bed and grabbed Bluie, the blue stuffed bear I'd had since I was, like, one—back when it was socially acceptable to name one's friends after their hue.

"You don't want to go to a movie with Kaitlyn or Matt or someone?" who were my friends.

That was an idea. "Sure," I said. "I'll text Kaitlyn and see if she wants to go to the mall or something after school."

Mom smiled, hugging the bear to her stomach. "Is it still cool to go to the mall?" she asked.

"I take quite a lot of pride in not knowing what's cool," I answered.

. . .

I texted Kaitlyn, took a shower, got dressed, and then Mom drove me to school. My class was American Literature, a lecture about Frederick Douglass in a mostly empty auditorium, and it was incredibly difficult to stay awake. Forty minutes into the ninety-minute class, Kaitlyn texted back.

> Awesomesauce. Happy Half Birthday. Castleton at 3:32?

Kaitlyn had the kind of packed social life that needs to be scheduled down to the minute. I responded:

> Sounds good. I'll be at the food court.

Mom drove me directly from school to the bookstore attached to the mall, where I purchased both *Midnight Dawns* and *Requiem for Mayhem*, the first two sequels to *The Price of Dawn*, and then I walked over to the huge food court and bought a Diet Coke. It was 3:21.

I watched these kids playing in the pirate-ship indoor playground while I read. There was this tunnel that these two kids kept crawling through over and over and they never seemed to get tired, which made me think of Augustus Waters and the existentially fraught free throws.

Mom was also in the food court, alone, sitting in

a corner where she thought I couldn't see her, eating a cheesesteak sandwich and reading through some papers. Medical stuff, probably. The paperwork was endless.

At 3:32 precisely, I noticed Kaitlyn striding confidently past the Wok House. She saw me the moment I raised my hand, flashed her very white and newly straightened teeth at me, and headed over.

She wore a knee-length charcoal coat that fit perfectly and sunglasses that dominated her face. She pushed them up onto the top of her head as she leaned down to hug me.

"Darling," she said, vaguely British. "How *are* you?" People didn't find the accent odd or off-putting. Kaitlyn just happened to be an extremely sophisticated twenty-five-year-old British socialite stuck inside a sixteen-year-old body in Indianapolis. Everyone accepted it.

"I'm good. How are you?"

"I don't even know anymore. Is that diet?" I nodded and handed it to her. She sipped through the straw. "I do wish you were at school these days. Some of the boys have become downright *edible*."

"Oh, yeah? Like who?" I asked. She proceeded to name five guys we'd attended elementary and middle school with, but I couldn't picture any of them.

"I've been dating Derek Wellington for a bit," she said, "but I don't think it will last. He's such a *boy*. But enough about me. What is new in the Hazelverse?"

"Nothing, really," I said.

"Health is good?"

"The same, I guess?"

"Phalanxifor!" she enthused, smiling. "So you could just live forever, right?"

"Probably not forever," I said.

"But basically," she said. "What else is new?"

I thought of telling her that I was seeing a boy, too, or at least that I'd watched a movie with one, just because I knew it would surprise and amaze her that anyone as disheveled and awkward and stunted as me could even briefly win the affections of a boy. But I didn't really have much to brag about, so I just shrugged.

"What in heaven is *that*?" asked Kaitlyn, gesturing to the book.

"Oh, it's sci-fi. I've gotten kinda into it. It's a series."

"I am alarmed. Shall we shop?"

We went to this shoe store. As we were shopping, Kaitlyn kept picking out all these open-toed flats for me and saying, "These would look cute on *you*," which reminded me that Kaitlyn never wore open-toed shoes on account of how she hated her feet because she felt her second toes were too long, as if the second toe was a window into the soul or something. So when I pointed out a pair of sandals that would suit her skin tone, she was like, "Yeah, but . . ." the but being *but they will expose my hideous second toes to the public*, and I said, "Kaitlyn, you're the only person I've ever known to have toe-specific dysmorphia," and she said, "What is that?"

"You know, like when you look in the mirror and the thing you see is not the thing as it really is."

"Oh. Oh," she said. "Do you like these?" She held up a pair of cute but unspectacular Mary Janes, and I nodded, and she found her size and tried them on, pacing up and down the aisle, watching her feet in the knee-high angled mirrors. Then she grabbed a pair of strappy hooker shoes and said, "Is it even possible to walk in these? I mean, I would just *die*—" and then stopped short, looking at me as if to say *I'm sorry*, as if it were a crime to mention death to the dying. "You should try them on," Kaitlyn continued, trying to paper over the awkwardness.

"I'd sooner die," I assured her.

I ended up just picking out some flip-flops so that I could have something to buy, and then I sat down on one of the benches opposite a bank of shoes and watched Kaitlyn snake her way through the aisles, shopping with the kind of intensity and focus that one usually associates with professional chess. I kind of wanted to take out *Midnight Dawns* and read for a while, but I knew that'd be rude, so I just watched Kaitlyn. Occasionally she'd circle back to me clutching some closed-toe prey and say, "This?" and I would try to make an intelligent comment about the shoe, and then finally she bought three pairs and I bought my flip-flops and then as we exited she said, "Anthropologie?"

"I should head home actually," I said. "I'm kinda tired."

"Sure, of course," she said. "I have to see you more often, darling." She placed her hands on my shoulders, kissed me on both cheeks, and marched off, her narrow hips swishing.

I didn't go home, though. I'd told Mom to pick me up at six, and while I figured she was either in the mall or in the parking lot, I still wanted the next two hours to myself.

I liked my mom, but her perpetual nearness sometimes made me feel weirdly nervous. And I liked Kaitlyn, too. I really did. But three years removed from proper full-time schoolic exposure to my peers, I felt a certain unbridgeable distance between us. I think my school friends wanted to help me through my cancer, but they eventually found out that they couldn't. For one thing, there was no *through*.

So I excused myself on the grounds of pain and fatigue, as I often had over the years when seeing Kaitlyn or any of my other friends. In truth, it always hurt. It always hurt not to breathe like a normal person, incessantly reminding your lungs to be lungs, forcing yourself to accept as unsolvable the clawing scraping inside-out ache of underoxygenation. So I wasn't lying, exactly. I was just choosing among truths.

I found a bench surrounded by an Irish Gifts store, the Fountain Pen Emporium, and a baseball-cap outlet—a corner of the mall even Kaitlyn would never shop, and started reading *Midnight Dawns*.

It featured a sentence-to-corpse ratio of nearly 1:1,

and I tore through it without ever looking up. I liked Staff Sergeant Max Mayhem, even though he didn't have much in the way of a technical personality, but mostly I liked that his adventures *kept happening*. There were always more bad guys to kill and more good guys to save. New wars started even before the old ones were won. I hadn't read a real series like that since I was a kid, and it was exciting to live again in an infinite fiction.

Twenty pages from the end of *Midnight Dawns*, things started to look pretty bleak for Mayhem when he was shot seventeen times while attempting to rescue a (blond, American) hostage from the Enemy. But as a reader, I did not despair. The war effort would go on without him. There could—and would—be sequels starring his cohorts: Specialist Manny Loco and Private Jasper Jacks and the rest.

I was just about to the end when this little girl with barretted braids appeared in front of me and said, "What's in your nose?"

And I said, "Um, it's called a cannula. These tubes give me oxygen and help me breathe." Her mother swooped in and said, "Jackie," disapprovingly, but I said, "No no, it's okay," because it totally was, and then Jackie asked, "Would they help me breathe, too?"

"I dunno. Let's try." I took it off and let Jackie stick the cannula in her nose and breathe. "Tickles," she said.

"I know, right?"

"I think I'm breathing better," she said.

"Yeah?"

"Yeah."

"Well," I said, "I wish I could give you my cannula but I kind of really need the help." I already felt the loss. I focused on my breathing as Jackie handed the tubes back to me. I gave them a quick swipe with my T-shirt, laced the tubes behind my ears, and put the nubbins back in place.

"Thanks for letting me try it," she said.

"No problem."

"Jackie," her mother said again, and this time I let her go.

I returned to the book, where Staff Sergeant Max Mayhem was regretting that he had but one life to give for his country, but I kept thinking about that little kid, and how much I liked her.

The other thing about Kaitlyn, I guess, was that it could never again feel natural to talk to her. Any attempts to feign normal social interactions were just depressing because it was so glaringly obvious that everyone I spoke to for the rest of my life would feel awkward and self-conscious around me, except maybe kids like Jackie who just didn't know any better.

Anyway, I really did like being alone. I liked being alone with poor Staff Sergeant Max Mayhem, who—oh, come on, he's not going to *survive* these seventeen bullet wounds, is he?

(Spoiler alert: He lives.)

CHAPTER FOUR

I went to bed a little early that night, changing into boy boxers and a T-shirt before crawling under the covers of my bed, which was queen size and pillow topped and one of my favorite places in the world. And then I started reading *An Imperial Affliction* for the millionth time.

AIA is about this girl named Anna (who narrates the story) and her one-eyed mom, who is a professional gardener obsessed with tulips, and they have a normal lower-middle-class life in a little central California town until Anna gets this rare blood cancer.

But it's not a *cancer book*, because cancer books suck. Like, in cancer books, the cancer person starts a charity that raises money to fight cancer, right? And this commitment to charity reminds the cancer person of the essential goodness of humanity and makes him/her feel loved and encouraged because s/he will leave a cancer-curing legacy. But in *AIA*, Anna decides that being a person with cancer who starts a cancer charity is a bit narcissistic, so she starts a charity called The Anna Foundation for People with Cancer Who Want to Cure Cholera.

Also, Anna is honest about all of it in a way no one else really is: Throughout the book, she refers to herself as *the side effect*, which is just totally correct. Cancer kids are essentially side effects of the relentless mutation that made the diversity of life on earth possible. So as the story goes on, she gets sicker, the treatments and disease racing to kill her, and her mom falls in love with this Dutch tulip trader Anna calls the Dutch Tulip Man. The Dutch Tulip Man has lots of money and very eccentric ideas about how to treat cancer, but Anna thinks this guy might be a con man and possibly not even Dutch, and then just as the possibly Dutch guy and her mom are about to get married and Anna is about to start this crazy new treatment regimen involving wheatgrass and low doses of arsenic, the book ends right in the middle of a

I know it's a very *literary* decision and everything and probably part of the reason I love the book so much, but there is something to recommend a story that *ends*. And if it can't end, then it should at least continue into perpetuity like the adventures of Staff Sergeant Max Mayhem's platoon.

I understood the story ended because Anna died or got too sick to write and this midsentence thing was supposed to reflect how life really ends and whatever, but there were characters other than Anna in the story, and it seemed unfair that I would never find out what happened to them. I'd written, care of his publisher, a dozen letters to Peter Van Houten, each asking for some answers about what happens after the end of the story: whether the Dutch Tulip Man is a con man, whether Anna's mother ends up married to him, what happens to Anna's stupid hamster (which her mom hates), whether Anna's friends graduate from high school—all that stuff. But he'd never responded to any of my letters.

AIA was the only book Peter Van Houten had written, and all anyone seemed to know about him was that after the book came out he moved from the United States to the Netherlands and became kind of reclusive. I imagined that he was working on a sequel set in the Netherlands—maybe Anna's mom and the Dutch Tulip Man end up moving there and trying to start a new life. But it had been ten years since *An Imperial Affliction* came out, and Van Houten hadn't published so much as a blog post. I couldn't wait forever.

As I reread that night, I kept getting distracted imagining Augustus Waters reading the same words. I wondered if he'd like it, or if he'd dismiss it as pretentious.

Then I remembered my promise to call him after reading *The Price of Dawn*, so I found his number on its title page and texted him.

> Price of Dawn review: Too many bodies. Not enough adjectives. How's AIA?

He replied a minute later:

> As I recall, you promised to CALL when you finished the book, not text.

So I called.

"Hazel Grace," he said upon picking up.

"So have you read it?"

"Well, I haven't finished it. It's six hundred fifty-one pages long and I've had twenty-four hours."

"How far are you?"

"Four fifty-three."

"And?"

"I will withhold judgment until I finish. However, I will say that I'm feeling a bit embarrassed to have given you *The Price of Dawn*."

"Don't be. I'm already on *Requiem for Mayhem*."

"A sparkling addition to the series. So, okay, is the tulip guy a crook? I'm getting a bad vibe from him."

"No spoilers," I said.

"If he is anything other than a total gentleman, I'm going to gouge his eyes out."

"So you're into it."

"Withholding judgment! When can I see you?"

"Certainly not until you finish *An Imperial Affliction*." I enjoyed being coy.

"Then I'd better hang up and start reading."

"You'd better," I said, and the line clicked dead without another word.

Flirting was new to me, but I liked it.

The next morning I had Twentieth-Century American Poetry at MCC. This old woman gave a lecture wherein she managed to talk for ninety minutes about Sylvia Plath without ever once quoting a single word of Sylvia Plath.

When I got out of class, Mom was idling at the curb in front of the building.

"Did you just wait here the entire time?" I asked as she hurried around to help me haul my cart and tank into the car.

"No, I picked up the dry cleaning and went to the post office."

"And then?"

"I have a book to read," she said.

"And *I'm* the one who needs to get a life." I smiled, and she tried to smile back, but there was something flimsy in it.

After a second, I said, "Wanna go to a movie?"

"Sure. Anything you've been wanting to see?"

"Let's just do the thing where we go and see whatever starts next." She closed the door for me and walked around to the driver's side. We drove over to the Castleton theater and watched a 3-D movie about talking gerbils. It was kind of funny, actually.

When I got out of the movie, I had four text messages from Augustus.

> Tell me my copy is missing the last twenty pages or something.

> Hazel Grace, tell me I have not reached the end of this book.

> OH MY GOD DO THEY GET MARRIED OR NOT OH MY GOD WHAT IS THIS

> I guess Anna died and so it just ends? CRUEL. Call me when you can. Hope all's okay.

So when I got home I went out into the backyard and sat down on this rusting latticed patio chair and called him. It was a cloudy day, typical Indiana: the kind of weather that boxes you in. Our little backyard was dominated by my childhood swing set, which was looking pretty waterlogged and pathetic.

Augustus picked up on the third ring. "Hazel Grace," he said.

"So welcome to the sweet torture of reading *An Imperial*—" I stopped when I heard violent sobbing on the other end of the line. "Are you okay?" I asked.

"I'm grand," Augustus answered. "I am, however, with Isaac, who seems to be decompensating." More wailing. Like the death cries of some injured animal. Gus turned his attention to Isaac. "Dude. Dude. Does Support Group Hazel make this better or worse? Isaac. Focus. On. Me." After a minute, Gus said to me, "Can you meet us at my house in, say, twenty minutes?"

"Sure," I said, and hung up.

If you could drive in a straight line, it would only take like five minutes to get from my house to Augustus's house, but you can't drive in a straight line because Holliday Park is between us.

Even though it was a geographic inconvenience, I really liked Holliday Park. When I was a little kid, I would wade in the White River with my dad and there was always this great moment when he would throw me up in the air, just toss me away from him, and I would reach out my arms as I flew and he would reach out his arms, and then we would both see that our arms were not going to touch and no one was going to catch me, and it would kind of scare the shit out of both of us in the best possible way, and then I would legs-flailingly hit the water and then come up for air uninjured and the current would bring me back to him as I said *again, Daddy, again.*

I pulled into the driveway right next to an old black Toyota sedan I figured was Isaac's car. Carting the tank behind me, I walked up to the door. I knocked. Gus's dad answered.

"Just Hazel," he said. "Nice to see you."

"Augustus said I could come over?"

"Yeah, he and Isaac are in the basement." At which point there was a wail from below. "That would be Isaac," Gus's dad said, and shook his head slowly. "Cindy had to go for a drive. The sound . . ." he said, drifting off. "Anyway, I guess you're wanted downstairs. Can I carry your, uh, tank?" he asked.

"Nah, I'm good. Thanks, though, Mr. Waters."

"Mark," he said.

I was kind of scared to go down there. Listening to people howl in misery is not among my favorite pastimes. But I went.

"Hazel Grace," Augustus said as he heard my footsteps. "Isaac, Hazel from Support Group is coming downstairs. Hazel, a gentle reminder: Isaac is in the midst of a psychotic episode."

Augustus and Isaac were sitting on the floor in gaming

chairs shaped like lazy *Ls*, staring up at a gargantuan television. The screen was split between Isaac's point of view on the left, and Augustus's on the right. They were soldiers fighting in a bombed-out modern city. I recognized the place from *The Price of Dawn*. As I approached, I saw nothing unusual: just two guys sitting in the lightwash of a huge television pretending to kill people.

Only when I got parallel to them did I see Isaac's face. Tears streamed down his reddened cheeks in a continual flow, his face a taut mask of pain. He stared at the screen, not even glancing at me, and howled, all the while pounding away at his controller. "How are you, Hazel?" asked Augustus.

"I'm okay," I said. "Isaac?" No response. Not even the slightest hint that he was aware of my existence. Just the tears flowing down his face onto his black T-shirt.

Augustus glanced away from the screen ever so briefly. "You look nice," he said. I was wearing this just-past-the-knees dress I'd had forever. "Girls think they're only allowed to wear dresses on formal occasions, but I like a woman who says, you know, *I'm going over to see a boy who is having a nervous breakdown, a boy whose connection to the sense of sight itself is tenuous, and gosh dang it, I am going to wear a dress for him.*"

"And yet," I said, "Isaac won't so much as glance over at me. Too in love with Monica, I suppose," which resulted in a catastrophic sob.

"Bit of a touchy subject," Augustus explained. "Isaac,

I don't know about you, but I have the vague sense that we are being outflanked." And then back to me, "Isaac and Monica are no longer a going concern, but he doesn't want to talk about it. He just wants to cry and play Counterinsurgence 2: The Price of Dawn."

"Fair enough," I said.

"Isaac, I feel a growing concern about our position. If you agree, head over to that power station, and I'll cover you." Isaac ran toward a nondescript building while Augustus fired a machine gun wildly in a series of quick bursts, running behind him.

"Anyway," Augustus said to me, "it doesn't hurt to *talk* to him. If you have any sage words of feminine advice."

"I actually think his response is probably appropriate," I said as a burst of gunfire from Isaac killed an enemy who'd peeked his head out from behind the burned-out husk of a pickup truck.

Augustus nodded at the screen. "Pain demands to be felt," he said, which was a line from *An Imperial Affliction*. "You're sure there's no one behind us?" he asked Isaac. Moments later, tracer bullets started whizzing over their heads. "Oh, goddamn it, Isaac," Augustus said. "I don't mean to criticize you in your moment of great weakness, but you've allowed us to be outflanked, and now there's nothing between the terrorists and the school." Isaac's character took off running toward the fire, zigging and zagging down a narrow alleyway.

"You could go over the bridge and circle back," I said, a tactic I knew about thanks to *The Price of Dawn*.

Augustus sighed. "Sadly, the bridge is already under insurgent control due to questionable strategizing by my bereft cohort."

"Me?" Isaac said, his voice breathy. "Me?! You're the one who suggested we hole up in the freaking power station."

Gus turned away from the screen for a second and flashed his crooked smile at Isaac. "I knew you could talk, buddy," he said. "Now let's go save some fictional schoolchildren."

Together, they ran down the alleyway, firing and hiding at the right moments, until they reached this one-story, single-room schoolhouse. They crouched behind a wall across the street and picked off the enemy one by one.

"Why do they want to get into the school?" I asked.

"They want the kids as hostages," Augustus answered. His shoulders rounded over his controller, slamming buttons, his forearms taut, veins visible. Isaac leaned toward the screen, the controller dancing in his thin-fingered hands. "Get it get it get it," Augustus said. The waves of terrorists continued, and they mowed down every one, their shooting astonishingly precise, as it had to be, lest they fire into the school.

"Grenade! Grenade!" Augustus shouted as something

arced across the screen, bounced in the doorway of the school, and then rolled against the door.

Isaac dropped his controller in disappointment. “If the bastards can’t take hostages, they just kill them and claim we did it.”

“Cover me!” Augustus said as he jumped out from behind the wall and raced toward the school. Isaac fumbled for his controller and then started firing while the bullets rained down on Augustus, who was shot once and then twice but still ran, Augustus shouting, *“YOU CAN’T KILL MAX MAYHEM!”* and with a final flurry of button combinations, he dove onto the grenade, which detonated beneath him. His dismembered body exploded like a geyser and the screen went red. A throaty voice said, “MISSION FAILURE,” but Augustus seemed to think otherwise as he smiled at his remnants on the screen. He reached into his pocket, pulled out a cigarette, and shoved it between his teeth. “Saved the kids,” he said.

“Temporarily,” I pointed out.

“All salvation is temporary,” Augustus shot back. “I bought them a minute. Maybe that’s the minute that buys them an hour, which is the hour that buys them a year. No one’s gonna buy them forever, Hazel Grace, but my life bought them a minute. And that’s not nothing.”

“Whoa, okay,” I said. “We’re just talking about pixels.”

He shrugged, as if he believed the game might be really

real. Isaac was wailing again. Augustus snapped his head back to him. "Another go at the mission, corporal?"

Isaac shook his head no. He leaned over Augustus to look at me and through tightly strung vocal cords said, "She didn't want to do it after."

"She didn't want to dump a blind guy," I said. He nodded, the tears not like tears so much as a quiet metronome—steady, endless.

"She said she couldn't handle it," he told me. "I'm about to lose my eyesight and *she* can't handle it."

I was thinking about the word *handle*, and all the unholdable things that get handled. "I'm sorry," I said.

He wiped his sopping face with a sleeve. Behind his glasses, Isaac's eyes seemed so big that everything else on his face kind of disappeared and it was just these disembodied floating eyes staring at me—one real, one glass. "It's unacceptable," he told me. "It's totally unacceptable."

"Well, to be fair," I said, "I mean, she probably *can't* handle it. Neither can you, but she doesn't *have* to handle it. And you do."

"I kept saying 'always' to her today, 'always always always,' and she just kept talking over me and not saying it back. It was like I was already gone, you know? 'Always' was a promise! How can you just break the promise?"

"Sometimes people don't understand the promises they're making when they make them," I said.

Isaac shot me a look. "Right, of course. But you keep the promise anyway. That's what love *is*. Love is keeping the promise anyway. Don't you believe in true love?"

I didn't answer. I didn't have an answer. But I thought that if true love *did* exist, that was a pretty good definition of it.

"Well, I believe in true love," Isaac said. "And I love her. And she promised. She *promised me always*." He stood and took a step toward me. I pushed myself up, thinking he wanted a hug or something, but then he just spun around, like he couldn't remember why he'd stood up in the first place, and then Augustus and I both saw this rage settle into his face.

"Isaac," Gus said.

"What?"

"You look a little . . . Pardon the double entendre, my friend, but there's something a little worrisome in your eyes."

Suddenly Isaac started kicking the crap out of his gaming chair, which somersaulted back toward Gus's bed. "Here we go," said Augustus. Isaac chased after the chair and kicked it again. "Yes," Augustus said. "Get it. Kick the shit out of that chair!" Isaac kicked the chair again, until it bounced against Gus's bed, and then he grabbed one of the pillows and started slamming it against the wall between the bed and the trophy shelf above.

Augustus looked over at me, cigarette still in his mouth, and half smiled. "I can't stop thinking about that book."

"I know, right?"

"He never said what happens to the other characters?"

"No," I told him. Isaac was still throttling the wall with the pillow. "He moved to Amsterdam, which makes me think maybe he is writing a sequel featuring the Dutch Tulip Man, but he hasn't published anything. He's never interviewed. He doesn't seem to be online. I've written him a bunch of letters asking what happens to everyone, but he never responds. So . . . yeah." I stopped talking because Augustus didn't appear to be listening. Instead, he was squinting at Isaac.

"Hold on," he mumbled to me. He walked over to Isaac and grabbed him by the shoulders. "Dude, pillows don't break. Try something that breaks."

Isaac reached for a basketball trophy from the shelf above the bed and then held it over his head as if waiting for permission. "Yes," Augustus said. "Yes!" The trophy smashed against the floor, the plastic basketball player's arm splintering off, still grasping its ball. Isaac stomped on the trophy. "Yes!" Augustus said. "Get it!"

And then back to me, "I've been looking for a way to tell my father that I actually sort of hate basketball, and I think we've found it." The trophies came down one after the other, and Isaac stomped on them and screamed while Augustus and I stood a few feet away, bearing witness to the madness. The poor, mangled bodies of plastic basketballers littered the carpeted ground: here, a ball palmed by a disembodied hand; there, two torsoless legs caught midjump. Isaac kept attacking the trophies, jumping on them with both feet, screaming, breathless, sweaty, until finally he collapsed on top of the jagged trophic remnants.

Augustus stepped toward him and looked down. "Feel better?" he asked.

"No," Isaac mumbled, his chest heaving.

"That's the thing about pain," Augustus said, and then glanced back at me. "It demands to be felt."

CHAPTER FIVE

I did not speak to Augustus again for about a week. I had called him on the Night of the Broken Trophies, so per tradition it was his turn to call. But he didn't. Now, it wasn't as if I held my phone in my sweaty hand all day, staring at it while wearing my Special Yellow Dress, patiently waiting for my gentleman caller to live up to his sobriquet. I went about my life: I met Kaitlyn and her (cute but frankly not Augustinian) boyfriend for coffee one afternoon; I ingested my recommended daily allowance of Phalanxifor; I attended classes three mornings that week at MCC; and every night, I sat down to dinner with my mom and dad.

Sunday night, we had pizza with green peppers and broccoli. We were seated around our little circular table in the kitchen when my phone started singing, but I wasn't allowed to check it because we have a strict no-phones-during-dinner rule.

So I ate a little while Mom and Dad talked about this earthquake that had just happened in Papua New Guinea. They met in the Peace Corps in Papua New Guinea, and so whenever anything happened there, even something terrible, it was like all of a sudden they were not large sedentary creatures, but the young and idealistic and self-sufficient and rugged people they had once been, and their rapture was such that they didn't even glance over at me as I ate faster than I'd ever eaten, transmitting items from my plate into my mouth with a speed and ferocity that left me quite out of breath, which of course made me worry that my lungs were again swimming in a rising pool of fluid. I banished the thought as best I could. I had a PET scan scheduled in a couple weeks. If something was wrong, I'd find out soon enough. Nothing to be gained by worrying between now and then.

And yet still I worried. I liked being a person. I wanted to keep at it. Worry is yet another side effect of dying.

Finally I finished and said, "Can I be excused?" and they hardly even paused from their conversation about the strengths and weaknesses of Guinean infrastructure. I grabbed my phone from my purse on the kitchen counter and checked my recent calls. *Augustus Waters.*

I went out the back door into the twilight. I could see

the swing set, and I thought about walking out there and swinging while I talked to him, but it seemed pretty far away given that *eating* tired me.

Instead, I lay down in the grass on the patio's edge, looked up at Orion, the only constellation I could recognize, and called him.

"Hazel Grace," he said.

"Hi," I said. "How are you?"

"Grand," he said. "I have been wanting to call you on a nearly minutely basis, but I have been waiting until I could form a coherent thought in re *An Imperial Affliction*." (He said "in re." He really did. That boy.)

"And?" I said.

"I think it's, like. Reading it, I just kept feeling like, like."

"Like?" I asked, teasing him.

"Like it was a gift?" he said askingly. "Like you'd given me something important."

"Oh," I said quietly.

"That's cheesy," he said. "I'm sorry."

"No," I said. "No. Don't apologize."

"But it doesn't end."

"Yeah," I said.

"Torture. I totally *get it*, like, I get that she died or whatever."

"Right, I assume so," I said.

"And okay, fair enough, but there is this unwritten contract between author and reader and I think not ending your book kind of violates that contract."

"I don't know," I said, feeling defensive of Peter Van Houten. "That's part of what I like about the book in some ways. It portrays death truthfully. You die in the middle of your life, in the middle of a sentence. But I do—God, I do really want to know what happens to everyone else. That's what I asked him in my letters. But he, yeah, he never answers."

"Right. You said he is a recluse?"

"Correct."

"Impossible to track down."

"Correct."

"Utterly unreachable," Augustus said.

"Unfortunately so," I said.

"'Dear Mr. Waters,'" he answered. "'I am writing to thank you for your electronic correspondence, received via Ms. Vliegenthart this sixth of April, from the United States of America, insofar as geography can be said to exist in our triumphantly digitized contemporaneity.'"

"Augustus, what the hell?"

"He has an assistant," Augustus said. "Lidewij Vliegenthart. I found her. I emailed her. She gave him the email. He responded via her email account."

"Okay, okay. Keep reading."

"'My response is being written with ink and paper in the glorious tradition of our ancestors and then transcribed by Ms. Vliegenthart into a series of 1s and 0s to travel through the insipid web which has lately ensnared our species, so I apologize for any errors or omissions that may result.

"'Given the entertainment bacchanalia at the disposal of young men and women of your generation, I am grateful to anyone anywhere who sets aside the hours necessary to read my little book. But I am particularly indebted to you, sir, both for your kind words about *An Imperial Affliction* and for taking the time to tell me that the book, and here I quote you directly, "meant a great deal" to you.

"'This comment, however, leads me to wonder: What do you mean by *meant*? Given the final futility of our struggle, is the fleeting jolt of meaning that art gives us valuable? Or is the only value in passing the time as comfortably as possible? What should a story seek to emulate, Augustus? A ringing alarm? A call to arms? A morphine drip? Of course, like all interrogation of the universe, this line of inquiry inevitably reduces us to asking what it means to be human and whether—to borrow a phrase from the angst-encumbered sixteen-year-olds you no doubt revile—*there is a point to it all.*

"'I fear there is not, my friend, and that you would receive scant encouragement from further encounters with my writing. But to answer your question: No, I have not written anything else, nor will I. I do not feel that continuing to share my thoughts with readers would benefit either them or me. Thank you again for your generous email.

"'Yours most sincerely, Peter Van Houten, via Lidewij Vliegenthart.'"

"Wow," I said. "Are you making this up?"

"Hazel Grace, could I, with my meager intellectual capacities, make up a letter from Peter Van Houten featuring phrases like 'our triumphantly digitized contemporaneity'?"

"You could not," I allowed. "Can I, can I have the email address?"

"Of course," Augustus said, like it was not the best gift ever.

I spent the next two hours writing an email to Peter Van Houten. It seemed to get worse each time I rewrote it, but I couldn't stop myself.

Dear Mr. Peter Van Houten
(c/o Lidewij Vliegenthart),

> My name is Hazel Grace Lancaster. My friend Augustus Waters, who read *An Imperial Affliction* at my recommendation, just received an email from you at this address. I hope you will not mind that Augustus shared that email with me.
>
> Mr. Van Houten, I understand from your email to Augustus that you are not planning to publish

any more books. In a way, I am disappointed, but I'm also relieved: I never have to worry whether your next book will live up to the magnificent perfection of the original. As a three-year survivor of Stage IV cancer, I can tell you that you got everything right in *An Imperial Affliction*. Or at least you got *me* right. Your book has a way of telling me what I'm feeling before I even feel it, and I've reread it dozens of times.

I wonder, though, if you would mind answering a couple questions I have about what happens after the end of the novel. I understand the book ends because Anna dies or becomes too ill to continue writing it, but I would really like to know what happens to Anna's mom—whether she married the Dutch Tulip Man, whether she ever has another child, and whether she stays at 917 W. Temple, etc. Also, is the Dutch Tulip Man a fraud or does he really love them? What happens to Anna's friends—particularly Claire and Jake? Do they stay together? And lastly—I realize that this is the kind of deep and thoughtful question you always hoped your readers would ask—what becomes of Sisyphus the Hamster? These questions have haunted me for years—and I don't know how long I have left to get answers to them.

I know these are not important literary questions and that your book is full of important literary questions, but I would just really like to know.

And of course, if you ever do decide to write anything else, even if you don't want to publish it, I'd love to read it. Frankly, I'd read your grocery lists.

Yours with great admiration,
Hazel Grace Lancaster
(age 16)

After I sent it, I called Augustus back, and we stayed up late talking about *An Imperial Affliction*, and I read him the Emily Dickinson poem that Van Houten had used for the title, and he said I had a good voice for reading and didn't pause too long for the line breaks, and then he told me that the sixth *Price of Dawn* book, *The Blood Approves*, begins with a quote from a poem. It took him a minute to find the book, but finally he read the quote to me. "'Say your life broke down. The last good kiss / You had was years ago.'"

"Not bad," I said. "Bit pretentious. I believe Max Mayhem would refer to that as 'sissy shit.'"

"Yes, with his teeth gritted, no doubt. God, Mayhem grits his teeth a lot in these books. He's definitely going to get TMJ, if he survives all this combat." And then after a second, Gus asked, "When was the last good kiss you had?"

I thought about it. My kissing—all prediagnosis—had been uncomfortable and slobbery, and on some level it always felt like kids playing at being grown. But of course it had been a while. "Years ago," I said finally. "You?"

"I had a few good kisses with my ex-girlfriend, Caroline Mathers."

"Years ago?"

"The last one was just less than a year ago."

"What happened?"

"During the kiss?"

"No, with you and Caroline."

"Oh," he said. And then after a second, "Caroline is no longer suffering from personhood."

"Oh," I said.

"Yeah," he said.

"I'm sorry," I said. I'd known plenty of dead people, of course. But I'd never dated one. I couldn't even imagine it, really.

"Not your fault, Hazel Grace. We're all just side effects, right?"

"'Barnacles on the container ship of consciousness,'" I said, quoting *AIA*.

"Okay," he said. "I gotta go to sleep. It's almost one."

"Okay," I said.

"Okay," he said.

I giggled and said, "Okay." And then the line was quiet but not dead. I almost felt like he was there in my room with me, but in a way it was better, like I was not in my room and he was not in his, but instead we were together in some invisible and tenuous third space that could only be visited on the phone.

"Okay," he said after forever. "Maybe *okay* will be our *always*."

"Okay," I said.

It was Augustus who finally hung up.

Peter Van Houten replied to Augustus's email four hours after he sent it, but two days later, Van Houten still hadn't replied to me. Augustus assured me it was because my email was better and required a more thoughtful response, that Van Houten was busy writing answers to my questions, and that brilliant prose took time. But still I worried.

On Wednesday during American Poetry for Dummies 101, I got a text from Augustus:

Isaac out of surgery. It went well. He's officially NEC.

NEC meant "no evidence of cancer." A second text came a few seconds later.

I mean, he's blind. So that's unfortunate.

That afternoon, Mom consented to loan me the car so I could drive down to Memorial to check in on Isaac.

I found my way to his room on the fifth floor, knocking even though the door was open, and a woman's voice said, "Come in." It was a nurse who was doing something to the bandages on Isaac's eyes. "Hey, Isaac," I said.

And he said, "Mon?"

"Oh, no. Sorry. No, it's, um, Hazel. Um, Support Group Hazel? Night-of-the-broken-trophies Hazel?"

"Oh," he said. "Yeah, people keep saying my other senses will improve to compensate, but CLEARLY NOT YET. Hi, Support Group Hazel. Come over here so I can examine your face with my hands and see deeper into your soul than a sighted person ever could."

"He's kidding," the nurse said.

"Yes," I said. "I realize."

I took a few steps toward the bed. I pulled a chair up and sat down, took his hand. "Hey," I said.

"Hey," he said back. Then nothing for a while.

"How you feeling?" I asked.

"Okay," he said. "I don't know."

"You don't know what?" I asked. I looked at his hand because I didn't want to look at his face blindfolded by bandages. Isaac bit his nails, and I could see some blood on the corners of a couple of his cuticles.

"She hasn't even visited," he said. "I mean, we were together fourteen months. Fourteen months is a long time. God, that hurts." Isaac let go of my hand to fumble for his pain pump, which you hit to give yourself a wave of narcotics.

The nurse, having finished the bandage change, stepped back. "It's only been a day, Isaac," she said, vaguely condescending. "You've gotta give yourself time to heal.

And fourteen months *isn't* that long, not in the scheme of things. You're just getting started, buddy. You'll see."

The nurse left. "Is she gone?"

I nodded, then realized he couldn't see me nod. "Yeah," I said.

"I'll *see*? Really? Did she seriously say that?"

"Qualities of a Good Nurse: Go," I said.

"1. Doesn't pun on your disability," Isaac said.

"2. Gets blood on the first try," I said.

"Seriously, that is huge. I mean is this my freaking arm or a dartboard? 3. No condescending voice."

"How are you doing, sweetie?" I asked, cloying. "I'm going to stick you with a needle now. There might be a little ouchie."

"Is my wittle fuffywump sickywicky?" he answered. And then after a second, "Most of them are good, actually. I just want the hell out of this place."

"This place as in the hospital?"

"That, too," he said. His mouth tightened. I could see the pain. "Honestly, I think a hell of a lot more about Monica than my eye. Is that crazy? That's crazy."

"It's a little crazy," I allowed.

"But I believe in true love, you know? I don't believe that everybody gets to keep their eyes or not get sick or whatever, but everybody *should* have true love, and it should last at least as long as your life does."

"Yeah," I said.

"I just wish the whole thing hadn't happened sometimes. The whole cancer thing." His speech was slowing down. The medicine working.

"I'm sorry," I said.

"Gus was here earlier. He was here when I woke up. Took off school. He . . ." His head turned to the side a little. "It's better," he said quietly.

"The pain?" I asked. He nodded a little.

"Good," I said. And then, like the bitch I am: "You were saying something about Gus?" But he was gone.

I went downstairs to the tiny windowless gift shop and asked the decrepit volunteer sitting on a stool behind a cash register what kind of flowers smell the strongest.

"They all smell the same. They get sprayed with Super Scent," she said.

"Really?"

"Yeah, they just squirt 'em with it."

I opened the cooler to her left and sniffed at a dozen roses, and then leaned over some carnations. Same smell, and lots of it. The carnations were cheaper, so I grabbed a dozen yellow ones. They cost fourteen dollars. I went back into the room; his mom was there, holding his hand. She was young and really pretty.

"Are you a friend?" she asked, which struck me as one of those unintentionally broad and unanswerable questions.

"Um, yeah," I said. "I'm from Support Group. These are for him."

She took them and placed them in her lap. "Do you know Monica?" she asked.

I shook my head no.

"Well, he's sleeping," she said.

"Yeah. I talked to him a little before, when they were doing the bandages or whatever."

"I hated leaving him for that but I had to pick up Graham at school," she said.

"He did okay," I told her. She nodded. "I should let him sleep." She nodded again. I left.

The next morning I woke up early and checked my email first thing.

lidewij.vliegenthart@gmail.com had finally replied.

Dear Ms. Lancaster,

> I fear your faith has been misplaced—but then, faith usually is. I cannot answer your questions, at least not in writing, because to write out such answers would constitute a sequel to *An Imperial Affliction*, which you might publish or otherwise share on the network that has replaced the brains of your generation. There is the telephone, but then you might record the

conversation. Not that I don't trust you, of course, but I don't trust you. Alas, dear Hazel, I could never answer such questions except in person, and you are there, while I am here.

That noted, I must confess that the unexpected receipt of your correspondence via Ms. Vliegenthart has delighted me: What a wondrous thing to know that I made something useful to you—even if that book seems so distant from me that I feel it was written by a different man altogether. (The author of that novel was so thin, so frail, so comparatively optimistic!)

Should you find yourself in Amsterdam, however, please do pay a visit at your leisure. I am usually home. I would even allow you a peek at my grocery lists.

Yours most sincerely,
Peter Van Houten
c/o Lidewij Vliegenthart

"WHAT?!" I shouted aloud. "WHAT IS THIS LIFE?"

Mom ran in. "What's wrong?"

"Nothing," I assured her.

Still nervous, Mom knelt down to check on Philip to ensure he was condensing oxygen appropriately. I imagined sitting at a sun-drenched café with Peter Van Houten as he leaned across the table on his elbows, speaking in a soft voice so no one else would hear the truth of what happened to the characters I'd spent years thinking about. He'd said he couldn't tell me *except in person*, and then *invited me to Amsterdam*. I explained this to Mom, and then said, "I have to go."

"Hazel, I love you, and you know I'd do anything for you, but we don't—we don't have the money for international travel, and the expense of getting equipment over there—love, it's just not—"

"Yeah," I said, cutting her off. I realized I'd been silly even to consider it. "Don't worry about it." But she looked worried.

"It's really important to you, yeah?" she asked, sitting down, a hand on my calf.

"It would be pretty amazing," I said, "to be the only person who knows what happens besides him."

"That would be amazing," she said. "I'll talk to your father."

"No, don't," I said. "Just, seriously, don't spend any money on it please. I'll think of something."

It occurred to me that the reason my parents had no money was me. I'd sapped the family savings with Phalanxifor copays, and Mom couldn't work because she had taken on the full-time profession of Hovering Over Me. I didn't want to put them even further into debt.

I told Mom I wanted to call Augustus to get her out of the room, because I couldn't handle her I-can't-make-my-daughter's-dreams-come-true sad face.

Augustus Waters–style, I read him the letter in lieu of saying hello.

"Wow," he said.

"I know, right?" I said. "How am I going to get to Amsterdam?"

"Do you have a Wish?" he asked, referring to this organization, The Genie Foundation, which is in the business of granting sick kids one wish.

"No," I said. "I used my Wish pre-Miracle."

"What'd you do?"

I sighed loudly. "I was thirteen," I said.

"Not Disney," he said.

I said nothing.

"You did not go to Disney World."

I said nothing.

"Hazel GRACE!" he shouted. "You *did not* use your one dying Wish to go to Disney World with your parents."

"Also Epcot Center," I mumbled.

"Oh, my God," Augustus said. "I can't believe I have a crush on a girl with such cliché wishes."

"I was *thirteen*," I said again, although of course I was only thinking *crush crush crush crush crush*. I was flattered but changed the subject immediately. "Shouldn't you be in school or something?"

"I'm playing hooky to hang out with Isaac, but he's sleeping, so I'm in the atrium doing geometry."

"How's he doing?" I asked.

"I can't tell if he's just not ready to confront the seriousness of his disability or if he really does care more about getting dumped by Monica, but he won't talk about anything else."

"Yeah," I said. "How long's he gonna be in the hospital?"

"Few days. Then he goes to this rehab or something for a while, but he gets to sleep at home, I think."

"Sucks," I said.

"I see his mom. I gotta go."

"Okay," I said.

"Okay," he answered. I could hear his crooked smile.

On Saturday, my parents and I went down to the farmers' market in Broad Ripple. It was sunny, a rarity for Indiana in April, and everyone at the farmers' market was wearing short sleeves even though the temperature didn't quite justify it. We Hoosiers are excessively optimistic about summer. Mom and I sat next to each other on a bench across from a goat-soap maker, a man in overalls who had to explain to every single person who walked by that yes, they were his goats, and no, goat soap does not smell like goats.

My phone rang. "Who is it?" Mom asked before I could even check.

"I don't know," I said. It was Gus, though.

"Are you currently at your house?" he asked.

"Um, no," I said.

"That was a trick question. I knew the answer, because I am currently at your house."

"Oh. Um. Well, we are on our way, I guess?"

"Awesome. See you soon."

Augustus Waters was sitting on the front step as we pulled into the driveway. He was holding a bouquet of bright orange tulips just beginning to bloom, and wearing an Indiana Pacers jersey under his fleece, a wardrobe choice that seemed utterly out of character, although it did look quite good on him. He pushed himself up off the stoop, handed me the tulips, and asked, "Wanna go on a picnic?" I nodded, taking the flowers.

My dad walked up behind me and shook Gus's hand.

"Is that a Rik Smits jersey?" my dad asked.

"Indeed it is."

"God, I loved that guy," Dad said, and immediately they were engrossed in a basketball conversation I could not (and did not want to) join, so I took my tulips inside.

"Do you want me to put those in a vase?" Mom asked as I walked in, a huge smile on her face.

"No, it's okay," I told her. If we'd put them in a vase in the living room, they would have been everyone's flowers. I wanted them to be my flowers.

I went to my room but didn't change. I brushed my

hair and teeth and put on some lip gloss and the smallest possible dab of perfume. I kept looking at the flowers. They were *aggressively* orange, almost too orange to be pretty. I didn't have a vase or anything, so I took my toothbrush out of my toothbrush holder and filled it halfway with water and left the flowers there in the bathroom.

When I reentered my room, I could hear people talking, so I sat on the edge of my bed for a while and listened through my hollow bedroom door:

Dad: "So you met Hazel at Support Group."

Augustus: "Yes, sir. This is a lovely house you've got. I like your artwork."

Mom: "Thank you, Augustus."

Dad: "You're a survivor yourself, then?"

Augustus: "I am. I didn't cut this fella off for the sheer unadulterated pleasure of it, although it is an excellent weight-loss strategy. Legs are heavy!"

Dad: "And how's your health now?"

Augustus: "NEC for fourteen months."

Mom: "That's wonderful. The treatment options these days—it really is remarkable."

Augustus: "I know. I'm lucky."

Dad: "You have to understand that Hazel is still sick, Augustus, and will be for the rest of her life. She'll want to keep up with you, but her lungs—"

At which point I emerged, silencing him.

"So where are you going?" asked Mom. Augustus stood

up and leaned over to her, whispering the answer, and then held a finger to his lips. "Shh," he told her. "It's a secret."

Mom smiled. "You've got your phone?" she asked me. I held it up as evidence, tilted my oxygen cart onto its front wheels, and started walking. Augustus hustled over, offering me his arm, which I took. My fingers wrapped around his biceps.

Unfortunately, he insisted upon driving, so the surprise could be a surprise. As we shuddered toward our destination, I said, "You nearly charmed the pants off my mom."

"Yeah, and your dad is a Smits fan, which helps. You think they liked me?"

"Sure they did. Who cares, though? They're just parents."

"They're *your* parents," he said, glancing over at me. "Plus, I like being liked. Is that crazy?"

"Well, you don't have to rush to hold doors open or smother me in compliments for me to like you." He slammed the brakes, and I flew forward hard enough that my breathing felt weird and tight. I thought of the PET scan. *Don't worry. Worry is useless.* I worried anyway.

We burned rubber, roaring away from a stop sign before turning left onto the misnomered Grandview (there's a view of a golf course, I guess, but nothing *grand*). The only thing I could think of in this direction was the cemetery. Augustus reached into the center console, flipped open a full pack of cigarettes, and removed one.

"Do you ever throw them away?" I asked him.

"One of the many benefits of not smoking is that packs of cigarettes last *forever*," he answered. "I've had this one for almost a year. A few of them are broken near the filters, but I think this pack could easily get me to my eighteenth birthday." He held the filter between his fingers, then put it in his mouth. "So, okay," he said. "Okay. Name some things that you never see in Indianapolis."

"Um. Skinny adults," I said.

He laughed. "Good. Keep going."

"Mmm, beaches. Family-owned restaurants. Topography."

"All excellent examples of things we lack. Also, culture."

"Yeah, we are a bit short on culture," I said, finally realizing where he was taking me. "Are we going to the museum?"

"In a manner of speaking."

"Oh, are we going to that park or whatever?"

Gus looked a bit deflated. "Yes, we are going to that park or whatever," he said. "You've figured it out, haven't you?"

"Um, figured what out?"

"Nothing."

There was this park behind the museum where a bunch of artists had made big sculptures. I'd heard about it but had never visited. We drove past the museum and parked right next to this basketball court filled with huge blue and red steel arcs that imagined the path of a bouncing ball.

We walked down what passes for a hill in Indianapolis to this clearing where kids were climbing all over this huge oversize skeleton sculpture. The bones were each about waist high, and the thighbone was longer than me. It looked like a child's drawing of a skeleton rising up out of the ground.

My shoulder hurt. I worried the cancer had spread from my lungs. I imagined the tumor metastasizing into my own bones, boring holes into my skeleton, a slithering eel of insidious intent. *"Funky Bones,"* Augustus said. "Created by Joep Van Lieshout."

"Sounds Dutch."

"He is," Gus said. "So is Rik Smits. So are tulips." Gus stopped in the middle of the clearing with the bones right in front of us and slipped his backpack off one shoulder, then the other. He unzipped it, producing an orange blanket, a pint of orange juice, and some sandwiches wrapped in plastic wrap with the crusts cut off.

"What's with all the orange?" I asked, still not wanting to let myself imagine that all this would lead to Amsterdam.

"National color of the Netherlands, of course. You remember William of Orange and everything?"

"He wasn't on the GED test." I smiled, trying to contain my excitement.

"Sandwich?" he asked.

"Let me guess," I said.

"Dutch cheese. And tomato. The tomatoes are from Mexico. Sorry."

"You're always such a *disappointment*, Augustus. Couldn't you have at least gotten orange tomatoes?"

He laughed, and we ate our sandwiches in silence, watching the kids play on the sculpture. I couldn't very well *ask* him about it, so I just sat there surrounded by Dutchness, feeling awkward and hopeful.

In the distance, soaked in the unblemished sunlight so rare and precious in our hometown, a gaggle of kids made a skeleton into a playground, jumping back and forth among the prosthetic bones.

"Two things I love about this sculpture," Augustus said. He was holding the unlit cigarette between his fingers, flicking at it as if to get rid of the ash. He placed it back in his mouth. "First, the bones are just far enough apart that if you're a kid, you *cannot resist the urge* to jump between them. Like, you just *have* to jump from rib cage to skull. Which means that, second, the sculpture essentially *forces children to play on bones*. The symbolic resonances are endless, Hazel Grace."

"You do love symbols," I said, hoping to steer the conversation back toward the many symbols of the Netherlands at our picnic.

"Right, about that. You are probably wondering why

you are eating a bad cheese sandwich and drinking orange juice and why I am wearing the jersey of a Dutchman who played a sport I have come to loathe."

"It has crossed my mind," I said.

"Hazel Grace, like so many children before you—and I say this with great affection—you spent your Wish hastily, with little care for the consequences. The Grim Reaper was staring you in the face and the fear of dying with your Wish still in your proverbial pocket, ungranted, led you to rush toward the first Wish you could think of, and you, like so many others, chose the cold and artificial pleasures of the theme park."

"I actually had a great time on that trip. I met Goofy and Minn—"

"I am in the midst of a soliloquy! I wrote this out and memorized it and if you interrupt me I will completely screw it up," Augustus interrupted. "Please to be eating your sandwich and listening." (The sandwich was inedibly dry, but I smiled and took a bite anyway.) "Okay, where was I?"

"The artificial pleasures."

He returned the cigarette to its pack. "Right, the cold and artificial pleasures of the theme park. But let me submit that the real heroes of the Wish Factory are the young men and women who wait like Vladimir and Estragon wait for Godot and good Christian girls wait for marriage. These young heroes wait stoically and without complaint for their one true Wish to come along. Sure, it may never come along, but at least they can rest easily in the grave knowing that they've done their little part to preserve the integrity of the Wish as an idea.

"But then again, maybe it *will* come along: Maybe you'll realize that your one true Wish is to visit the brilliant Peter Van Houten in his Amsterdamian exile, and you will be glad indeed to have saved your Wish."

Augustus stopped speaking long enough that I figured the soliloquy was over. "But I didn't save my Wish," I said.

"Ah," he said. And then, after what felt like a practiced pause, he added, "But I saved mine."

"Really?" I was surprised that Augustus was Wish-eligible, what with being still in school and a year into remission. You had to be pretty sick for the Genies to hook you up with a Wish.

"I got it in exchange for the leg," he explained. There was all this light on his face; he had to squint to look at me, which made his nose crinkle adorably. "Now, I'm not going to *give* you my Wish or anything. But I also have an interest in meeting Peter Van Houten, and it wouldn't make sense to meet him without the girl who introduced me to his book."

"It definitely wouldn't," I said.

"So I talked to the Genies, and they are in total agreement. They said Amsterdam is lovely in the beginning of May. They proposed leaving May third and returning May seventh."

"Augustus, really?"

He reached over and touched my cheek and for a moment I thought he might kiss me. My body tensed, and I think he saw it, because he pulled his hand away.

"Augustus," I said. "Really. You don't have to do this."

"Sure I do," he said. "I found my Wish."

"God, you're the best," I told him.

"I bet you say that to all the boys who finance your international travel," he answered.

CHAPTER SIX

Mom was folding my laundry while watching this TV show called *The View* when I got home. I told her that the tulips and the Dutch artist and everything were all because Augustus was using his Wish to take me to Amsterdam. "That's too much," she said, shaking her head. "We can't accept that from a virtual stranger."

"He's not a stranger. He's easily my second best friend."

"Behind Kaitlyn?"

"Behind you," I said. It was true, but I'd mostly said it because I wanted to go to Amsterdam.

"I'll ask Dr. Maria," she said after a moment.

...

Dr. Maria said I couldn't go to Amsterdam without an adult intimately familiar with my case, which more or less meant either Mom or Dr. Maria herself. (My dad understood my cancer the way I did: in the vague and incomplete way people understand electrical circuits and ocean tides. But my mom knew more about differentiated thyroid carcinoma in adolescents than most oncologists.)

"So you'll come," I said. "The Genies will pay for it. The Genies are loaded."

"But your father," she said. "He would miss us. It wouldn't be fair to him, and he can't get time off work."

"Are you kidding? You don't think Dad would enjoy a few days of watching TV shows that are not about aspiring models and ordering pizza every night, using paper towels as plates so he doesn't have to do the dishes?"

Mom laughed. Finally, she started to get excited, typing tasks into her phone: She'd have to call Gus's parents and talk to the Genies about my medical needs and do they have a hotel yet and what are the best guidebooks and we should do our research if we only have three days, and so on. I kind of had a headache, so I downed a couple Advil and decided to take a nap.

But I ended up just lying in bed and replaying the whole picnic with Augustus. I couldn't stop thinking about the little moment when I'd tensed up as he touched me. The gentle familiarity felt wrong, somehow. I thought maybe it was how orchestrated the whole thing had been: Augustus was amazing, but he'd overdone everything at the picnic, right down to the sandwiches that were metaphorically resonant but tasted terrible and the memorized soliloquy that prevented conversation. It all felt Romantic, but not romantic.

But the truth is that I had never wanted him to kiss me, not in the way you are supposed to want these things. I mean, he was gorgeous. I was attracted to him. I thought about him *in that way*, to borrow a phrase from the middle school vernacular. But the actual touch, the realized touch . . . it was all wrong.

Then I found myself worrying I would *have* to make out with him to get to Amsterdam, which is not the kind of thing you want to be thinking, because (a) It shouldn't've even been a *question* whether I wanted to kiss him, and (b) Kissing someone so that you can get a free trip is perilously close to full-on hooking, and I have to confess that while I did not fancy myself a particularly good person, I never thought my first real sexual action would be prostitutional.

But then again, he hadn't tried to kiss me; he'd only touched my face, which is not even *sexual*. It was not a move designed to elicit arousal, but it was certainly a designed move, because Augustus Waters was no improviser. So what had he been trying to convey? And why hadn't I wanted to accept it?

At some point, I realized I was Kaitlyning the encounter, so I decided to text Kaitlyn and ask for some advice. She called immediately.

"I have a boy problem," I said.

"DELICIOUS," Kaitlyn responded. I told her all about it, complete with the awkward face touching, leaving out only Amsterdam and Augustus's name. "You're sure he's hot?" she asked when I was finished.

"Pretty sure," I said.

"Athletic?"

"Yeah, he used to play basketball for North Central."

"Wow. How'd you meet him?"

"This hideous Support Group."

"Huh," Kaitlyn said. "Out of curiosity, how many legs does this guy have?"

"Like, 1.4," I said, smiling. Basketball players were famous in Indiana, and although Kaitlyn didn't go to North Central, her social connectivity was endless.

"Augustus Waters," she said.

"Um, maybe?"

"Oh, my God. I've seen him at parties. The things I would do to that boy. I mean, not now that I know you're interested in him. But, oh, sweet holy Lord, I would ride that one-legged pony all the way around the corral."

"Kaitlyn," I said.

"Sorry. Do you think you'd have to be on top?"

"Kaitlyn," I said.

"What were we talking about. Right, you and Augustus Waters. Maybe . . . are you gay?"

"I don't think so? I mean, I definitely like him."

"Does he have ugly hands? Sometimes beautiful people have ugly hands."

"No, he has kind of amazing hands."

"Hmm," she said.

"Hmm," I said.

After a second, Kaitlyn said, "Remember Derek? He broke up with me last week because he'd decided there was something fundamentally incompatible about us deep down and that we'd only get hurt more if we played it out. He called it *preemptive dumping*. So maybe you have this premonition that there is something fundamentally incompatible and you're preempting the preemption."

"Hmm," I said.

"I'm just thinking out loud here."

"Sorry about Derek."

"Oh, I got over it, darling. It took me a sleeve of Girl Scout Thin Mints and forty minutes to get over that boy."

I laughed. "Well, thanks, Kaitlyn."

"In the event you do hook up with him, I expect lascivious details."

"But of course," I said, and then Kaitlyn made a kissy sound into the phone and I said, "Bye," and she hung up.

...

I realized while listening to Kaitlyn that I didn't have a premonition of hurting him. I had a postmonition.

I pulled out my laptop and looked up Caroline Mathers. The physical similarities were striking: same steroidally round face, same nose, same approximate overall body shape. But her eyes were dark brown (mine are green) and her complexion was much darker—Italian or something.

Thousands of people—literally thousands—had left condolence messages for her. It was an endless scroll of people who missed her, so many that it took me an hour of clicking to get past the *I'm sorry you're dead* wall posts to the *I'm praying for you* wall posts. She'd died a year ago of brain cancer. I was able to click through to some of her pictures. Augustus was in a bunch of the earlier ones: pointing with a thumbs-up to the jagged scar across her bald skull; arm in arm at Memorial Hospital's playground, with their backs facing the camera; kissing while Caroline held the camera out, so you could only see their noses and closed eyes.

The most recent pictures were all of her before, when she was healthy, uploaded postmortem by friends: a beautiful girl, wide-hipped and curvy, with long, straight deadblack hair falling over her face. My healthy self looked very little like her healthy self. But our cancer selves might've been sisters. No wonder he'd stared at me the first time he saw me.

I kept clicking back to this one wall post, written two months ago, nine months after she died, by one of her friends. *We all miss you so much. It just never ends. It feels like we were all wounded in your battle, Caroline. I miss you. I love you.*

After a while, Mom and Dad announced it was time for dinner. I shut down the computer and got up, but I couldn't get the wall post out of my mind, and for some reason it made me nervous and unhungry.

I kept thinking about my shoulder, which hurt, and also I still had the headache, but maybe only because I'd been thinking about a girl who'd died of brain cancer. I kept telling myself to compartmentalize, to be here now at the circular table (arguably too large in diameter for three people and definitely too large for two) with this soggy broccoli and a black-bean burger that all the ketchup in the world could not adequately moisten. I told myself that imagining a met in my brain or my shoulder would not affect the invisible reality going on inside of me, and that therefore all such thoughts were wasted moments in a life composed of a definitionally finite set of such moments. I even tried to tell myself to live my best life today.

For the longest time I couldn't figure out why something a stranger had written on the Internet to a different (and deceased) stranger was bothering me so much and making me worry that there was something inside my brain—which really did hurt, although I knew from years of experience that pain is a blunt and nonspecific diagnostic instrument.

Because there had not been an earthquake in Papua New Guinea that day, my parents were all hyperfocused on me, and so I could not hide this flash flood of anxiety.

"Is everything all right?" asked Mom as I ate.

"Uh-huh," I said. I took a bite of burger. Swallowed. Tried to say something that a normal person whose brain was not drowning in panic would say. "Is there broccoli in the burgers?"

"A little," Dad said. "Pretty exciting that you might go to Amsterdam."

"Yeah," I said. I tried not to think about the word *wounded*, which of course is a way of thinking about it.

"Hazel," Mom said. "Where are you right now?"

"Just thinking, I guess," I said.

"Twitterpated," my dad said, smiling.

"I am not a bunny, and I am not in love with Gus Waters or anyone," I answered, way too defensively. *Wounded*. Like Caroline Mathers had been a bomb and when she blew up everyone around her was left with embedded shrapnel.

Dad asked me if I was working on anything for school. "I've got some very advanced Algebra homework," I told him. "So advanced that I couldn't possibly explain it to a layperson."

"And how's your friend Isaac?"

"Blind," I said.

"You're being very teenagery today," Mom said. She seemed annoyed about it.

"Isn't this what you wanted, Mom? For me to be teenagery?"

"Well, not necessarily *this* kinda teenagery, but of course your father and I are excited to see you become a young woman, making friends, going on dates."

"I'm not going on dates," I said. "I don't want to go on dates with anyone. It's a terrible idea and a huge waste of time and–"

"Honey," my mom said. "What's wrong?"

"I'm like. Like. I'm like a *grenade*, Mom. I'm a grenade and at some point I'm going to blow up and I would like to minimize the casualties, okay?"

My dad tilted his head a little to the side, like a scolded puppy.

"I'm a grenade," I said again. "I just want to stay away from people and read books and think and be with you guys because there's nothing I can do about hurting you; you're too invested, so just please let me do that, okay? I'm not depressed. I don't need to get out more. And I can't be a regular teenager, because I'm a grenade."

"Hazel," Dad said, and then choked up. He cried a lot, my dad.

"I'm going to go to my room and read for a while, okay?

I'm fine. I really am fine; I just want to go read for a while."

I started out trying to read this novel I'd been assigned, but we lived in a tragically thin-walled home, so I could hear much of the whispered conversation that ensued. My dad saying, "It kills me," and my mom saying, "That's exactly what she *doesn't* need to hear," and my dad saying, "I'm sorry but—" and my mom saying, "Are you not grateful?" And him saying, "God, of course I'm grateful." I kept trying to get into this story but I couldn't stop hearing them.

So I turned on my computer to listen to some music, and with Augustus's favorite band, The Hectic Glow, as my sound track, I went back to Caroline Mathers's tribute pages, reading about how heroic her fight was, and how much she was missed, and how she was in a better place, and how she would live *forever* in their memories, and how everyone who knew her—everyone—was laid low by her leaving.

Maybe I was supposed to hate Caroline Mathers or something because she'd been with Augustus, but I didn't. I couldn't see her very clearly amid all the tributes, but there didn't seem to be much to hate—she seemed to be mostly a professional sick person, like me, which made me worry that when I died they'd have nothing to say about me except that I fought heroically, as if the only thing I'd ever done was Have Cancer.

Anyway, eventually I started reading Caroline Mathers's little notes, which were mostly actually written by her parents, because I guess her brain cancer was of the variety that makes you not you before it makes you not alive.

So it was all like, *Caroline continues to have behavioral problems. She's struggling a lot with anger and frustration over not being able to speak (we are frustrated about these things, too, of course, but we have more socially acceptable ways of dealing with our anger). Gus has taken to calling Caroline HULK SMASH, which resonates with the doctors. There's nothing easy about this for any of us, but you take your humor where you can get it. Hoping to go home on Thursday. We'll let you know . . .*

She didn't go home on Thursday, needless to say.

So of course I tensed up when he touched me. To be with him was to hurt him—inevitably. And that's what I'd felt as he reached for me: I'd felt as though I were committing an act of violence against him, because I was.

I decided to text him. I wanted to avoid a whole conversation about it.

> Hi, so okay, I don't know if you'll understand this but I can't kiss you or anything. Not that you'd necessarily want to, but I can't.
>
> When I try to look at you like that, all I see is what I'm going to put you through. Maybe that doesn't make sense to you.
>
> Anyway, sorry.

He responded a few minutes later.

> Okay.

I wrote back.

> Okay.

He responded:

> Oh, my God, stop flirting with me!

I just said:

> Okay.

My phone buzzed moments later.

> I was kidding, Hazel Grace. I understand. (But we both know that okay is a very flirty word. Okay is BURSTING with sensuality.)

I was very tempted to respond *Okay* again, but I pictured him at my funeral, and that helped me text properly.

> Sorry.

. . .

I tried to go to sleep with my headphones still on, but then after a while my mom and dad came in, and my mom grabbed Bluie from the shelf and hugged him to her stomach, and my dad sat down in my desk chair, and without crying he said, "You are not a grenade, not to us. Thinking about you dying makes us sad, Hazel, but you are not a grenade. You are amazing. You can't know, sweetie, because you've never had a baby become a brilliant young reader with a side interest in horrible television shows, but the joy you bring us is so much greater than the sadness we feel about your illness."

"Okay," I said.

"Really," my dad said. "I wouldn't bullshit you about this. If you were more trouble than you're worth, we'd just toss you out on the streets."

"We're not sentimental people," Mom added, deadpan. "We'd leave you at an orphanage with a note pinned to your pajamas."

I laughed.

"You don't have to go to Support Group," Mom added. "You don't have to do anything. Except go to school." She handed me the bear.

"I think Bluie can sleep on the shelf tonight," I said. "Let me remind you that I am more than thirty-three half years old."

"Keep him tonight," she said.

"Mom," I said.

“He’s *lonely*,” she said.

“Oh, my God, Mom,” I said. But I took stupid Bluie and kind of cuddled with him as I fell asleep.

I still had one arm draped over Bluie, in fact, when I awoke just after four in the morning with an apocalyptic pain fingering out from the unreachable center of my head.

CHAPTER SEVEN

I screamed to wake up my parents, and they burst into the room, but there was nothing they could do to dim the supernovae exploding inside my brain, an endless chain of intracranial firecrackers that made me think that I was once and for all going, and I told myself—as I've told myself before—that the body shuts down when the pain gets too bad, that consciousness is temporary, that this will pass. But just like always, I didn't slip away. I was left on the shore with the waves washing over me, unable to drown.

Dad drove, talking on the phone with the hospital, while I lay in the back with my head in Mom's lap. There was nothing to do: Screaming made it worse. All stimuli made it worse, actually.

The only solution was to try to unmake the world, to make it black and silent and uninhabited again, to return to the moment before the Big Bang, in the beginning when there was the Word, and to live in that vacuous uncreated space alone with the Word.

People talk about the courage of cancer patients, and I do not deny that courage. I had been poked and stabbed and poisoned for years, and still I trod on. But make no mistake: In that moment, I would have been very, very happy to die.

I woke up in the ICU. I could tell I was in the ICU because I didn't have my own room, and because there was so much beeping, and because I was alone: They don't let your family stay with you 24/7 in the ICU at Children's because it's an infection risk. There was wailing down the hall. Somebody's kid had died. I was alone. I hit the red call button.

A nurse came in seconds later. "Hi," I said.

"Hello, Hazel. I'm Alison, your nurse," she said.

"Hi, Alison My Nurse," I said.

Whereupon I started to feel pretty tired again. But I woke up a bit when my parents came in, crying and kissing my face repeatedly, and I reached up for them and tried to squeeze, but my everything hurt when I squeezed, and Mom and Dad told me that I did not have a brain tumor, but that my headache was caused by poor oxygenation, which was caused by my lungs swimming in fluid, a liter and a half (!!!!)

of which had been successfully drained from my chest, which was why I might feel a slight discomfort in my side, where there was, *hey look at that*, a tube that went from my chest into a plastic bladder half full of liquid that for all the world resembled my dad's favorite amber ale. Mom told me I was going to go home, that I really was, that I would just have to get this drained every now and again and get back on the BiPAP, this nighttime machine that forces air in and out of my crap lungs. But I'd had a total body PET scan on the first night in the hospital, they told me, and the news was good: no tumor growth. No new tumors. My shoulder pain had been lack-of-oxygen pain. Heart-working-too-hard pain.

"Dr. Maria said this morning that she remains optimistic," Dad said. I liked Dr. Maria, and she didn't bullshit you, so that felt good to hear.

"This is just a thing, Hazel," my mom said. "It's a thing we can live with."

I nodded, and then Alison My Nurse kind of politely made them leave. She asked me if I wanted some ice chips, and I nodded, and then she sat at the bed with me and spooned them into my mouth.

"So you've been gone a couple days," Alison said. "Hmm, what'd you miss . . . A celebrity did drugs. Politicians disagreed. A different celebrity wore a bikini that revealed a bodily imperfection. A team won a sporting event, but another team lost." I smiled. "You can't go disappearing on everybody like this, Hazel. You miss too much."

"More?" I asked, nodding toward the white Styrofoam cup in her hand.

"I shouldn't," she said, "but I'm a rebel." She gave me another plastic spoonful of crushed ice. I mumbled a thank-you. Praise God for good nurses. "Getting tired?" she asked. I nodded. "Sleep for a while," she said. "I'll try to run interference and give you a couple hours before somebody comes in to check vitals and the like." I said Thanks again. You say thanks a lot in a hospital. I tried to settle into the bed. "You're not gonna ask about your boyfriend?" she asked.

"Don't have one," I told her.

"Well, there's a kid who has hardly left the waiting room since you got here," she said.

"He hasn't seen me like this, has he?"

"No. Family only."

I nodded and sank into an aqueous sleep.

It would take me six days to get home, six undays of staring at acoustic ceiling tile and watching television and sleeping and pain and wishing for time to pass. I did not see Augustus or anyone other than my parents. My hair looked like a bird's nest; my shuffling gait like a dementia patient's. I felt a little better each day, though: Each sleep ended to reveal a person who seemed a bit more like me. Sleep fights cancer, Regular Dr. Jim said for the thousandth time as he hovered over me one morning surrounded by a coterie of medical students.

"Then I am a cancer-fighting machine," I told him.

"That you are, Hazel. Keep resting, and hopefully we'll get you home soon."

On Tuesday, they told me I'd go home on Wednesday. On Wednesday, two minimally supervised medical students removed my chest tube, which felt like getting stabbed in reverse and generally didn't go very well, so they decided I'd have to stay until Thursday. I was beginning to think that I was the subject of some existentialist experiment in permanently delayed gratification when Dr. Maria showed up on Friday morning, sniffed around me for a minute, and told me I was good to go.

So Mom opened her oversize purse to reveal that she'd had my Go Home Clothes with her all along. A nurse came in and took out my IV. I felt untethered even though I still had the oxygen tank to carry around with me. I went into the bathroom, took my first shower in a week, got dressed, and when I got out, I was so tired I had to lie down and get my breath. Mom asked, "Do you want to see Augustus?"

"I guess," I said after a minute. I stood up and shuffled over to one of the molded plastic chairs against the wall, tucking my tank beneath the chair. It wore me out.

Dad came back with Augustus a few minutes later. His hair was messy, sweeping down over his forehead. He lit up with a real Augustus Waters Goofy Smile when he saw me, and I couldn't help but smile back. He sat down in the blue faux-leather recliner next to my chair. He leaned in toward me, seemingly incapable of stifling the smile.

Mom and Dad left us alone, which felt awkward. I worked hard to meet his eyes, even though they were the kind of pretty that's hard to look at. "I missed you," Augustus said.

My voice was smaller than I wanted it to be. "Thanks for not trying to see me when I looked like hell."

"To be fair, you still look pretty bad."

I laughed. "I missed you, too. I just don't want you to see . . . all this. I just want, like . . . It doesn't matter. You don't always get what you want."

"Is that so?" he asked. "I'd always thought the world was a wish-granting factory."

"Turns out that is not the case," I said. He was so beautiful. He reached for my hand but I shook my head. "No," I said quietly. "If we're gonna hang out, it has to be, like, not that."

"Okay," he said. "Well, I have good news and bad news on the wish-granting front."

"Okay?" I said.

"The bad news is that we obviously can't go to Amsterdam until you're better. The Genies will, however, work their famous magic when you're well enough."

"That's the good news?"

"No, the good news is that while you were sleeping, Peter Van Houten shared a bit more of his brilliant brain with us."

He reached for my hand again, but this time to slip into it a heavily folded sheet of stationery on the letterhead of *Peter Van Houten, Novelist Emeritus.*

I didn't read it until I got home, situated in my own huge and empty bed with no chance of medical interruption. It took me forever to decode Van Houten's sloped, scratchy script.

Dear Mr. Waters,

> I am in receipt of your electronic mail dated the 14th of April and duly impressed by the Shakespearean complexity of your tragedy. Everyone in this tale has a rock-solid *hamartia*: hers, that she is so sick; yours, that you are so well. Were she better or you sicker, then the stars would not be so terribly crossed, but it is the nature of stars to cross, and never was Shakespeare more wrong than when he had Cassius note, "The fault, dear Brutus, is not in our stars / But in ourselves." Easy enough to say when you're a Roman nobleman (or Shakespeare!),

but there is no shortage of fault to be found amid our stars.

While we're on the topic of old Will's insufficiencies, your writing about young Hazel reminds me of the Bard's Fifty-fifth sonnet, which of course begins, "Not marble, nor the gilded monuments / Of princes, shall outlive this powerful rhyme; / But you shall shine more bright in these contents / Than unswept stone, besmear'd with sluttish time." (Off topic, but: What a slut time is. She screws everybody.) It's a fine poem but a deceitful one: We do indeed remember Shakespeare's powerful rhyme, but what do we remember about the person it commemorates? Nothing. We're pretty sure he was male; everything else is guesswork. Shakespeare told us precious little of the man whom he entombed in his linguistic sarcophagus. (Witness also that when we talk about literature, we do so in the present tense. When we speak of the dead, we are not so kind.) You do not immortalize the lost by writing about them. Language buries, but does not resurrect. (Full disclosure: I am not the first to make this observation. cf, the MacLeish poem "Not Marble, Nor the Gilded Monuments," which contains the heroic line "I shall say you will die and none will remember you.")

> I digress, but here's the rub: The dead are visible only in the terrible lidless eye of memory. The living, thank heaven, retain the ability to surprise and to disappoint. Your Hazel is alive, Waters, and you mustn't impose your will upon another's decision, particularly a decision arrived at thoughtfully. She wishes to spare you pain, and you should let her. You may not find young Hazel's logic persuasive, but I have trod through this vale of tears longer than you, and from where I'm sitting, she's not the lunatic.

Yours truly,
Peter Van Houten

It was really written by him. I licked my finger and dabbed the paper and the ink bled a little, so I knew it was really real.

"Mom," I said. I did not say it loudly, but I didn't have to. She was always waiting. She peeked her head around the door.

"You okay, sweetie?"

"Can we call Dr. Maria and ask if international travel would kill me?"

CHAPTER EIGHT

We had a big Cancer Team Meeting a couple days later. Every so often, a bunch of doctors and social workers and physical therapists and whoever else got together around a big table in a conference room and discussed my situation. (Not the Augustus Waters situation or the Amsterdam situation. The cancer situation.)

Dr. Maria led the meeting. She hugged me when I got there. She was a hugger.

I felt a little better, I guess. Sleeping with the BiPAP all night made my lungs feel almost normal, although, then again, I did not really remember lung normality.

Everyone got there and made a big show of turning off

their pagers and everything so it would be *all about me*, and then Dr. Maria said, "So the great news is that Phalanxifor continues to control your tumor growth, but obviously we're still seeing serious problems with fluid accumulation. So the question is, how should we proceed?"

And then she just looked at me, like she was waiting for an answer. "Um," I said, "I feel like I am not the most qualified person in the room to answer that question?"

She smiled. "Right, I was waiting for Dr. Simons. Dr. Simons?" He was another cancer doctor of some kind.

"Well, we know from other patients that most tumors eventually evolve a way to grow in spite of Phalanxifor, but if that were the case, we'd see tumor growth on the scans, which we don't see. So it's not that yet."

Yet, I thought.

Dr. Simons tapped at the table with his forefinger. "The thought around here is that it's possible the Phalanxifor is worsening the edema, but we'd face far more serious problems if we discontinued its use."

Dr. Maria added, "We don't really understand the long-term effects of Phalanxifor. Very few people have been on it as long as you have."

"So we're gonna do nothing?"

"We're going to stay the course," Dr. Maria said, "but we'll need to do more to keep that edema from building up." I felt kind of sick for some reason, like I was going to throw up. I hated Cancer Team Meetings in general, but I hated this one in particular. "Your cancer is not going away, Hazel. But we've seen people live with your level of tumor penetration for a long time." (I did not ask what constituted a long time. I'd made that mistake before.) "I know that coming out of the ICU, it doesn't feel this way, but this fluid is, at least for the time being, manageable."

"Can't I just get like a lung transplant or something?" I asked.

Dr. Maria's lips shrank into her mouth. "You would not be considered a strong candidate for a transplant, unfortunately," she said. I understood: No use wasting good lungs on a hopeless case. I nodded, trying not to look like that comment hurt me. My dad started crying a little. I didn't look over at him, but no one said anything for a long time, so his hiccuping cry was the only sound in the room.

I hated hurting him. Most of the time, I could forget about it, but the inexorable truth is this: They might be glad to have me around, but I was the alpha and the omega of my parents' suffering.

Just before the Miracle, when I was in the ICU and it looked like I was going to die and Mom was telling me it was okay to let go, and I was trying to let go but my lungs kept searching for air, Mom sobbed something into Dad's chest that I wish I hadn't heard, and that I hope she never finds out that I did hear. She said, "I won't be a mom anymore." It gutted me pretty badly.

I couldn't stop thinking about that during the whole Cancer Team Meeting. I couldn't get it out of my head, how she sounded when she said that, like she would never be okay again, which probably she wouldn't.

Anyway, eventually we decided to keep things the same only with more frequent fluid drainings. At the end, I asked if I could travel to Amsterdam, and Dr. Simons actually and literally laughed, but then Dr. Maria said, "Why not?" And Simons said, dubiously, "Why not?" And Dr. Maria said, "Yeah, I don't see why not. They've got oxygen on the planes, after all." Dr. Simons said, "Are they just going to gate-check a BiPAP?" And Maria said, "Yeah, or have one waiting for her."

"Placing a patient—one of the most promising Phalanxifor survivors, no less—an eight-hour flight from the only physicians intimately familiar with her case? That's a recipe for disaster."

Dr. Maria shrugged. "It would increase some risks," she acknowledged, but then turned to me and said, "But it's your life."

Except not really. On the car ride home, my parents agreed: I would not be going to Amsterdam unless and until there was medical agreement that it would be safe.

. . .

Augustus called that night after dinner. I was already in bed—after dinner had become my bedtime for the moment—propped up with a gajillion pillows and also Bluie, with my computer on my lap.

I picked up, saying, "Bad news," and he said, "Shit, what?"

"I can't go to Amsterdam. One of my doctors thinks it's a bad idea."

He was quiet for a second. "God," he said. "I should've just paid for it myself. Should've just taken you straight from the *Funky Bones* to Amsterdam."

"But then I would've had a probably fatal episode of deoxygenation in Amsterdam, and my body would have been shipped home in the cargo hold of an airplane," I said.

"Well, yeah," he said. "But before that, my grand romantic gesture would have totally gotten me laid."

I laughed pretty hard, hard enough that I felt where the chest tube had been.

"You laugh because it's true," he said.

I laughed again.

"It's true, isn't it!"

"Probably not," I said, and then after a moment added, "although you never know."

He moaned in misery. "I'm gonna die a virgin," he said.

"You're a virgin?" I asked, surprised.

"Hazel Grace," he said, "do you have a pen and a piece of paper?" I said I did. "Okay, please draw a circle." I did. "Now draw a smaller circle within that circle." I did. "The larger circle is virgins. The smaller circle is seventeen-year-old guys with one leg."

I laughed again, and told him that having most of your social engagements occur at a children's hospital also did not encourage promiscuity, and then we talked about Peter Van Houten's amazingly brilliant comment about the sluttiness of time, and even though I was in bed and he was in his basement, it really felt like we were back in that uncreated third space, which was a place I really liked visiting with him.

Then I got off the phone and my mom and dad came into my room, and even though it was really not big enough for all three of us, they lay on either side of the bed with me and we all watched *ANTM* on the little TV in my room. This girl I didn't like, Selena, got kicked off, which made me really happy for some reason. Then Mom hooked me up to the BiPAP and tucked me in, and Dad kissed me on the forehead, the kiss all stubble, and then I closed my eyes.

The BiPAP essentially took control of my breathing away from me, which was intensely annoying, but the great thing about it was that it made all this noise, rumbling with each inhalation and whirring as I exhaled. I kept thinking that it sounded like a dragon breathing in time with me, like I had this pet dragon who was cuddled up next to me and cared enough about me to time his breaths to mine. I was thinking about that as I sank into sleep.

I got up late the next morning. I watched TV in bed and checked my email and then after a while started crafting an email to Peter Van Houten about how I couldn't come to Amsterdam but I swore upon the life of my mother that I would never share any information about the characters with anyone, that I didn't even *want* to share it, because I was a terribly selfish person, and could he please just tell me if the Dutch Tulip Man is for real and if Anna's mom marries him and also about Sisyphus the Hamster.

But I didn't send it. It was too pathetic even for me.

Around three, when I figured Augustus would be home from school, I went into the backyard and called him. As the phone rang, I sat down on the grass, which was all overgrown and dandeliony. That swing set was still back there, weeds growing out of the little ditch I'd created from kicking myself higher as a little kid. I remembered Dad bringing home the kit from Toys "R" Us and building it in the backyard with a neighbor. He'd insisted on swinging on it first to test it, and the thing damn near broke.

The sky was gray and low and full of rain but not yet raining. I hung up when I got Augustus's voice mail and then put the phone down in the dirt beside me and kept looking at the swing set, thinking that I would give up all the sick days I had left for a few healthy ones. I tried to tell myself that it could be worse, that the world was not a wish-granting factory, that I was living with cancer not dying of it, that I mustn't let it kill me before it kills me, and then I just started muttering *stupid stupid stupid stupid stupid stupid* over and over again until the sound unhinged from its meaning. I was still saying it when he called back.

"Hi," I said.

"Hazel Grace," he said.

"Hi," I said again.

"Are you crying, Hazel Grace?"

"Kind of?"

"Why?" he asked.

"'Cause I'm just—I want to go to Amsterdam, and I want him to tell me what happens after the book is over, and I just don't want my particular life, and also the sky is depressing me, and there is this old swing set out here that my dad made for me when I was a kid."

"I must see this old swing set of tears immediately," he said. "I'll be over in twenty minutes."

I stayed in the backyard because Mom was always really smothery and concerned when I was crying, because I did not cry often, and I knew she'd want to *talk* and discuss whether I shouldn't consider adjusting my medication, and the thought of that whole conversation made me want to throw up.

It's not like I had some utterly poignant, well-lit memory of a healthy father pushing a healthy child and the child saying *higher higher higher* or some other metaphorically resonant moment. The swing set was just sitting there, abandoned, the two little swings hanging still and sad from a grayed plank of wood, the outline of the seats like a kid's drawing of a smile.

Behind me, I heard the sliding-glass door open. I turned around. It was Augustus, wearing khaki pants and a short-sleeve plaid button-down. I wiped my face with my sleeve and smiled. "Hi," I said.

It took him a second to sit down on the ground next to me, and he grimaced as he landed rather ungracefully on his ass. "Hi," he said finally. I looked over at him. He was looking past me, into the backyard. "I see your point," he said as he put an arm around my shoulder. "That is one sad goddamned swing set."

I nudged my head into his shoulder. "Thanks for offering to come over."

"You realize that trying to keep your distance from me will not lessen my affection for you," he said.

"I guess?" I said.

"All efforts to save me from you will fail," he said.

"Why? Why would you even like me? Haven't you put

yourself through enough of this?" I asked, thinking of Caroline Mathers.

Gus didn't answer. He just held on to me, his fingers strong against my left arm. "We gotta do something about this frigging swing set," he said. "I'm telling you, it's ninety percent of the problem."

Once I'd recovered, we went inside and sat down on the couch right next to each other, the laptop half on his (fake) knee and half on mine. "Hot," I said of the laptop's base.

"Is it now?" He smiled. Gus loaded this giveaway site called Free No Catch and together we wrote an ad.

"Headline?" he asked.

"'Swing Set Needs Home,'" I said.

"'Desperately Lonely Swing Set Needs Loving Home,'" he said.

"'Lonely, Vaguely Pedophilic Swing Set Seeks the Butts of Children,'" I said.

He laughed. "That's why."

"What?"

"That's why I like you. Do you realize how rare it is to come across a hot girl who creates an adjectival version of the word *pedophile*? You are so busy being you that you have no idea how utterly unprecedented you are."

I took a deep breath through my nose. There was never enough air in the world, but the shortage was particularly acute in that moment.

We wrote the ad together, editing each other as we went. In the end, we settled upon this:

> **Desperately Lonely Swing Set Needs Loving Home**
>
> One swing set, well worn but structurally sound, seeks new home. Make memories with your kid or kids so that someday he or she or they will look into the backyard and feel the ache of sentimentality as desperately as I did this afternoon. It's all fragile and fleeting, dear reader, but with this swing set, your child(ren) will be introduced to the ups and downs of human life gently and safely, and may also learn the most important lesson of all: No matter how hard you kick, no matter how high you get, you can't go all the way around.
>
> Swing set currently resides near 83rd and Spring Mill.

After that, we turned on the TV for a little while, but we couldn't find anything to watch, so I grabbed *An Imperial Affliction* off the bedside table and brought it back into the living room and Augustus Waters read to me while Mom, making lunch, listened in.

"'*Mother's glass eye turned inward,*'" Augustus began. As

he read, I fell in love the way you fall asleep: slowly, and then all at once.

When I checked my email an hour later, I learned that we had plenty of swing-set suitors to choose from. In the end, we picked a guy named Daniel Alvarez who'd included a picture of his three kids playing video games with the subject line *I just want them to go outside*. I emailed him back and told him to pick it up at his leisure.

Augustus asked if I wanted to go with him to Support Group, but I was really tired from my busy day of Having Cancer, so I passed. We were sitting there on the couch together, and he pushed himself up to go but then fell back down onto the couch and sneaked a kiss onto my cheek.

"Augustus!" I said.

"Friendly," he said. He pushed himself up again and really stood this time, then took two steps over to my mom and said, "Always a pleasure to see you," and my mom opened her arms to hug him, whereupon Augustus leaned in and kissed my mom on the cheek. He turned back to me. "See?" he asked.

I went to bed right after dinner, the BiPAP drowning out the world beyond my room.

I never saw the swing set again.

I slept for a long time, ten hours, possibly because of the slow recovery and possibly because sleep fights cancer and possibly because I was a teenager with no particular wake-up time. I wasn't strong enough yet to go back to classes at MCC. When I finally felt like getting up, I removed the BiPAP snout from my nose, put my oxygen nubbins in, turned them on, and then grabbed my laptop from beneath my bed, where I'd stashed it the night before.

I had an email from Lidewij Vliegenthart.

Dear Hazel,

> I have received word via the Genies that you will be visiting us with Augustus Waters and your mother beginning on 4th of May. Only a week away! Peter and I are delighted and cannot wait to make your acquaintance. Your hotel, the Filosoof, is just one street away from Peter's home. Perhaps we should give you one day for the jet lag, yes? So if convenient, we will meet you at Peter's home on the morning of 5th May at perhaps ten o'clock for a cup of coffee and for him to answer questions you have about his book. And then perhaps afterward we can tour a museum or the Anne Frank House?

With all best wishes,
Lidewij Vliegenthart
Executive Assistant to Mr. Peter Van Houten,
author of *An Imperial Affliction*

. . .

"Mom," I said. She didn't answer. "MOM!" I shouted. Nothing. Again, louder, "MOM!"

She ran in wearing a threadbare pink towel under her armpits, dripping, vaguely panicked. "What's wrong?"

"Nothing. Sorry, I didn't know you were in the shower," I said.

"Bath," she said. "I was just . . ." She closed her eyes. "Just trying to take a bath for five seconds. Sorry. What's going on?"

"Can you call the Genies and tell them the trip is off? I just got an email from Peter Van Houten's assistant. She thinks we're coming."

She pursed her lips and squinted past me.

"What?" I asked.

"I'm not supposed to tell you until your father gets home."

"What?" I asked again.

"Trip's on," she said finally. "Dr. Maria called us last night and made a convincing case that you need to live your—"

"MOM, I LOVE YOU SO MUCH!" I shouted, and she came to the bed and let me hug her.

I texted Augustus because I knew he was in school:

Still free May three? :-)

He texted back immediately.

Everything's coming up Waters.

If I could just stay alive for a week, I'd know the unwritten secrets of Anna's mom and the Dutch Tulip Guy. I looked down my blouse at my chest.

"Keep your shit together," I whispered to my lungs.

CHAPTER NINE

The day before we left for Amsterdam, I went back to Support Group for the first time since meeting Augustus. The cast had rotated a bit down there in the Literal Heart of Jesus. I arrived early, enough time for perennially strong appendiceal cancer survivor Lida to bring me up-to-date on everyone as I ate a grocery-store chocolate chip cookie while leaning against the dessert table.

Twelve-year-old leukemic Michael had passed away. He'd fought hard, Lida told me, as if there were another way to fight. Everyone else was still around. Ken was NEC after radiation. Lucas had relapsed, and she said it with a sad smile and a little shrug, the way you might say an alcoholic had relapsed.

A cute, chubby girl walked over to the table and said hi to Lida, then introduced herself to me as Susan. I didn't know what was wrong with her, but she had a scar extending from the side of her nose down her lip and across her cheek. She had put makeup over the scar, which only served to emphasize it. I was feeling a little out of breath from all the standing, so I said, "I'm gonna go sit," and then the elevator opened, revealing Isaac and his mom. He wore sunglasses and clung to his mom's arm with one hand, a cane in the other.

"Support Group Hazel not Monica," I said when he got close enough, and he smiled and said, "Hey, Hazel. How's it going?"

"Good. I've gotten *really hot* since you went blind."

"I bet," he said. His mom led him to a chair, kissed the top of his head, and shuffled back toward the elevator. He felt around beneath him and then sat. I sat down in the chair next to him. "So how's it going?"

"Okay. Glad to be home, I guess. Gus told me you were in the ICU?"

"Yeah," I said.

"Sucks," he said.

"I'm a lot better now," I said. "I'm going to Amsterdam tomorrow with Gus."

"I know. I'm pretty well up-to-date on your life, because Gus never. Talks. About. Anything. Else."

I smiled. Patrick cleared his throat and said, "If we could all take a seat?" He caught my eye. "Hazel!" he said. "I'm so glad to see you!"

Everyone sat and Patrick began his retelling of his ball-lessness, and I fell into the routine of Support Group: communicating through sighs with Isaac, feeling sorry for everyone in the room and also everyone outside of it, zoning out of the conversation to focus on my breathlessness and the aching. The world went on, as it does, without my full participation, and I only woke up from the reverie when someone said my name.

It was Lida the Strong. Lida in remission. Blond, healthy, stout Lida, who swam on her high school swim team. Lida, missing only her appendix, saying my name, saying, "Hazel is such an inspiration to me; she really is. She just keeps fighting the battle, waking up every morning and going to war without complaint. She's so strong. She's so much stronger than I am. I just wish I had her strength."

"Hazel?" Patrick asked. "How does that make you feel?"

I shrugged and looked over at Lida. "I'll give you my strength if I can have your remission." I felt guilty as soon as I said it.

"I don't think that's what Lida meant," Patrick said. "I think she . . ." But I'd stopped listening.

After the prayers for the living and the endless litany of the dead (with Michael tacked on to the end), we held hands and said, "Living our best life today!"

Lida immediately rushed up to me full of apology and explanation, and I said, "No, no, it's really fine," waving her off, and I said to Isaac, "Care to accompany me upstairs?"

He took my arm, and I walked with him to the elevator, grateful to have an excuse to avoid the stairs. I'd almost made it all the way to the elevator when I saw his mom standing in a corner of the Literal Heart. "I'm here," she said to Isaac, and he switched from my arm to hers before asking, "You want to come over?"

"Sure," I said. I felt bad for him. Even though I hated the sympathy people felt toward me, I couldn't help but feel it toward him.

Isaac lived in a small ranch house in Meridian Hills next to this fancy private school. We sat down in the living room while his mom went off to the kitchen to make dinner, and then he asked if I wanted to play a game.

"Sure," I said. So he asked for the remote. I gave it to him, and he turned on the TV and then a computer attached to it. The TV screen stayed black, but after a few seconds a deep voice spoke from it.

"Deception," the voice said. "One player or two?"

"Two," Isaac said. "Pause." He turned to me. "I play this game with Gus all the time, but it's infuriating because he is a completely suicidal video-game player. He's, like, way too aggressive about saving civilians and whatnot."

"Yeah," I said, remembering the night of the broken trophies.

"Unpause," Isaac said.

"Player one, identify yourself."

"This is player one's sexy sexy voice," Isaac said.

"Player two, identify yourself."

"I would be player two, I guess," I said.

Staff Sergeant Max Mayhem and Private Jasper Jacks awake in a dark, empty room approximately twelve feet square.

Isaac pointed toward the TV, like I should talk to it or something. "Um," I said. "Is there a light switch?"

No.

"Is there a door?"

Private Jacks locates the door. It is locked.

Isaac jumped in. "There's a key above the door frame."

Yes, there is.

"Mayhem opens the door."

The darkness is still complete.

"Take out knife," Isaac said.

"Take out knife," I added.

A kid–Isaac's brother, I assume–darted out from the kitchen. He was maybe ten, wiry and overenergetic, and he kind of skipped across the living room before shouting in a really good imitation of Isaac's voice, "KILL MYSELF."

Sergeant Mayhem places his knife to his neck. Are you sure you—

"No," Isaac said. "Pause. Graham, don't make me kick your ass." Graham laughed giddily and skipped off down a hallway.

As Mayhem and Jacks, Isaac and I felt our way forward in the cavern until we bumped into a guy whom we stabbed after getting him to tell us that we were in a Ukrainian prison cave, more than a mile beneath the ground. As we continued, sound effects—a raging underground river, voices speaking in Ukrainian and accented English—led you through the cave, but there was nothing to see in this game. After playing for an hour, we began to hear the cries of a desperate prisoner, pleading, "God, help me. God, help me."

"Pause," Isaac said. "This is when Gus always insists on finding the prisoner, even though that keeps you from winning the game, and the only way to *actually free* the prisoner is to win the game."

"Yeah, he takes video games too seriously," I said. "He's a bit too enamored with metaphor."

"Do you like him?" Isaac asked.

"Of course I like him. He's great."

"But you don't want to hook up with him?"

I shrugged. "It's complicated."

"I know what you're trying to do. You don't want to give him something he can't handle. You don't want him to Monica you," he said.

"Kinda," I said. But it wasn't that. The truth was, I didn't want to Isaac him. "To be fair to Monica," I said, "what you did to her wasn't very nice either."

"What'd *I* do to her?" he asked, defensive.

"You know, going blind and everything."

"But that's not my fault," Isaac said.

"I'm not saying it was your *fault*. I'm saying it wasn't *nice*."

CHAPTER TEN

We could only take one suitcase. I couldn't carry one, and Mom insisted that she couldn't carry two, so we had to jockey for space in this black suitcase my parents had gotten as a wedding present a million years ago, a suitcase that was supposed to spend its life in exotic locales but ended up mostly going back and forth to Dayton, where Morris Property, Inc., had a satellite office that Dad often visited.

I argued with Mom that I should have slightly more than half of the suitcase, since without me and my cancer, we'd never be going to Amsterdam in the first place. Mom countered that since she was twice as large as me and therefore required more physical fabric to preserve her modesty, she deserved at least two-thirds of the suitcase.

In the end, we both lost. So it goes.

Our flight didn't leave until noon, but Mom woke me up at five thirty, turning on the light and shouting, "AMSTERDAM!" She ran around all morning making sure we had international plug adapters and quadruple-checking that we had the right number of oxygen tanks to get there and that they were all full, etc., while I just rolled out of bed, put on my Travel to Amsterdam Outfit (jeans, a pink tank top, and a black cardigan in case the plane was cold).

The car was packed by six fifteen, whereupon Mom insisted that we eat breakfast with Dad, although I had a moral opposition to eating before dawn on the grounds that I was not a nineteenth-century Russian peasant fortifying myself for a day in the fields. But anyway, I tried to stomach down some eggs while Mom and Dad enjoyed these homemade versions of Egg McMuffins they liked.

"Why are breakfast foods breakfast foods?" I asked them. "Like, why don't we have curry for breakfast?"

"Hazel, eat."

"But *why*?" I asked. "I mean, seriously: How did scrambled eggs get stuck with breakfast exclusivity? You can put bacon on a sandwich without anyone freaking out. But the moment your sandwich has an egg, boom, it's a *breakfast* sandwich."

Dad answered with his mouth full. "When you come back, we'll have breakfast for dinner. Deal?"

"I don't want to have 'breakfast for dinner,'" I answered, crossing knife and fork over my mostly full plate. "I want to have scrambled eggs for dinner without this ridiculous construction that a scrambled egg–inclusive meal is *breakfast* even when it occurs at dinnertime."

"You've gotta pick your battles in this world, Hazel," my mom said. "But if this is the issue you want to champion, we will stand behind you."

"Quite a bit behind you," my dad added, and Mom laughed.

Anyway, I knew it was stupid, but I felt kind of *bad* for scrambled eggs.

After they finished eating, Dad did the dishes and walked us to the car. Of course, he started crying, and he kissed my cheek with his wet stubbly face. He pressed his nose against my cheekbone and whispered, "I love you. I'm so proud of you." (*For what,* I wondered.)

"Thanks, Dad."

"I'll see you in a few days, okay, sweetie? I love you so much."

"I love you, too, Dad." I smiled. "And it's only three days."

As we backed out of the driveway, I kept waving at him. He was waving back, and crying. It occurred to me that he was probably thinking he might never see me again, which he probably thought every single morning of his entire weekday life as he left for work, which probably sucked.

Mom and I drove over to Augustus's house, and when we got there, she wanted me to stay in the car to rest, but I went to the door with her anyway. As we approached the house, I could hear someone crying inside. I didn't think it was Gus at first, because it didn't sound anything like the low rumble of his speaking, but then I heard a voice that was definitely a twisted version of his say, "BECAUSE IT IS MY LIFE, MOM. IT BELONGS TO ME." And quickly my mom put her arm around my shoulders and spun me back toward the car, walking quickly, and I was like, "Mom, what's wrong?"

And she said, "We can't eavesdrop, Hazel."

We got back into the car and I texted Augustus that we were outside whenever he was ready.

We stared at the house for a while. The weird thing about houses is that they almost always look like nothing is happening inside of them, even though they contain most of our lives. I wondered if that was sort of the point of architecture.

"Well," Mom said after a while, "we are pretty early, I guess."

"Almost as if I didn't have to get up at five thirty," I said. Mom reached down to the console between us, grabbed her coffee mug, and took a sip. My phone buzzed. A text from Augustus.

> Just CAN'T decide what to wear. Do you like me better in a polo or a button-down?

I replied:

> Button-down.

Thirty seconds later, the front door opened, and a smiling Augustus appeared, a roller bag behind him. He wore a pressed sky-blue button-down tucked into his jeans. A Camel Light dangled from his lips. My mom got out to say hi to him. He took the cigarette out momentarily and spoke in the confident voice to which I was accustomed. "Always a pleasure to see you, ma'am."

I watched them through the rearview mirror until Mom opened the trunk. Moments later, Augustus opened a door behind me and engaged in the complicated business of entering the backseat of a car with one leg.

"Do you want shotgun?" I asked.

"Absolutely not," he said. "And hello, Hazel Grace."

"Hi," I said. "Okay?" I asked.

"Okay," he said.

"Okay," I said.

My mom got in and closed the car door. "Next stop, Amsterdam," she announced.

Which was not quite true. The next stop was the airport parking lot, and then a bus took us to the terminal, and then an open-air electric car took us to the security line. The TSA guy at the front of the line was shouting about how our bags had better not contain explosives or firearms or anything liquid over three ounces, and I said to Augustus, "Observation: Standing in line is a form of oppression," and he said, "Seriously."

Rather than be searched by hand, I chose to walk through the metal detector without my cart or my tank or even the plastic nubbins in my nose. Walking through the X-ray machine marked the first time I'd taken a step without oxygen in some months, and it felt pretty amazing to walk unencumbered like that, stepping across the Rubicon, the machine's silence acknowledging that I was, however briefly, a nonmetallicized creature.

I felt a bodily sovereignty that I can't really describe except to say that when I was a kid I used to have a really heavy backpack that I carried everywhere with all my books in it, and if I walked around with the backpack for long enough, when I took it off I felt like I was floating.

After about ten seconds, my lungs felt like they were folding in upon themselves like flowers at dusk. I sat down on a gray bench just past the machine and tried to catch my breath, my cough a rattling drizzle, and I felt pretty miserable until I got the cannula back into place.

Even then, it hurt. The pain was always there, pulling me inside of myself, demanding to be felt. It always felt like I was waking up from the pain when something in the world outside of me suddenly required my comment or attention. Mom was looking at me, concerned. She'd just said something. What had she just said? Then I remembered. She'd asked what was wrong.

"Nothing," I said.

"Amsterdam!" she half shouted.

I smiled. "Amsterdam," I answered. She reached her hand down to me and pulled me up.

We got to the gate an hour before our scheduled boarding time. "Mrs. Lancaster, you are an impressively punctual person," Augustus said as he sat down next to me in the mostly empty gate area.

"Well, it helps that I am not technically very busy," she said.

"You're plenty busy," I told her, although it occurred to me that Mom's business was mostly me. There was also the business of being married to my dad—he was kind of clueless about, like, banking and hiring plumbers and cooking and doing things other than working for Morris

Property, Inc.—but it was mostly me. Her primary reason for living and my primary reason for living were awfully entangled.

As the seats around the gate started to fill, Augustus said, "I'm gonna get a hamburger before we leave. Can I get you anything?"

"No," I said, "but I really appreciate your refusal to give in to breakfasty social conventions."

He tilted his head at me, confused. "Hazel has developed an issue with the ghettoization of scrambled eggs," Mom said.

"It's embarrassing that we all just walk through life blindly accepting that scrambled eggs are fundamentally associated with mornings."

"I want to talk about this more," Augustus said. "But I am starving. I'll be right back."

When Augustus hadn't showed up after twenty minutes, I asked Mom if she thought something was wrong, and she looked up from her awful magazine only long enough to say, "He probably just went to the bathroom or something."

A gate agent came over and switched my oxygen container out with one provided by the airline. I was embarrassed to have this lady kneeling in front of me while everyone watched, so I texted Augustus while she did it.

He didn't reply. Mom seemed unconcerned, but I

was imagining all kinds of Amsterdam trip-ruining fates (arrest, injury, mental breakdown) and I felt like there was something noncancery wrong with my chest as the minutes ticked away.

And just when the lady behind the ticket counter announced they were going to start preboarding people who might need a bit of extra time and every single person in the gate area turned squarely to me, I saw Augustus fast-limping toward us with a McDonald's bag in one hand, his backpack slung over his shoulder.

"Where were you?" I asked.

"Line got superlong, sorry," he said, offering me a hand up. I took it, and we walked side by side to the gate to preboard.

I could feel everybody watching us, wondering what was wrong with us, and whether it would kill us, and how heroic my mom must be, and everything else. That was the worst part about having cancer, sometimes: The physical evidence of disease separates you from other people. We were irreconcilably other, and never was it more obvious than when the three of us walked through the empty plane, the stewardess nodding sympathetically and gesturing us toward our row in the distant back. I sat in the middle of our three-person row with Augustus in the window seat and Mom in the aisle. I felt a little hemmed in by Mom, so of course I scooted over toward Augustus. We were right behind the plane's wing. He opened up his bag and unwrapped his burger.

"The thing about eggs, though," he said, "is that breakfastization gives the scrambled egg a certain *sacrality*, right? You can get yourself some bacon or Cheddar cheese anywhere anytime, from tacos to breakfast sandwiches to grilled cheese, but scrambled eggs—they're *important.*"

"Ludicrous," I said. The people were starting to file into the plane now. I didn't want to look at them, so I looked away, and to look away was to look at Augustus.

"I'm just saying: Maybe scrambled eggs are ghettoized, but they're also special. They have a place and a time, like church does."

"You couldn't be more wrong," I said. "You are buying into the cross-stitched sentiments of your parents' throw pillows. You're arguing that the fragile, rare thing is beautiful simply because it is fragile and rare. But that's a lie, and you know it."

"You're a hard person to comfort," Augustus said.

"Easy comfort isn't comforting," I said. "You were a rare and fragile flower once. You remember."

For a moment, he said nothing. "You do know how to shut me up, Hazel Grace."

"It's my privilege and my responsibility," I answered.

Before I broke eye contact with him, he said, "Listen, sorry I avoided the gate area. The McDonald's line wasn't really that long; I just . . . I just didn't want to sit there with all those people looking at us or whatever."

"At me, mostly," I said. You could glance at Gus and never know he'd been sick, but I carried my disease with me on the outside, which is part of why I'd become a homebody in the first place. "Augustus Waters, noted charismatist, is embarrassed to sit next to a girl with an oxygen tank."

"Not embarrassed," he said. "They just piss me off sometimes. And I don't want to be pissed off today." After a minute, he dug into his pocket and flipped open his pack of smokes.

About nine seconds later, a blond stewardess rushed over to our row and said, "Sir, you can't smoke on this plane. Or any plane."

"I don't smoke," he explained, the cigarette dancing in his mouth as he spoke.

"But—"

"It's a metaphor," I explained. "He puts the killing thing in his mouth but doesn't give it the power to kill him."

The stewardess was flummoxed for only a moment. "Well, that metaphor is prohibited on today's flight," she said. Gus nodded and rejoined the cigarette to its pack.

We finally taxied out to the runway and the pilot said, *Flight attendants, prepare for departure*, and then two tremendous jet engines roared to life and we began to accelerate. "This is what it feels like to drive in a car with you," I said, and he smiled, but kept his jaw clenched tight and I said, "Okay?"

We were picking up speed and suddenly Gus's hand grabbed the armrest, his eyes wide, and I put my hand on top of his and said, "Okay?" He didn't say anything, just stared at me wide-eyed, and I said, "Are you scared of flying?"

"I'll tell you in a minute," he said. The nose of the plane rose up and we were aloft. Gus stared out the window, watching the planet shrink beneath us, and then I felt his hand relax beneath mine. He glanced at me and then back out the window. "We are *flying*," he announced.

"You've never been on a plane before?"

He shook his head. "LOOK!" he half shouted, pointing at the window.

"Yeah," I said. "Yeah, I see it. It looks like we're in an airplane."

"NOTHING HAS EVER LOOKED LIKE THAT EVER IN ALL OF HUMAN HISTORY," he said. His enthusiasm was adorable. I couldn't resist leaning over to kiss him on the cheek.

"Just so you know, I'm right here," Mom said. "Sitting next to you. Your mother. Who held your hand as you took your first infantile steps."

"It's friendly," I reminded her, turning to kiss her on the cheek.

"Didn't feel too friendly," Gus mumbled just loud

enough for me to hear. When surprised and excited and innocent Gus emerged from Grand Gesture Metaphorically Inclined Augustus, I literally could not resist.

It was a quick flight to Detroit, where the little electric car met us as we disembarked and drove us to the gate for Amsterdam. That plane had TVs in the back of each seat, and once we were above the clouds, Augustus and I timed it so that we started watching the same romantic comedy at the same time on our respective screens. But even though we were perfectly synchronized in our pressing of the play button, his movie started a couple seconds before mine, so at every funny moment, he'd laugh just as I started to hear whatever the joke was.

Mom had this big plan that we would sleep for the last several hours of the flight, so when we landed at eight A.M., we'd hit the city ready to suck the marrow out of life or whatever. So after the movie was over, Mom and Augustus and I all took sleeping pills. Mom conked out within seconds, but Augustus and I stayed up to look out the window for a while. It was a clear day, and although we couldn't see the sun setting, we could see the sky's response.

"God, that is beautiful," I said mostly to myself.

"'The risen sun too bright in her losing eyes,'" he said, a line from *An Imperial Affliction*.

"But it's not rising," I said.

"It's rising somewhere," he answered, and then after a moment said, "Observation: It would be awesome to fly in a superfast airplane that could chase the sunrise around the world for a while."

"Also I'd live longer." He looked at me askew. "You know, because of relativity or whatever." He still looked confused. "We age slower when we move quickly versus standing still. So right now time is passing slower for us than for people on the ground."

"College chicks," he said. "They're so smart."

I rolled my eyes. He hit his (real) knee with my knee and I hit his knee back with mine. "Are you sleepy?" I asked him.

"Not at all," he answered.

"Yeah," I said. "Me neither." Sleeping meds and narcotics didn't do for me what they did for normal people.

"Want to watch another movie?" he asked. "They've got a Portman movie from her Hazel Era."

"I want to watch something you haven't seen."

In the end we watched *300*, a war movie about 300 Spartans who protect Sparta from an invading army of like a billion Persians. Augustus's movie started before mine again, and after a few minutes of hearing him go, "Dang!" or "Fatality!" every time someone was killed in some badass way, I leaned over the armrest and put my head on his shoulder so I could see his screen and we could actually watch the movie together.

300 featured a sizable collection of shirtless and well-oiled strapping young lads, so it was not particularly difficult on the eyes, but it was mostly a lot of sword wielding to no real effect. The bodies of the Persians and the Spartans piled up, and I couldn't quite figure out why the Persians were so evil or the Spartans so awesome. "Contemporaneity," to quote *AIA*, "specializes in the kind of battles wherein no one loses anything of any value, except arguably their lives." And so it was with these titans clashing.

Toward the end of the movie, almost everyone is dead, and there is this insane moment when the Spartans start stacking the bodies of the dead up to form a wall of corpses. The dead become this massive roadblock standing between the Persians and the road to Sparta. I found the gore a bit gratuitous, so I looked away for a second, asking Augustus, "How many dead people do you think there are?"

He dismissed me with a wave. "*Shh. Shh.* This is getting awesome."

When the Persians attacked, they had to climb up the wall of death, and the Spartans were able to occupy the high ground atop the corpse mountain, and as the bodies piled up, the wall of martyrs only became higher and therefore harder to climb, and everybody swung swords/shot arrows, and the rivers of blood poured down Mount Death, etc.

I took my head off his shoulder for a moment to get

a break from the gore and watched Augustus watch the movie. He couldn't contain his goofy grin. I watched my own screen through squinted eyes as the mountain grew with the bodies of Persians and Spartans. When the Persians finally overran the Spartans, I looked over at Augustus again. Even though the good guys had just lost, Augustus seemed downright *joyful.* I nuzzled up to him again, but kept my eyes closed until the battle was finished.

As the credits rolled, he took off his headphones and said, "Sorry, I was awash in the nobility of sacrifice. What were you saying?"

"How many dead people do you think there are?"

"Like, how many fictional people died in that fictional movie? Not enough," he joked.

"No, I mean, like, ever. Like, how many people do you think have ever died?"

"I happen to know the answer to that question," he said. "There are seven billion living people, and about ninety-eight billion dead people."

"Oh," I said. I'd thought that maybe since population growth had been so fast, there were more people alive than all the dead combined.

"There are about fourteen dead people for every living person," he said. The credits continued rolling. It took a long time to identify all those corpses, I guess. My head was still on his shoulder. "I did some research on this a couple years ago," Augustus continued. "I was wondering if everybody could be remembered. Like, if we got organized, and assigned a certain number of corpses to each living person, would there be enough living people to remember all the dead people?"

"And are there?"

"Sure, anyone can name fourteen dead people. But we're disorganized mourners, so a lot of people end up remembering Shakespeare, and no one ends up remembering the person he wrote Sonnet Fifty-five about."

"Yeah," I said.

It was quiet for a minute, and then he asked, "You want to read or something?" I said sure. I was reading this long poem called *Howl* by Allen Ginsberg for my poetry class, and Gus was rereading *An Imperial Affliction*.

After a while he said, "Is it any good?"

"The poem?" I asked.

"Yeah."

"Yeah, it's great. The guys in this poem take even more drugs than I do. How's *AIA*?"

"Still perfect," he said. "Read to me."

"This isn't really a poem to read aloud when you are sitting next to your sleeping mother. It has, like, sodomy and angel dust in it," I said.

"You just named two of my favorite pastimes," he said. "Okay, read me something else then?"

"Um," I said. "I don't *have* anything else?"

"That's too bad. I am so in the mood for poetry. Do you have anything memorized?"

"'Let us go then, you and I,'" I started nervously, "'When the evening is spread out against the sky / Like a patient etherized upon a table.'"

"Slower," he said.

I felt bashful, like I had when I'd first told him of *An Imperial Affliction*. "Um, okay. Okay. 'Let us go, through certain half-deserted streets, / The muttering retreats / Of restless nights in one-night cheap hotels / And sawdust restaurants with oyster-shells: / Streets that follow like a tedious argument / Of insidious intent / To lead you to an overwhelming question . . . / Oh, do not ask, "What is it?" / Let us go and make our visit.'"

"I'm in love with you," he said quietly.

"Augustus," I said.

"I am," he said. He was staring at me, and I could see the corners of his eyes crinkling. "I'm in love with you, and I'm not in the business of denying myself the simple pleasure of saying true things. I'm in love with you, and I know that love is just a shout into the void, and that oblivion is inevitable, and that we're all doomed and that there will come a day when all our labor has been returned to dust, and I know the sun will swallow the only earth we'll ever have, and I am in love with you."

"Augustus," I said again, not knowing what else to

say. It felt like everything was rising up in me, like I was drowning in this weirdly painful joy, but I couldn't say it back. I couldn't say anything back. I just looked at him and let him look at me until he nodded, lips pursed, and turned away, placing the side of his head against the window.

CHAPTER ELEVEN

I think he must have fallen asleep. I did, eventually, and woke to the landing gear coming down. My mouth tasted horrible, and I tried to keep it shut for fear of poisoning the airplane.

I looked over at Augustus, who was staring out the window, and as we dipped below the low-hung clouds, I straightened my back to see the Netherlands. The land seemed sunk into the ocean, little rectangles of green surrounded on all sides by canals. We landed, in fact, parallel to a canal, like there were two runways: one for us and one for waterfowl.

After getting our bags and clearing customs, we all

piled into a taxi driven by this doughy bald guy who spoke perfect English—like better English than I do. "The Hotel Filosoof?" I said.

And he said, "You are Americans?"

"Yes," Mom said. "We're from *Indiana*."

"Indiana," he said. "They steal the land from the Indians and leave the name, yes?"

"Something like that," Mom said. The cabbie pulled out into traffic and we headed toward a highway with lots of blue signs featuring double vowels: Oosthuizen, Haarlem. Beside the highway, flat empty land stretched for miles, interrupted by the occasional huge corporate headquarters. In short, Holland looked like Indianapolis, only with smaller cars. "This is Amsterdam?" I asked the cabdriver.

"Yes and no," he answered. "Amsterdam is like the rings of a tree: It gets older as you get closer to the center."

It happened all at once: We exited the highway and there were the row houses of my imagination leaning precariously toward canals, ubiquitous bicycles, and coffeeshops advertising LARGE SMOKING ROOM. We drove over a canal and from atop the bridge I could see dozens of houseboats moored along the water. It looked nothing like America. It looked like an old painting, but real—everything achingly idyllic in the morning light—and I thought about how wonderfully strange it would be to live in a place where almost everything had been built by the dead.

"Are these houses very old?" asked my mom.

"Many of the canal houses date from the Golden Age, the seventeenth century," he said. "Our city has a rich history, even though many tourists are only wanting to see the Red Light District." He paused. "Some tourists think Amsterdam is a city of sin, but in truth it is a city of freedom. And in freedom, most people find sin."

All the rooms in the Hotel Filosoof were named after filosoofers: Mom and I were staying on the ground floor in the Kierkegaard; Augustus was on the floor above us, in the Heidegger. Our room was small: a double bed pressed against a wall with my BiPAP machine, an oxygen concentrator, and a dozen refillable oxygen tanks at the foot of the bed. Past the equipment, there was a dusty old paisley chair with a sagging seat, a desk, and a bookshelf above the bed containing the collected works of Søren Kierkegaard. On the desk we found a wicker basket full of presents from the Genies: wooden shoes, an orange Holland T-shirt, chocolates, and various other goodies.

The Filosoof was right next to the Vondelpark, Amsterdam's most famous park. Mom wanted to go on a walk, but I was supertired, so she got the BiPAP working and placed its snout on me. I hated talking with that thing on, but I said, "Just go to the park and I'll call you when I wake up."

"Okay," she said. "Sleep tight, honey."

But when I woke up some hours later, she was sitting in the ancient little chair in the corner, reading a guidebook.

"Morning," I said.

"Actually late afternoon," she answered, pushing herself out of the chair with a sigh. She came to the bed, placed a tank in the cart, and connected it to the tube while I took off the BiPAP snout and placed the nubbins into my nose. She set it for 2.5 liters a minute–six hours before I'd need a change–and then I got up. "How are you feeling?" she asked.

"Good," I said. "Great. How was the Vondelpark?"

"I skipped it," she said. "Read all about it in the guidebook, though."

"Mom," I said, "you didn't have to stay here."

She shrugged. "I know. I wanted to. I like watching you sleep."

"Said the creeper." She laughed, but I still felt bad. "I just want you to have fun or whatever, you know?"

"Okay. I'll have fun tonight, okay? I'll go do crazy mom stuff while you and Augustus go to dinner."

"Without you?" I asked.

"Yes without me. In fact, you have reservations at a

place called Oranjee," she said. "Mr. Van Houten's assistant set it up. It's in this neighborhood called the Jordaan. Very fancy, according to the guidebook. There's a tram station right around the corner. Augustus has directions. You can eat outside, watch the boats go by. It'll be lovely. Very romantic."

"Mom."

"I'm just saying," she said. "You should get dressed. The sundress, maybe?"

One might marvel at the insanity of the situation: A mother sends her sixteen-year-old daughter alone with a seventeen-year-old boy out into a foreign city famous for its permissiveness. But this, too, was a side effect of dying: I could not run or dance or eat foods rich in nitrogen, but in the city of freedom, I was among the most liberated of its residents.

I did indeed wear the sundress—this blue print, flowey knee-length Forever 21 thing—with tights and Mary Janes because I liked being quite a lot shorter than him. I went into the hilariously tiny bathroom and battled my bedhead for a while until everything looked suitably mid-2000s Natalie Portman. At six P.M. on the dot (noon back home), there was a knock.

"Hello?" I said through the door. There was no peephole at the Hotel Filosoof.

"Okay," Augustus answered. I could hear the cigarette

in his mouth. I looked down at myself. The sundress offered the most in the way of my rib cage and collarbone that Augustus had seen. It wasn't obscene or anything, but it was as close as I ever got to showing some skin. (My mother had a motto on this front that I agreed with: "Lancasters don't bare midriffs.")

I pulled the door open. Augustus wore a black suit, narrow lapels, perfectly tailored, over a light blue dress shirt and a thin black tie. A cigarette dangled from the unsmiling corner of his mouth. "Hazel Grace," he said, "you look gorgeous."

"I," I said. I kept thinking the rest of my sentence would emerge from the air passing through my vocal cords, but nothing happened. Then finally, I said, "I feel underdressed."

"Ah, this old thing?" he said, smiling down at me.

"Augustus," my mom said behind me, "you look *extremely* handsome."

"Thank you, ma'am," he said. He offered me his arm. I took it, glancing back to Mom.

"See you by eleven," she said.

Waiting for the number one tram on a wide street busy with traffic, I said to Augustus, "The suit you wear to funerals, I assume?"

"Actually, no," he said. "That suit isn't nearly this nice."

The blue-and-white tram arrived, and Augustus handed our cards to the driver, who explained that we needed to wave them at this circular sensor. As we walked through the crowded tram, an old man stood up to give us seats together, and I tried to tell him to sit, but he gestured toward the seat insistently. We rode the tram for three stops, me leaning over Gus so we could look out the window together.

Augustus pointed up at the trees and asked, "Do you see that?"

I did. There were elm trees everywhere along the canals, and these seeds were blowing out of them. But they didn't look like seeds. They looked for all the world like miniaturized rose petals drained of their color. These pale petals were gathering in the wind like flocking birds—thousands of them, like a spring snowstorm.

The old man who'd given up his seat saw us noticing and said, in English, "Amsterdam's spring snow. The *iepen* throw confetti to greet the spring."

We switched trams, and after four more stops we arrived at a street split by a beautiful canal, the reflections of the ancient bridge and picturesque canal houses rippling in water.

Oranjee was just steps from the tram. The restaurant was on one side of the street; the outdoor seating on the other, on a concrete outcropping right at the edge of the canal. The hostess's eyes lit up as Augustus and I walked toward her. "Mr. and Mrs. Waters?"

"I guess?" I said.

"Your table," she said, gesturing across the street to a narrow table inches from the canal. "The champagne is our gift."

Gus and I glanced at each other, smiling. Once we'd crossed the street, he pulled out a seat for me and helped me scoot it back in. There were indeed two flutes of champagne at our white-tableclothed table. The slight chill in the air was balanced magnificently by the sunshine; on one side of us, cyclists pedaled past—well-dressed men and women on their way home from work, improbably attractive blond girls riding sidesaddle on the back of a friend's bike, tiny helmetless kids bouncing around in plastic seats behind their parents. And on our other side, the canal water was choked with millions of the confetti seeds. Little boats were moored at the brick banks, half full of rainwater, some of them near sinking. A bit farther down the canal, I could see houseboats floating on pontoons, and in the middle of the canal, an open-air, flat-bottomed boat decked out with lawn chairs and a portable stereo idled toward us. Augustus took his flute of champagne and raised it. I took mine, even though I'd never had a drink aside from sips of my dad's beer.

"Okay," he said.

"Okay," I said, and we clinked glasses. I took a sip. The tiny bubbles melted in my mouth and journeyed northward into my brain. Sweet. Crisp. Delicious. "That is really good," I said. "I've never drunk champagne."

A sturdy young waiter with wavy blond hair appeared. He was maybe even taller than Augustus. "Do you know," he asked in a delicious accent, "what Dom Pérignon said after inventing champagne?"

"No?" I said.

"He called out to his fellow monks, 'Come quickly: I am tasting the stars.' Welcome to Amsterdam. Would you like to see a menu, or will you have the chef's choice?"

I looked at Augustus and he at me. "The chef's choice sounds lovely, but Hazel is a vegetarian." I'd mentioned this to Augustus precisely once, on the first day we met.

"This is not a problem," the waiter said.

"Awesome. And can we get more of this?" Gus asked, of the champagne.

"Of course," said our waiter. "We have bottled all the stars this evening, my young friends. Gah, the confetti!" he said, and lightly brushed a seed from my bare shoulder. "It hasn't been so bad in many years. It's everywhere. Very annoying."

The waiter disappeared. We watched the confetti fall from the sky, skip across the ground in the breeze, and tumble into the canal. "Kind of hard to believe anyone could ever find that annoying," Augustus said after a while.

"People always get used to beauty, though."

"I haven't gotten used to you just yet," he answered, smiling. I felt myself blushing. "Thank you for coming to Amsterdam," he said.

"Thank you for letting me hijack your wish," I said.

"Thank you for wearing that dress which is like whoa," he said. I shook my head, trying not to smile at him. I didn't want to be a grenade. But then again, he knew what he was doing, didn't he? It was his choice, too. "Hey, how's that poem end?" he asked.

"Huh?"

"The one you recited to me on the plane."

"Oh, 'Prufrock'? It ends, 'We have lingered in the chambers of the sea / By sea-girls wreathed with seaweed red and brown / Till human voices wake us, and we drown.'"

Augustus pulled out a cigarette and tapped the filter against the table. "Stupid human voices always ruining everything."

The waiter arrived with two more glasses of champagne and what he called "Belgian white asparagus with a lavender infusion."

"I've never had champagne either," Gus said after he left. "In case you were wondering or whatever. Also, I've never had white asparagus."

I was chewing my first bite. "It's amazing," I promised.

He took a bite, swallowed. "God. If asparagus tasted like that all the time, I'd be a vegetarian, too." Some people in a lacquered wooden boat approached us on the canal below. One of them, a woman with curly blond hair, maybe thirty, drank from a beer then raised her glass toward us and shouted something.

"We don't speak Dutch," Gus shouted back.

One of the others shouted a translation: "The beautiful couple is beautiful."

The food was so good that with each passing course, our conversation devolved further into fragmented celebrations of its deliciousness: "I want this dragon carrot risotto to become a person so I can take it to Las Vegas and marry it." "Sweet-pea sorbet, you are so unexpectedly magnificent." I wish I'd been hungrier.

After green garlic gnocchi with red mustard leaves, the waiter said, "Dessert next. More stars first?" I shook my head. Two glasses was enough for me. Champagne was no exception to my high tolerance for depressants and pain relievers; I felt warm but not intoxicated. But I didn't want to get drunk. Nights like this one didn't come along often, and I wanted to remember it.

"Mmmm," I said after the waiter left, and Augustus smiled crookedly as he stared down the canal while I stared up it. We had plenty to look at, so the silence didn't feel awkward really, but I wanted everything to be perfect. It *was* perfect, I guess, but it felt like someone had tried to stage the Amsterdam of my imagination, which made it hard to forget that this dinner, like the trip itself, was a cancer perk. I just wanted us to be talking and joking comfortably, like we were on the couch together back home, but some tension underlay everything.

"It's not my funeral suit," he said after a while. "When I first found out I was sick—I mean, they told me I had like an eighty-five percent chance of cure. I know those are great odds, but I kept thinking it was a game of Russian roulette. I mean, I was going to have to go through hell for six months or a year and lose my leg and then at the end, it *still* might not work, you know?"

"I know," I said, although I didn't, not really. I'd never been anything but terminal; all my treatment had been in pursuit of extending my life, not curing my cancer. Phalanxifor had introduced a measure of ambiguity to my cancer story, but I was different from Augustus: My final chapter was written upon diagnosis. Gus, like most cancer survivors, lived with uncertainty.

"Right," he said. "So I went through this whole thing about wanting to be ready. We bought a plot in Crown Hill, and I walked around with my dad one day and picked out a spot. And I had my whole funeral planned out and everything, and then right before the surgery, I asked my parents if I could buy a suit, like a really nice suit, just in case I bit it. Anyway, I've never had occasion to wear it. Until tonight."

"So it's your death suit."

"Correct. Don't you have a death outfit?"

"Yeah," I said. "It's a dress I bought for my fifteenth birthday party. But I don't wear it on dates."

His eyes lit up. "We're on a date?" he asked.

I looked down, feeling bashful. "Don't push it."

We were both really full, but dessert—a succulently rich *crémeux* surrounded by passion fruit—was too good not to at least nibble, so we lingered for a while over dessert, trying to get hungry again. The sun was a toddler insistently refusing to go to bed: It was past eight thirty and still light.

Out of nowhere, Augustus asked, "Do you believe in an afterlife?"

"I think forever is an incorrect concept," I answered.

He smirked. "You're an incorrect concept."

"I know. That's why I'm being taken out of the rotation."

"That's not funny," he said, looking at the street. Two girls passed on a bike, one riding sidesaddle over the back wheel.

"Come on," I said. "That was a joke."

"The thought of you being removed from the rotation

is not funny to me," he said. "Seriously, though: afterlife?"

"No," I said, and then revised. "Well, maybe I wouldn't go so far as no. You?"

"Yes," he said, his voice full of confidence. "Yes, absolutely. Not like a heaven where you ride unicorns, play harps, and live in a mansion made of clouds. But yes. I believe in Something with a capital *S*. Always have."

"Really?" I asked. I was surprised. I'd always associated belief in heaven with, frankly, a kind of intellectual disengagement. But Gus wasn't dumb.

"Yeah," he said quietly. "I believe in that line from *An Imperial Affliction*. 'The risen sun too bright in her losing eyes.' That's God, I think, the rising sun, and the light is too bright and her eyes are losing but they aren't lost. I don't believe we return to haunt or comfort the living or anything, but I think something becomes of us."

"But you fear oblivion."

"Sure, I fear earthly oblivion. But, I mean, not to sound like my parents, but I believe humans have souls, and I believe in the conservation of souls. The oblivion fear is something else, fear that I won't be able to give anything in exchange for my life. If you don't live a life in service of a greater good, you've gotta at least die a death in service of a greater good, you know? And I fear that I won't get either a life or a death that means anything."

I just shook my head.

"What?" he asked.

"Your obsession with, like, dying for something or leaving behind some great sign of your heroism or whatever. It's just weird."

"Everyone wants to lead an extraordinary life."

"Not everyone," I said, unable to disguise my annoyance.

"Are you mad?"

"It's just," I said, and then couldn't finish my sentence. "Just," I said again. Between us flickered the candle. "It's really mean of you to say that the only lives that matter are the ones that are lived for something or die for something. That's a really mean thing to say to me."

I felt like a little kid for some reason, and I took a bite of dessert to make it appear like it was not that big of a deal to me. "Sorry," he said. "I didn't mean it like that. I was just thinking about myself."

"Yeah, you were," I said. I was too full to finish. I worried I might puke, actually, because I often puked after eating. (Not bulimia, just cancer.) I pushed my dessert plate toward Gus, but he shook his head.

"I'm sorry," he said again, reaching across the table for my hand. I let him take it. "I could be worse, you know."

"How?" I asked, teasing.

"I mean, I have a work of calligraphy over my toilet that reads, 'Bathe Yourself Daily in the Comfort of God's Words,' Hazel. I could be way worse."

"Sounds unsanitary," I said.

"I could be worse."

"You could be worse." I smiled. He really did like me. Maybe I was a narcissist or something, but when I realized it there in that moment at Oranjee, it made me like him even more.

When our waiter appeared to take dessert away, he said, "Your meal has been paid for by Mr. Peter Van Houten."

Augustus smiled. "This Peter Van Houten fellow ain't half bad."

We walked along the canal as it got dark. A block up from Oranjee, we stopped at a park bench surrounded by old rusty bicycles locked to bike racks and to each other. We sat down hip to hip facing the canal, and he put his arm around me.

I could see the halo of light coming from the Red Light District. Even though it was the *Red* Light District, the glow coming from up there was an eerie sort of green. I imagined thousands of tourists getting drunk and stoned and pinballing around the narrow streets.

"I can't believe he's going to tell us tomorrow," I said. "Peter Van Houten is going to tell us the famously unwritten end of the best book ever."

"Plus he paid for our dinner," Augustus said.

"I keep imagining that he is going to search us for

recording devices before he tells us. And then he will sit down between us on the couch in his living room and whisper whether Anna's mom married the Dutch Tulip Man."

"Don't forget Sisyphus the Hamster," Augustus added.

"Right, and also of course what fate awaited Sisyphus the Hamster." I leaned forward, to see into the canal. There were so many of those pale elm petals in the canals, it was ridiculous. "A sequel that will exist just for us," I said.

"So what's your guess?" he asked.

"I really don't know. I've gone back and forth like a thousand times about it all. Each time I reread it, I think something different, you know?" He nodded. "You have a theory?"

"Yeah. I don't think the Dutch Tulip Man is a con man, but he's also not rich like he leads them to believe. And I think after Anna dies, Anna's mom goes to Holland with him and thinks they will live there forever, but it doesn't work out, because she wants to be near where her daughter was."

I hadn't realized he'd thought about the book so much, that *An Imperial Affliction* mattered to Gus independently of me mattering to him.

The water lapped quietly at the stone canal walls beneath us; a group of friends biked past in a clump, shouting over each other in rapid-fire, guttural Dutch; the tiny boats, not much longer than me, half drowned in the canal; the smell of water that had stood too still for too long; his arm pulling me in; his real leg against my real leg all the way from hip to foot. I leaned in to his body a little. He winced. "Sorry, you okay?"

He breathed out a *yeah* in obvious pain.

"Sorry," I said. "Bony shoulder."

"It's okay," he said. "Nice, actually."

We sat there for a long time. Eventually his hand abandoned my shoulder and rested against the back of the park bench. Mostly we just stared into the canal. I was thinking a lot about how they'd made this place exist even though it should've been underwater, and how I was for Dr. Maria a kind of Amsterdam, a half-drowned anomaly, and that made me think about dying. "Can I ask you about Caroline Mathers?"

"And you say there's no afterlife," he answered without looking at me. "But yeah, of course. What do you want to know?"

I wanted to know that he would be okay if I died. I wanted to not be a grenade, to not be a malevolent force in the lives of people I loved. "Just, like, what happened."

He sighed, exhaling for so long that to my crap lungs it seemed like he was bragging. He popped a fresh cigarette into his mouth. "You know how there is famously no place less played in than a hospital playground?" I nodded. "Well,

I was at Memorial for a couple weeks when they took off the leg and everything. I was up on the fifth floor and I had a view of the playground, which was always of course utterly desolate. I was all awash in the metaphorical resonance of the empty playground in the hospital courtyard. But then this girl started showing up alone at the playground, every day, swinging on a swing completely alone, like you'd see in a movie or something. So I asked one of my nicer nurses to get the skinny on the girl, and the nurse brought her up to visit, and it was Caroline, and I used my immense charisma to win her over." He paused, so I decided to say something.

"You're not that charismatic," I said. He scoffed, disbelieving. "You're mostly just hot," I explained.

He laughed it off. "The thing about dead people," he said, and then stopped himself. "The thing is you sound like a bastard if you don't romanticize them, but the truth is . . . complicated, I guess. Like, you are familiar with the trope of the stoic and determined cancer victim who heroically fights her cancer with inhuman strength and never complains or stops smiling even at the very end, etcetera?"

"Indeed," I said. "They are kindhearted and generous souls whose every breath is an Inspiration to Us All. They're so strong! We admire them so!"

"Right, but really, I mean aside from us obviously, cancer kids are not statistically more likely to be awesome or compassionate or perseverant or whatever. Caroline was always moody and miserable, but I liked it. I liked feeling as if she had chosen me as the only person in the world not to hate, and so we spent all this time together just ragging on everyone, you know? Ragging on the nurses and the other kids and our families and whatever else. But I don't know if that was her or the tumor. I mean, one of her nurses told me once that the kind of tumor Caroline had is known among medical types as the Asshole Tumor, because it just turns you into a monster. So here's this girl missing a fifth of her brain who's just had a recurrence of the Asshole Tumor, and so she was not, you know, the paragon of stoic cancer-kid heroism. She was . . . I mean, to be honest, she was a bitch. But you can't say that, because she had this tumor, and also she's, I mean, she's dead. And she had plenty of reason to be unpleasant, you know?"

I knew.

"You know that part in *An Imperial Affliction* when Anna's walking across the football field to go to PE or whatever and she falls and goes face-first into the grass and that's when she knows that the cancer is back and in her nervous system and she can't get up and her face is like an inch from the football-field grass and she's just stuck there looking at this grass up close, noticing the way the light hits it and . . . I don't remember the line but it's something like Anna having the Whitmanesque revelation that the definition of humanness is the opportunity to marvel at the majesty of creation or whatever. You know that part?"

"I know that part," I said.

"So afterward, while I was getting eviscerated by chemo, for some reason I decided to feel really hopeful. Not about survival specifically, but I felt like Anna does in the book, that feeling of excitement and gratitude about just being able to marvel at it all.

"But meanwhile Caroline got worse every day. She went home after a while and there were moments where I thought we could have, like, a regular relationship, but we couldn't, really, because she had no filter between her thoughts and her speech, which was sad and unpleasant and frequently hurtful. But, I mean, you can't dump a girl with a brain tumor. And her parents liked me, and she has this little brother who is a really cool kid. I mean, how can you dump her? She's *dying*.

"It took forever. It took almost a year, and it was a year of me hanging out with this girl who would, like, just start laughing out of nowhere and point at my prosthetic and call me Stumpy."

"No," I said.

"Yeah. I mean, it was the tumor. It ate her brain, you know? Or it wasn't the tumor. I have no way of knowing, because they were inseparable, she and the tumor. But as she got sicker, I mean, she'd just repeat the same stories and laugh at her own comments even if she'd already said the same thing a hundred times that day. Like, she made the same joke over and over again for weeks: 'Gus has great legs. I mean leg.' And then she would just laugh like a maniac."

"Oh, Gus," I said. "That's . . ." I didn't know what to say. He wasn't looking at me, and it felt invasive of me to look at him. I felt him scoot forward. He took the cigarette out of his mouth and stared at it, rolling it between his thumb and forefinger, then put it back.

"Well," he said, "to be fair, I *do* have great leg."

"I'm sorry," I said. "I'm really sorry."

"It's all good, Hazel Grace. But just to be clear, when I thought I saw Caroline Mathers's ghost in Support Group, I was not entirely happy. I was staring, but I wasn't yearning, if you know what I mean." He pulled the pack out of his pocket and placed the cigarette back in it.

"I'm sorry," I said again.

"Me too," he said.

"I don't ever want to do that to you," I told him.

"Oh, I wouldn't mind, Hazel Grace. It would be a privilege to have my heart broken by you."

CHAPTER TWELVE

I woke up at four in the Dutch morning ready for the day. All attempts to go back to sleep failed, so I lay there with the BiPAP pumping the air in and urging it out, enjoying the dragon sounds but wishing I could choose my breaths.

I reread *An Imperial Affliction* until Mom woke up and rolled over toward me around six. She nuzzled her head against my shoulder, which felt uncomfortable and vaguely Augustinian.

The hotel brought a breakfast to our room that, much to my delight, featured *deli meat* among many other denials of American breakfast constructions. The dress I'd planned to wear to meet Peter Van Houten had been moved up in the rotation for the Oranjee dinner, so after I showered and got my hair to lie halfway flat, I spent like thirty minutes debating with Mom the various benefits and drawbacks of the available outfits before deciding to dress as much like Anna in *AIA* as possible: Chuck Taylors and dark jeans like she always wore, and a light blue T-shirt.

The shirt was a screen print of a famous Surrealist artwork by René Magritte in which he drew a pipe and then beneath it wrote in cursive *Ceci n'est pas une pipe.* ("This is not a pipe.")

"I just don't get that shirt," Mom said.

"Peter Van Houten will get it, trust me. There are like seven thousand Magritte references in *An Imperial Affliction*."

"But it *is* a pipe."

"No, it's not," I said. "It's a *drawing* of a pipe. Get it? All representations of a thing are inherently abstract. It's very clever."

"How did you get so grown up that you understand things that confuse your ancient mother?" Mom asked. "It seems like just yesterday that I was telling seven-year-old Hazel why the sky was blue. You thought I was a genius back then."

"Why *is* the sky blue?" I asked.

"Cuz," she answered. I laughed.

As it got closer to ten, I grew more and more nervous: nervous to see Augustus; nervous to meet Peter Van Houten;

nervous that my outfit was not a good outfit; nervous that we wouldn't find the right house since all the houses in Amsterdam looked pretty similar; nervous that we would get lost and never make it back to the Filosoof; nervous nervous nervous. Mom kept trying to talk to me, but I couldn't really listen. I was about to ask her to go upstairs and make sure Augustus was up when he knocked.

I opened the door. He looked down at the shirt and smiled. "Funny," he said.

"Don't call my boobs funny," I answered.

"Right here," Mom said behind us. But I'd made Augustus blush and put him enough off his game that I could finally bear to look up at him.

"You sure you don't want to come?" I asked Mom.

"I'm going to the Rijksmuseum and the Vondelpark today," she said. "Plus, I just don't get his book. No offense. Thank him and Lidewij for us, okay?"

"Okay," I said. I hugged Mom, and she kissed my head just above my ear.

Peter Van Houten's white row house was just around the corner from the hotel, on the Vondelstraat, facing the park. Number 158. Augustus took me by one arm and grabbed the oxygen cart with the other, and we walked up the three steps to the lacquered blue-black front door. My heart pounded. One closed door away from the answers I'd dreamed of ever since I first read that last unfinished page.

Inside, I could hear a bass beat thumping loud enough to rattle the windowsills. I wondered whether Peter Van Houten had a kid who liked rap music.

I grabbed the lion's-head door knocker and knocked tentatively. The beat continued. "Maybe he can't hear over the music?" Augustus asked. He grabbed the lion's head and knocked much louder.

The music disappeared, replaced by shuffled footsteps. A dead bolt slid. Another. The door creaked open. A potbellied man with thin hair, sagging jowls, and a week-old beard squinted into the sunlight. He wore baby-blue man pajamas like guys in old movies. His face and belly were so round, and his arms so skinny, that he looked like a dough ball with four sticks stuck into it. "Mr. Van Houten?" Augustus asked, his voice squeaking a bit.

The door slammed shut. Behind it, I heard a stammering, reedy voice shout, "LEEE-DUH-VIGH!" (Until then, I'd pronounced his assistant's name like lid-uh-widge.)

We could hear everything through the door. "Are they here, Peter?" a woman asked.

"There are—Lidewij, there are two adolescent apparitions outside the door."

"Apparitions?" she asked with a pleasant Dutch lilt.

Van Houten answered in a rush. "Phantasms specters

ghouls visitants post-terrestrials *apparitions*, Lidewij. How can someone pursuing a postgraduate degree in American literature display such abominable English-language skills?"

"Peter, those are not post-terrestrials. They are Augustus and Hazel, the young fans with whom you have been corresponding."

"They are—what? They—I thought they were in America!"

"Yes, but you invited them here, you will remember."

"Do you know why I left America, Lidewij? So that I would never again have to encounter Americans."

"But you are an American."

"Incurably so, it seems. But as to *these* Americans, you must tell them to leave at once, that there has been a terrible mistake, that the blessed Van Houten was making a rhetorical offer to meet, not an actual one, that such offers must be read symbolically."

I thought I might throw up. I looked over at Augustus, who was staring intently at the door, and saw his shoulders slacken.

"I will not do this, Peter," answered Lidewij. "You *must* meet them. You must. You need to see them. You need to see how your work matters."

"Lidewij, did you knowingly deceive me to arrange this?"

A long silence ensued, and then finally the door opened again. He turned his head metronomically from Augustus to me, still squinting. "Which of you is Augustus Waters?" he asked. Augustus raised his hand tentatively. Van Houten nodded and said, "Did you close the deal with that chick yet?"

Whereupon I encountered for the first and only time a truly speechless Augustus Waters. "I," he started, "um, I, Hazel, um. Well."

"This boy appears to have some kind of developmental delay," Peter Van Houten said to Lidewij.

"Peter," she scolded.

"Well," Peter Van Houten said, extending his hand to me. "It is at any rate a pleasure to meet such ontologically improbable creatures." I shook his swollen hand, and then he shook hands with Augustus. I was wondering what *ontologically* meant. Regardless, I liked it. Augustus and I were together in the Improbable Creatures Club: us and duck-billed platypuses.

Of course, I had hoped that Peter Van Houten would be sane, but the world is not a wish-granting factory. The important thing was that the door was open and I was crossing the threshold to learn what happens after the end of *An Imperial Affliction*. That was enough. We followed him and Lidewij inside, past a huge oak dining room table with only two chairs, into a creepily sterile living room. It looked like a museum, except there was no art on the empty white walls. Aside from one couch and one lounge chair, both a mix of steel and black leather, the room seemed empty. Then I noticed two large black garbage bags, full and twist-tied, behind the couch.

"Trash?" I mumbled to Augustus soft enough that I thought no one else would hear.

"Fan mail," Van Houten answered as he sat down in the lounge chair. "Eighteen years' worth of it. Can't open it. Terrifying. Yours are the first missives to which I have replied, and look where that got me. I frankly find the reality of readers wholly unappetizing."

That explained why he'd never replied to my letters: He'd never read them. I wondered why he kept them at all, let alone in an otherwise empty formal living room. Van Houten kicked his feet up onto the ottoman and crossed his slippers. He motioned toward the couch. Augustus and I sat down next to each other, but not *too* next.

"Would you care for some breakfast?" asked Lidewij.

I started to say that we'd already eaten when Peter interrupted. "It is far too early for breakfast, Lidewij."

"Well, they are from America, Peter, so it is past noon in their bodies."

"Then it's too late for breakfast," he said. "However, it being after noon in the body and whatnot, we should enjoy a cocktail. Do you drink Scotch?" he asked me.

"Do I—um, no, I'm fine," I said.

"Augustus Waters?" Van Houten asked, nodding toward Gus.

"Uh, I'm good."

"Just me, then, Lidewij. Scotch and water, please." Peter turned his attention to Gus, asking, "You know how we make a Scotch and water in this home?"

"No, sir," Gus said.

"We pour Scotch into a glass and then call to mind thoughts of water, and then we mix the actual Scotch with the abstracted idea of water."

Lidewij said, "Perhaps a bit of breakfast first, Peter."

He looked toward us and stage-whispered, "She thinks I have a drinking problem."

"And I think that the sun has risen," Lidewij responded. Nonetheless, she turned to the bar in the living room, reached up for a bottle of Scotch, and poured a glass half full. She carried it to him. Peter Van Houten took a sip, then sat up straight in his chair. "A drink this good deserves one's best posture," he said.

I became conscious of my own posture and sat up a little on the couch. I rearranged my cannula. Dad always told me that you can judge people by the way they treat waiters and assistants. By this measure, Peter Van Houten was possibly the world's douchiest douche. "So you like my book," he said to Augustus after another sip.

"Yeah," I said, speaking up on Augustus's behalf. "And yes, we—well, Augustus, he made meeting you his Wish so that we could come here, so that you could tell us what happens after the end of *An Imperial Affliction*."

Van Houten said nothing, just took a long pull on his drink.

After a minute, Augustus said, "Your book is sort of the thing that brought us together."

"But you aren't together," he observed without looking at me.

"The thing that brought us nearly together," I said.

Now he turned to me. "Did you dress like her on purpose?"

"Anna?" I asked.

He just kept staring at me.

"Kind of," I said.

He took a long drink, then grimaced. "I do not have a drinking problem," he announced, his voice needlessly loud. "I have a Churchillian relationship with alcohol: I can crack jokes and govern England and do anything I want to do. Except not drink." He glanced over at Lidewij and nodded toward his glass. She took it, then walked back to the bar. "Just the *idea* of water, Lidewij," he instructed.

"Yah, got it," she said, the accent almost American.

The second drink arrived. Van Houten's spine stiffened again out of respect. He kicked off his slippers. He had really ugly feet. He was rather ruining the whole business of authorial genius for me. But he had the answers.

"Well, um," I said, "first, we do want to say thank you for dinner last night and—"

"We bought them dinner last night?" Van Houten asked Lidewij.

"Yes, at Oranjee."

"Ah, yes. Well, believe me when I say that you do not have me to thank but rather Lidewij, who is exceptionally talented in the field of spending my money."

"It was our pleasure," Lidewij said.

"Well, thanks, at any rate," Augustus said. I could hear annoyance in his voice.

"So here I am," Van Houten said after a moment. "What are your questions?"

"Um," Augustus said.

"He seemed so intelligent in print," Van Houten said to Lidewij regarding Augustus. "Perhaps the cancer has established a beachhead in his brain."

"Peter," Lidewij said, duly horrified.

I was horrified, too, but there was something pleasant about a guy so despicable that he wouldn't treat us deferentially. "We do have some questions, actually," I said. "I talked about them in my email. I don't know if you remember."

"I do not."

"His memory is compromised," Lidewij said.

"If only my memory would compromise," Van Houten responded.

"So, our questions," I repeated.

"She uses the royal we," Peter said to no one in particular. Another sip. I didn't know what Scotch tasted like, but if it tasted anything like champagne, I couldn't imagine how he could drink so much, so quickly, so early in the morning. "Are you familiar with Zeno's tortoise paradox?" he asked me.

"We have questions about what happens to the characters after the end of the book, specifically Anna's—"

"You wrongly assume that I need to hear your question in order to answer it. You are familiar with the philosopher Zeno?" I shook my head vaguely. "Alas. Zeno was a pre-Socratic philosopher who is said to have discovered forty paradoxes within the worldview put forth by Parmenides—surely you know Parmenides," he said, and I nodded that I knew Parmenides, although I did not. "Thank God," he said. "Zeno professionally specialized in revealing the inaccuracies and oversimplifications of Parmenides, which wasn't difficult, since Parmenides was spectacularly wrong everywhere and always. Parmenides is valuable in precisely the way that it is valuable to have an acquaintance who reliably picks the wrong horse each and every time you take him to the racetrack. But Zeno's most important—wait, give me a sense of your familiarity with Swedish hip-hop."

I could not tell if Peter Van Houten was kidding. After a moment, Augustus answered for me. "Limited," he said.

"Okay, but presumably you know Afasi och Filthy's seminal album *Fläcken*."

"We do not," I said for the both of us.

"Lidewij, play 'Bomfalleralla' immediately." Lidewij walked over to an MP3 player, spun the wheel a bit, then hit a button. A rap song boomed from every direction. It sounded like a fairly regular rap song, except the words were in Swedish.

After it was over, Peter Van Houten looked at us expectantly, his little eyes as wide as they could get. "Yeah?" he asked. "Yeah?"

I said, "I'm sorry, sir, but we don't speak Swedish."

"Well, of course you don't. Neither do I. Who the hell speaks Swedish? The important thing is not whatever nonsense the voices are *saying*, but what the voices are *feeling*. Surely you know that there are only two emotions, love and fear, and that Afasi och Filthy navigate between them with the kind of facility that one simply does not find in hip-hop music outside of Sweden. Shall I play it for you again?"

"Are you joking?" Gus said.

"Pardon?"

"Is this some kind of performance?" He looked up at Lidewij and asked, "Is it?"

"I'm afraid not," Lidewij answered. "He's not always—this is unusually—"

"Oh, shut up, Lidewij. Rudolf Otto said that if you had not encountered the numinous, if you have not experienced a nonrational encounter with the *mysterium tremendum*, then his work was not for you. And I say to you, young friends, that if you cannot hear Afasi och Filthy's bravadic response to fear, then my work is not for you."

I cannot emphasize this enough: It was a completely normal rap song, except in Swedish. "Um," I said. "So about *An Imperial Affliction*. Anna's mom, when the book ends, is about to—"

Van Houten interrupted me, tapping his glass as he talked until Lidewij refilled it again. "So Zeno is most famous for his tortoise paradox. Let us imagine that you are in a race with a tortoise. The tortoise has a ten-yard head start. In the time it takes you to run that ten yards, the tortoise has maybe moved one yard. And then in the time it takes you to make up that distance, the tortoise goes a bit farther, and so on forever. You are faster than the tortoise but you can never catch him; you can only decrease his lead.

"Of course, you just run past the tortoise without contemplating the mechanics involved, but the question of how you are able to do this turns out to be incredibly complicated, and no one really solved it until Cantor showed us that some infinities are bigger than other infinities."

"Um," I said.

"I assume that answers your question," he said

confidently, then sipped generously from his glass.

"Not really," I said. "We were wondering, after the end of *An Imperial Affliction*—"

"I disavow everything in that putrid novel," Van Houten said, cutting me off.

"No," I said.

"Excuse me?"

"No, that is not acceptable," I said. "I understand that the story ends midnarrative because Anna dies or becomes too sick to continue, but you said you would tell us what happens to everybody, and that's why we're here, and we, *I* need you to tell me."

Van Houten sighed. After another drink, he said, "Very well. Whose story do you seek?"

"Anna's mom, the Dutch Tulip Man, Sisyphus the Hamster, I mean, just—what happens to everyone."

Van Houten closed his eyes and puffed his cheeks as he exhaled, then looked up at the exposed wooden beams crisscrossing the ceiling. "The hamster," he said after a while. "The hamster gets adopted by Christine"—who was one of Anna's presickness friends. That made sense. Christine and Anna played with Sisyphus in a few scenes. "He is adopted by Christine and lives for a couple years after the end of the novel and dies peacefully in his hamster sleep."

Now we were getting somewhere. "Great," I said. "Great. Okay, so the Dutch Tulip Man. Is he a con man? Do he and Anna's mom get married?"

Van Houten was still staring at the ceiling beams. He took a drink. The glass was almost empty again. "Lidewij, I can't do it. I can't. I *can't.*" He leveled his gaze to me. "*Nothing* happens to the Dutch Tulip Man. He isn't a con man or not a con man; he's *God.* He's an obvious and unambiguous metaphorical representation of *God*, and asking what becomes of him is the intellectual equivalent of asking what becomes of the disembodied eyes of Dr. T. J. Eckleburg in *Gatsby*. Do he and Anna's mom get married? We are speaking of a novel, dear child, not some historical enterprise."

"Right, but surely you must have thought about what happens to them, I mean as characters, I mean independent of their metaphorical meanings or whatever."

"They're fictions," he said, tapping his glass again. "Nothing happens to them."

"You said you'd tell me," I insisted. I reminded myself to be assertive. I needed to keep his addled attention on my questions.

"Perhaps, but I was under the misguided impression that you were incapable of transatlantic travel. I was trying . . . to provide you some comfort, I suppose, which I should know better than to attempt. But to be perfectly frank, this childish idea that the author of a novel has some special insight into the characters in the novel . . . it's ridiculous. That novel was composed of scratches on a page, dear. The characters inhabiting it have no life outside of those scratches. What *happened* to them? They all ceased to exist the moment the novel ended."

"No," I said. I pushed myself up off the couch. "No, I understand that, but it's impossible not to imagine a future for them. You are the most qualified person to imagine that future. Something happened to Anna's mother. She either got married or didn't. She either moved to Holland with the Dutch Tulip Man or didn't. She either had more kids or didn't. I need to know what happens to her."

Van Houten pursed his lips. "I regret that I cannot indulge your childish whims, but I refuse to pity you in the manner to which you are well accustomed."

"I don't want your pity," I said.

"Like all sick children," he answered dispassionately, "you say you don't want pity, but your very existence depends upon it."

"Peter," Lidewij said, but he continued as he reclined there, his words getting rounder in his drunken mouth. "Sick children inevitably become arrested: You are fated to live out your days as the child you were when diagnosed, the child who believes there is life after a novel ends. And we, as adults, we pity this, so we pay for your treatments, for your oxygen machines. We give you food and water though you are unlikely to live long enough–"

"PETER!" Lidewij shouted.

"You are a side effect," Van Houten continued, "of an

evolutionary process that cares little for individual lives. You are a failed experiment in mutation."

"I RESIGN!" Lidewij shouted. There were tears in her eyes. But I wasn't angry. He was looking for the most hurtful way to tell the truth, but of course I already knew the truth. I'd had years of staring at ceilings from my bedroom to the ICU, and so I'd long ago found the most hurtful ways to imagine my own illness. I stepped toward him. "Listen, douchepants," I said, "you're not going to tell me anything about disease I don't already know. I need one and only one thing from you before I walk out of your life forever: WHAT HAPPENS TO ANNA'S MOTHER?"

He raised his flabby chins vaguely toward me and shrugged his shoulders. "I can no more tell you what happens to her than I can tell you what becomes of Proust's Narrator or Holden Caulfield's sister or Huckleberry Finn after he lights out for the territories."

"BULLSHIT! That's bullshit. Just tell me! Make something up!"

"No, and I'll thank you not to curse in my house. It isn't becoming of a lady."

I still wasn't angry, exactly, but I was very focused on getting the thing I'd been promised. Something inside me welled up and I reached down and smacked the swollen hand that held the glass of Scotch. What remained of the Scotch splashed across the vast expanse of his face, the glass bouncing off his nose and then spinning balletically through the air, landing with a shattering crash on the ancient hardwood floors.

"Lidewij," Van Houten said calmly, "I'll have a martini, if you please. Just a whisper of vermouth."

"I have resigned," Lidewij said after a moment.

"Don't be ridiculous."

I didn't know what to do. Being nice hadn't worked. Being mean hadn't worked. I needed an answer. I'd come all this way, hijacked Augustus's Wish. I needed to know.

"Have you ever stopped to wonder," he said, his words slurring now, "why you care so much about your silly questions?"

"YOU PROMISED!" I shouted, hearing Isaac's impotent wailing echoing from the night of the broken trophies. Van Houten didn't reply.

I was still standing over him, waiting for him to say something to me when I felt Augustus's hand on my arm. He pulled me away toward the door, and I followed him while Van Houten ranted to Lidewij about the ingratitude of contemporary teenagers and the death of polite society, and Lidewij, somewhat hysterical, shouted back at him in rapid-fire Dutch.

"You'll have to forgive my former assistant," he said. "Dutch is not so much a language as an ailment of the throat."

Augustus pulled me out of the room and through the

door to the late spring morning and the falling confetti of the elms.

For me there was no such thing as a quick getaway, but we made our way down the stairs, Augustus holding my cart, and then started to walk back toward the Filosoof on a bumpy sidewalk of interwoven rectangular bricks. For the first time since the swing set, I started crying.

"Hey," he said, touching my waist. "Hey. It's okay." I nodded and wiped my face with the back of my hand. "He sucks." I nodded again. "I'll write you an epilogue," Gus said. That made me cry harder. "I will," he said. "I will. Better than any shit that drunk could write. His brain is Swiss cheese. He doesn't even remember writing the book. I can write ten times the story that guy can. There will be blood and guts and sacrifice. *An Imperial Affliction* meets *The Price of Dawn*. You'll love it." I kept nodding, faking a smile, and then he hugged me, his strong arms pulling me into his muscular chest, and I sogged up his polo shirt a little but then recovered enough to speak.

"I spent your Wish on that doucheface," I said into his chest.

"Hazel Grace. No. I will grant you that you did spend my one and only Wish, but you did not spend it on him. You spent it on us."

Behind us, I heard the *plonk plonk* of high heels running.

I turned around. It was Lidewij, her eyeliner running down her cheeks, duly horrified, chasing us up the sidewalk. "Perhaps we should go to the Anne Frank Huis," Lidewij said.

"I'm not going anywhere with that monster," Augustus said.

"He is not invited," Lidewij said.

Augustus kept holding me, protective, his hand on the side of my face. "I don't think—" he started, but I cut him off.

"We should go." I still wanted answers from Van Houten. But it wasn't all I wanted. I only had two days left in Amsterdam with Augustus Waters. I wouldn't let a sad old man ruin them.

Lidewij drove a clunky gray Fiat with an engine that sounded like an excited four-year-old girl. As we drove through the streets of Amsterdam, she repeatedly and profusely apologized. "I am very sorry. There is no excuse. He is very sick," she said. "I thought meeting you would help him, if he would see that his work has shaped real lives, but . . . I'm very sorry. It is very, very embarrassing." Neither Augustus nor I said anything. I was in the backseat behind him. I snuck my hand between the side of the car and his seat, feeling for his hand, but I couldn't find it. Lidewij continued, "I have continued this work because I believe he is a genius and because the pay is very good, but he has become a monster."

"I guess he got pretty rich on that book," I said after a while.

"Oh, no no, he is of the Van Houtens," she said. "In the seventeenth century, his ancestor discovered how to mix cocoa into water. Some Van Houtens moved to the United States long ago, and Peter is of those, but he moved to Holland after his novel. He is an embarrassment to a great family."

The engine screamed. Lidewij shifted and we shot up a canal bridge. "It is circumstance," she said. "Circumstance has made him so cruel. He is not an evil man. But this day, I did not think–when he said these terrible things, I could not believe it. I am very sorry. Very very sorry."

We had to park a block away from the Anne Frank House, and then while Lidewij stood in line to get tickets for us, I sat with my back against a little tree, looking at all the moored houseboats in the Prinsengracht canal. Augustus was standing above me, rolling my oxygen cart in lazy circles, just watching the wheels spin. I wanted him to sit next to me, but I knew it was hard for him to sit, and harder still to stand back up. "Okay?" he asked, looking down at me. I shrugged and reached a hand for his calf. It was his fake calf, but I held on to it. He looked down at me.

"I wanted . . ." I said.

"I know," he said. "I know. Apparently the world is not

a wish-granting factory." That made me smile a little.

Lidewij returned with tickets, but her thin lips were pursed with worry. "There is no elevator," she said. "I am very very sorry."

"It's okay," I said.

"No, there are many stairs," she said. "Steep stairs."

"It's okay," I said again. Augustus started to say something, but I interrupted. "It's okay. I can do it."

We began in a room with a video about Jews in Holland and the Nazi invasion and the Frank family. Then we walked upstairs into the canal house where Otto Frank's business had been. The stairs were slow, for me and Augustus both, but I felt strong. Soon I was staring at the famous bookcase that had hid Anne Frank, her family, and four others. The bookcase was half open, and behind it was an even steeper set of stairs, only wide enough for one person. There were fellow visitors all around us, and I didn't want to hold up the procession, but Lidewij said, "If everyone could be patient, please," and I began the walk up, Lidewij carrying the cart behind me, Gus behind her.

It was fourteen steps. I kept thinking about the people behind me—they were mostly adults speaking a variety of languages—and feeling embarrassed or whatever, feeling like a ghost that both comforts and haunts, but finally I made it up, and then I was in an eerily empty room, leaning against the wall, my brain telling my lungs *it's okay it's okay calm down it's okay* and my lungs telling my brain *oh, God, we're dying here.* I didn't even see Augustus come upstairs, but he came over and wiped his brow with the back of his hand like *whew* and said, "You're a champion."

After a few minutes of wall-leaning, I made it to the next room, which Anne had shared with the dentist Fritz Pfeffer. It was tiny, empty of all furniture. You'd never know anyone had ever lived there except that the pictures Anne had pasted onto the wall from magazines and newspapers were still there.

Another staircase led up to the room where the van Pels family had lived, this one steeper than the last and eighteen steps, essentially a glorified ladder. I got to the threshold and looked up and figured I could not do it, but also knew the only way through was up.

"Let's go back," Gus said behind me.

"I'm okay," I answered quietly. It's stupid, but I kept thinking I *owed* it to her—to Anne Frank, I mean—because she was dead and I wasn't, because she had stayed quiet and kept the blinds drawn and done everything right and still died, and so I should go up the steps and see the rest of the world she'd lived in those years before the Gestapo came.

I began to climb the stairs, crawling up them like a little kid would, slow at first so I could breathe, but then faster because I knew I couldn't breathe and wanted to get to the top before everything gave out. The blackness encroached around my field of vision as I pulled myself up, eighteen steps, steep as hell. I finally crested the staircase mostly blind and nauseated, the muscles in my arms and legs screaming for oxygen. I slumped seated against a wall, heaving watered-down coughs. There was an empty glass case bolted to the wall above me and I stared up through it to the ceiling and tried not to pass out.

Lidewij crouched down next to me, saying, "You are at the top, that is it," and I nodded. I had a vague awareness of the adults all around glancing down at me worriedly; of Lidewij speaking quietly in one language and then another and then another to various visitors; of Augustus standing above me, his hand on the top of my head, stroking my hair along the part.

After a long time, Lidewij and Augustus pulled me to my feet and I saw what was protected by the glass case: pencil marks on the wallpaper measuring the growth of all the children in the annex during the period they lived there, inch after inch until they would grow no more.

From there, we left the Franks' living area, but we were still in the museum: A long narrow hallway showed pictures of each of the annex's eight residents and described how and where and when they died.

"The only member of his whole family who survived the war," Lidewij told us, referring to Anne's father, Otto. Her voice was hushed like we were in church.

"But he didn't survive a war, not really," Augustus said. "He survived a genocide."

"True," Lidewij said. "I do not know how you go on,

without your family. I do not know." As I read about each of the seven who died, I thought of Otto Frank not being a father anymore, left with a diary instead of a wife and two daughters. At the end of the hallway, a huge book, bigger than a dictionary, contained the names of the 103,000 dead from the Netherlands in the Holocaust. (Only 5,000 of the deported Dutch Jews, a wall label explained, had survived. 5,000 Otto Franks.) The book was turned to the page with Anne Frank's name, but what got me about it was the fact that right beneath her name there were four Aron Franks. *Four.* Four Aron Franks without museums, without historical markers, without anyone to mourn them. I silently resolved to remember and pray for the four Aron Franks as long as I was around. (Maybe some people need to believe in a proper and omnipotent God to pray, but I don't.)

As we got to the end of the room, Gus stopped and said, "You okay?" I nodded.

He gestured back toward Anne's picture. "The worst part is that she almost lived, you know? She died weeks away from liberation."

Lidewij took a few steps away to watch a video, and I grabbed Augustus's hand as we walked into the next room. It was an A-frame room with some letters Otto Frank had written to people during his months-long search for his daughters. On the wall in the middle of the room, a video of Otto Frank played. He was speaking in English.

"Are there any Nazis left that I could hunt down and

bring to justice?" Augustus asked while we leaned over the vitrines reading Otto's letters and the gutting replies that no, no one had seen his children after the liberation.

"I think they're all dead. But it's not like the Nazis had a monopoly on evil."

"True," he said. "That's what we should do, Hazel Grace: We should team up and be this disabled vigilante duo roaring through the world, righting wrongs, defending the weak, protecting the endangered."

Although it was his dream and not mine, I indulged it. He'd indulged mine, after all. "Our fearlessness shall be our secret weapon," I said.

"The tales of our exploits will survive as long as the human voice itself," he said.

"And even after that, when the robots recall the human absurdities of sacrifice and compassion, they will remember us."

"They will robot-laugh at our courageous folly," he said. "But something in their iron robot hearts will yearn to have lived and died as we did: on the hero's errand."

"Augustus Waters," I said, looking up at him, thinking that you cannot kiss anyone in the Anne Frank House, and then thinking that Anne Frank, after all, kissed someone in the Anne Frank House, and that she would probably like nothing more than for her home to have become a place where the young and irreparably broken sink into love.

"I must say," Otto Frank said on the video in his

accented English, "I was very much surprised by the deep thoughts Anne had."

And then we were kissing. My hand let go of the oxygen cart and I reached up for his neck, and he pulled me up by my waist onto my tiptoes. As his parted lips met mine, I started to feel breathless in a new and fascinating way. The space around us evaporated, and for a weird moment I really liked my body; this cancer-ruined thing I'd spent years dragging around suddenly seemed worth the struggle, worth the chest tubes and the PICC lines and the ceaseless bodily betrayal of the tumors.

"It was quite a different Anne I had known as my daughter. She never really showed this kind of inner feeling," Otto Frank continued.

The kiss lasted forever as Otto Frank kept talking from behind me. "And my conclusion is," he said, "since I had been in very good terms with Anne, that most parents don't know really their children."

I realized that my eyes were closed and opened them. Augustus was staring at me, his blue eyes closer to me than they'd ever been, and behind him, a crowd of people three deep had sort of circled around us. They were angry, I thought. Horrified. These teenagers, with their hormones, making out beneath a video broadcasting the shattered voice of a former father.

I pulled away from Augustus, and he snuck a peck onto my forehead as I stared down at my Chuck Taylors.

And then they started clapping. All the people, all these adults, just started clapping, and one shouted "Bravo!" in a European accent. Augustus, smiling, bowed. Laughing, I curtsied ever so slightly, which was met with another round of applause.

We made our way downstairs, letting all the adults go down first, and right before we got to the café (where blessedly an elevator took us back down to ground level and the gift shop) we saw pages of Anne's diary, and also her unpublished book of quotations. The quote book happened to be turned to a page of Shakespeare quotations. *For who so firm that cannot be seduced?* she'd written.

Lidewij drove us back to the Filosoof. Outside the hotel, it was drizzling and Augustus and I stood on the brick sidewalk slowly getting wet.

Augustus: "You probably need some rest."

Me: "I'm okay."

Augustus: "Okay." (Pause.) "What are you thinking about?"

Me: "You."

Augustus: "What about me?"

Me: "'I do not know which to prefer, / The beauty of inflections / Or the beauty of innuendos, / The blackbird whistling / Or just after.'"

Augustus: "God, you are sexy."

Me: "We could go to your room."
Augustus: "I've heard worse ideas."

We squeezed into the tiny elevator together. Every surface, including the floor, was mirrored. We had to pull the door to shut ourselves in and then the old thing creaked slowly up to the second floor. I was tired and sweaty and worried that I generally looked and smelled gross, but even so I kissed him in that elevator, and then he pulled away and pointed at the mirror and said, "Look, infinite Hazels."

"Some infinities are larger than other infinities," I drawled, mimicking Van Houten.

"What an assclown," Augustus said, and it took all that time and more just to get us to the second floor. Finally the elevator lurched to a halt, and he pushed the mirrored door open. When it was half open, he winced in pain and lost his grip on the door for a second.

"You okay?" I asked.

After a second, he said, "Yeah, yeah, door's just heavy, I guess." He pushed again and got it open. He let me walk out first, of course, but then I didn't know which direction to walk down the hallway, and so I just stood there outside the elevator and he stood there, too, his face still contorted, and I said again, "Okay?"

"Just out of shape, Hazel Grace. All is well."

We were just standing there in the hallway, and he

wasn't leading the way to his room or anything, and I didn't know where his room was, and as the stalemate continued, I became convinced he was trying to figure out a way not to hook up with me, that I never should have suggested the idea in the first place, that it was unladylike and therefore had disgusted Augustus Waters, who was standing there looking at me unblinking, trying to think of a way to extricate himself from the situation politely. And then, after forever, he said, "It's above my knee and it just tapers a little and then it's just skin. There's a nasty scar, but it just looks like—"

"What?" I asked.

"My leg," he said. "Just so you're prepared in case, I mean, in case you see it or what—"

"Oh, get over yourself," I said, and took the two steps I needed to get to him. I kissed him, hard, pressing him against the wall, and I kept kissing him as he fumbled for the room key.

We crawled into the bed, my freedom circumscribed some by the oxygen, but even so I could get on top of him and take his shirt off and taste the sweat on the skin below his collarbone as I whispered into his skin, "I love you, Augustus Waters," his body relaxing beneath mine as he heard me say it. He reached down and tried to pull my shirt off, but it got tangled in the tube. I laughed.

...

"How do you do this every day?" he asked as I disentangled my shirt from the tubes. Idiotically, it occurred to me that my pink underwear didn't match my purple bra, as if boys even notice such things. I crawled under the covers and kicked out of my jeans and socks and then watched the comforter dance as beneath it, Augustus removed first his jeans and then his leg.

We were lying on our backs next to each other, everything hidden by the covers, and after a second I reached over for his thigh and let my hand trail downward to the stump, the thick scarred skin. I held the stump for a second. He flinched. "It hurts?" I asked.

"No," he said.

He flipped himself onto his side and kissed me. "You're so hot," I said, my hand still on his leg.

"I'm starting to think you have an amputee fetish," he answered, still kissing me. I laughed.

"I have an Augustus Waters fetish," I explained.

The whole affair was the precise opposite of what I figured it would be: slow and patient and quiet and neither particularly painful nor particularly ecstatic. There were a lot of condomy problems that I did not get a particularly good look at. No headboards were broken. No screaming. Honestly, it was probably the longest time we'd ever spent together without talking.

Only one thing followed type: Afterward, when I had my face resting against Augustus's chest, listening to his heart pound, Augustus said, "Hazel Grace, I literally cannot keep my eyes open."

"Misuse of literality," I said.

"No," he said. "So. Tired."

His face turned away from me, my ear pressed to his chest, listening to his lungs settle into the rhythm of sleep. After a while, I got up, dressed, found the Hotel Filosoof stationery, and wrote him a love letter:

Dearest Augustus,

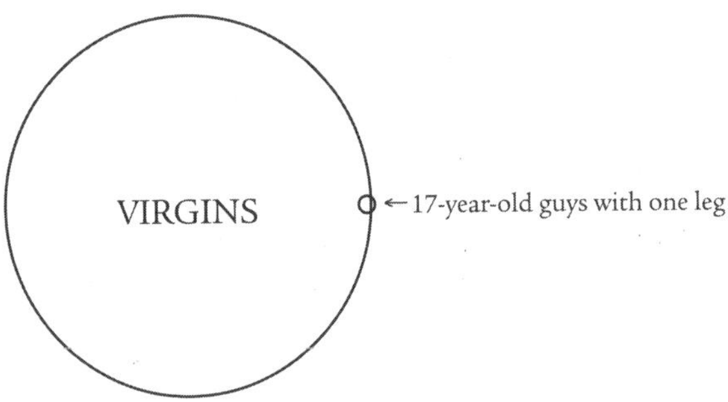

yrs,
Hazel Grace

CHAPTER THIRTEEN

The next morning, our last full day in Amsterdam, Mom and Augustus and I walked the half block from the hotel to the Vondelpark, where we found a café in the shadow of the Dutch national film museum. Over lattes—which, the waiter explained to us, the Dutch called "wrong coffee" because it had more milk than coffee—we sat in the lacy shade of a huge chestnut tree and recounted for Mom our encounter with the great Peter Van Houten. We made the story funny. You have a choice in this world, I believe, about how to tell sad stories, and we made the funny choice: Augustus, slumped in the café chair, pretended to be the tongue-tied, word-slurring Van Houten who could not so much as push himself out of his chair; I stood up to play a me all full of bluster and machismo, shouting, "Get up, you fat ugly old man!"

"Did you call him ugly?" Augustus asked.

"Just go with it," I told him.

"I'm naht uggy. You're the uggy one, nosetube girl."

"You're a coward!" I rumbled, and Augustus broke character to laugh. I sat down. We told Mom about the Anne Frank House, leaving out the kissing.

"Did you go back to chez Van Houten afterward?" Mom asked.

Augustus didn't even give me time to blush. "Nah, we just hung out at a café. Hazel amused me with some Venn diagram humor." He glanced at me. God, he was sexy.

"Sounds lovely," she said. "Listen, I'm going to go for a walk. Give the two of you time to talk," she said at Gus, an edge in it. "Then maybe later we can go for a tour on a canal boat."

"Um, okay?" I said. Mom left a five-euro note under her saucer and then kissed me on the top of the head, whispering, "I love love love you," which was two more loves than usual.

Gus motioned down to the shadows of the branches intersecting and coming apart on the concrete. "Beautiful, huh?"

"Yeah," I said.

"Such a good metaphor," he mumbled.

"Is it now?" I asked.

"The negative image of things blown together and then blown apart," he said. Before us, hundreds of people passed, jogging and biking and Rollerblading. Amsterdam was a city designed for movement and activity, a city that would rather not travel by car, and so inevitably I felt excluded from it. But God, was it beautiful, the creek carving a path around the huge tree, a heron standing still at the water's edge, searching for a breakfast amid the millions of elm petals floating in the water.

But Augustus didn't notice. He was too busy watching the shadows move. Finally, he said, "I could look at this all day, but we should go to the hotel."

"Do we have time?" I asked.

He smiled sadly. "If only," he said.

"What's wrong?" I asked.

He nodded back in the direction of the hotel.

We walked in silence, Augustus a half step in front of me. I was too scared to ask if I had reason to be scared.

So there is this thing called Maslow's Hierarchy of Needs. Basically, this guy Abraham Maslow became famous for his theory that certain needs must be met before you can even have other kinds of needs. It looks like this:

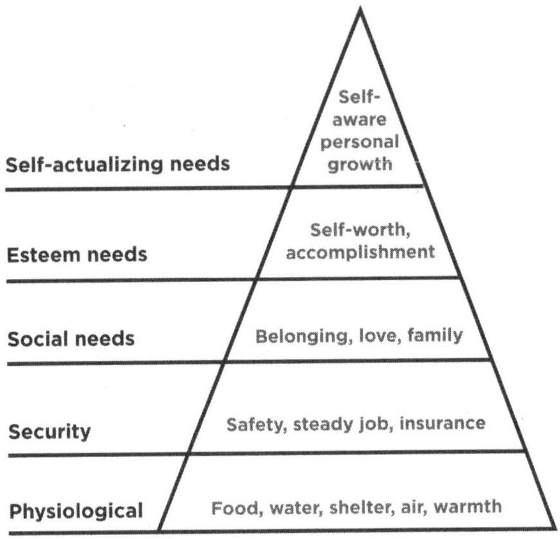

MASLOW'S HIERARCHY OF NEEDS

Once your needs for food and water are fulfilled, you move up to the next set of needs, security, and then the next and the next, but the important thing is that, according to Maslow, until your physiological needs are satisfied, you can't even *worry* about security or social needs, let alone "self-actualization," which is when you start to, like, make art and think about morality and quantum physics and stuff.

According to Maslow, I was stuck on the second level of the pyramid, unable to feel secure in my health and therefore unable to reach for love and respect and art and whatever else, which is, of course, utter horseshit: The urge to make art or contemplate philosophy does not go away when you are sick. Those urges just become transfigured by illness.

Maslow's pyramid seemed to imply that I was less human than other people, and most people seemed to agree with him. But not Augustus. I always thought he could love me because he'd once been sick. Only now did it occur to me that maybe he still was.

We arrived in my room, the Kierkegaard. I sat down on the bed expecting him to join me, but he hunkered down in the dusty paisley chair. That chair. How old was it? Fifty years?

I felt the ball in the base of my throat hardening as I watched him pull a cigarette from his pack and stick it between his lips. He leaned back and sighed. "Just before you went into the ICU, I started to feel this ache in my hip."

"No," I said. Panic rolled in, pulled me under.

He nodded. "So I went in for a PET scan." He stopped. He yanked the cigarette out of his mouth and clenched his teeth.

Much of my life had been devoted to trying not to cry in front of people who loved me, so I knew what Augustus was doing. You clench your teeth. You look up. You tell yourself that if they see you cry, it will hurt them, and you will be nothing but A Sadness in their lives, and you must not become a mere sadness, so you will not cry, and you say all of this to yourself while looking up at the ceiling, and then you swallow even though your throat does not want to close and you look at the person who loves you and smile.

He flashed his crooked smile, then said, "I lit up like a Christmas tree, Hazel Grace. The lining of my chest, my left hip, my liver, everywhere."

Everywhere. That word hung in the air awhile. We both knew what it meant. I got up, dragging my body and the cart across carpet that was older than Augustus would ever be, and I knelt at the base of the chair and put my head in his lap and hugged him by the waist.

He was stroking my hair. "I'm so sorry," I said.

"I'm sorry I didn't tell you," he said, his voice calm. "Your mom must know. The way she looked at me. My mom must've just told her or something. I should've told you. It was stupid. Selfish."

I knew why he hadn't said anything, of course: the same reason I hadn't wanted him to see me in the ICU. I couldn't be mad at him for even a moment, and only now that I loved a grenade did I understand the foolishness of trying to save others from my own impending fragmentation: I couldn't unlove Augustus Waters. And I didn't want to.

"It's not fair," I said. "It's just so goddamned unfair."

"The world," he said, "is not a wish-granting factory,"

and then he broke down, just for one moment, his sob roaring impotent like a clap of thunder unaccompanied by lightning, the terrible ferocity that amateurs in the field of suffering might mistake for weakness. Then he pulled me to him and, his face inches from mine, resolved, "I'll fight it. I'll fight it for you. Don't you worry about me, Hazel Grace. I'm okay. I'll find a way to hang around and annoy you for a long time."

I was crying. But even then he was strong, holding me tight so that I could see the sinewy muscles of his arms wrapped around me as he said, "I'm sorry. You'll be okay. It'll be okay. I promise," and smiled his crooked smile.

He kissed my forehead, and then I felt his powerful chest deflate just a little. "I guess I had a *hamartia* after all."

After a while, I pulled him over to the bed and we lay there together as he told me they'd started palliative chemo, but he gave it up to go to Amsterdam, even though his parents were furious. They'd tried to stop him right up until that morning, when I heard him screaming that his body belonged to him. "We could have rescheduled," I said.

"No, we couldn't have," he answered. "Anyway, it wasn't working. I could tell it wasn't working, you know?"

I nodded. "It's just bullshit, the whole thing," I said.

"They'll try something else when I get home. They've always got a new idea."

"Yeah," I said, having been the experimental pincushion myself.

"I kind of conned you into believing you were falling in love with a healthy person," he said.

I shrugged. "I'd have done the same to you."

"No, you wouldn't've, but we can't all be as awesome as you." He kissed me, then grimaced.

"Does it hurt?" I asked.

"No. Just." He stared at the ceiling for a long time before saying, "I like this world. I like drinking champagne. I like not smoking. I like the sound of Dutch people speaking Dutch. And now . . . I don't even get a battle. I don't get a fight."

"You get to battle cancer," I said. "That is your battle. And you'll keep fighting," I told him. I hated it when people tried to build me up to prepare for battle, but I did it to him, anyway. "You'll . . . you'll . . . live your best life today. This is your war now." I despised myself for the cheesy sentiment, but what else did I have?

"Some war," he said dismissively. "What am I at war with? My cancer. And what is my cancer? My cancer is me. The tumors are made of me. They're made of me as surely as my brain and my heart are made of me. It is a civil war, Hazel Grace, with a predetermined winner."

"Gus," I said. I couldn't say anything else. He was too smart for the kinds of solace I could offer.

"Okay," he said. But it wasn't. After a moment, he said,

"If you go to the Rijksmuseum, which I really wanted to do—but who are we kidding, neither of us can walk through a museum. But anyway, I looked at the collection online before we left. If you were to go, and hopefully someday you will, you would see a lot of paintings of dead people. You'd see Jesus on the cross, and you'd see a dude getting stabbed in the neck, and you'd see people dying at sea and in battle and a parade of martyrs. But Not. One. Single. Cancer. Kid. Nobody biting it from the plague or smallpox or yellow fever or whatever, because there is no glory in illness. There is no meaning to it. There is no honor in dying *of*."

Abraham Maslow, I present to you Augustus Waters, whose existential curiosity dwarfed that of his well-fed, well-loved, healthy brethren. While the mass of men went on leading thoroughly unexamined lives of monstrous consumption, Augustus Waters examined the collection of the Rijksmuseum from afar.

"What?" Augustus asked after a while.

"Nothing," I said. "I'm just . . ." I couldn't finish the sentence, didn't know how to. "I'm just very, very fond of you."

He smiled with half his mouth, his nose inches from mine. "The feeling is mutual. I don't suppose you can forget about it and treat me like I'm not dying."

"I don't think you're dying," I said. "I think you've just got a touch of cancer."

He smiled. Gallows humor. “I’m on a roller coaster that only goes up,” he said.

“And it is my privilege and my responsibility to ride all the way up with you,” I said.

“Would it be absolutely ludicrous to try to make out?”

“There is no try,” I said. “There is only do.”

CHAPTER FOURTEEN

On the flight home, twenty thousand feet above clouds that were ten thousand feet above the ground, Gus said, "I used to think it would be fun to live on a cloud."

"Yeah," I said. "Like it would be like one of those inflatable moonwalk machines, except for always."

"But then in middle school science, Mr. Martinez asked who among us had ever fantasized about living in the clouds, and everyone raised their hand. Then Mr. Martinez told us that up in the clouds the wind blew one hundred and fifty miles an hour and the temperature was thirty below zero and there was no oxygen and we'd all die within seconds."

"Sounds like a nice guy."

"He specialized in the murder of dreams, Hazel Grace, let me tell you. You think volcanoes are awesome? Tell that to the ten thousand screaming corpses at Pompeii. You still secretly believe that there is an element of magic to this world? It's all just soulless molecules bouncing against each other randomly. Do you worry about who will take care of you if your parents die? As well you should, because they will be worm food in the fullness of time."

"Ignorance is bliss," I said.

A flight attendant walked through the aisle with a beverage cart, half whispering, "Drinks? Drinks? Drinks? Drinks?" Gus leaned over me, raising his hand. "Could we have some champagne, please?"

"You're twenty-one?" she asked dubiously. I conspicuously rearranged the nubbins in my nose. The stewardess smiled, then glanced down at my sleeping mother. "She won't mind?" she asked of Mom.

"Nah," I said.

So she poured champagne into two plastic cups. Cancer Perks.

Gus and I toasted. "To you," he said.

"To you," I said, touching my cup to his.

We sipped. Dimmer stars than we'd had at Oranjee, but still good enough to drink.

"You know," Gus said to me, "everything Van Houten said was true."

"Maybe, but he didn't have to be such a douche about it. I can't believe he imagined a future for Sisyphus the Hamster but not for Anna's mom."

Augustus shrugged. He seemed to zone out all of a sudden. "Okay?" I asked.

He shook his head microscopically. "Hurts," he said.

"Chest?"

He nodded. Fists clenched. Later, he would describe it as a one-legged fat man wearing a stiletto heel standing on the middle of his chest. I returned my seat-back tray to its upright and locked position and bent forward to dig pills out of his backpack. He swallowed one with champagne. "Okay?" I asked again.

Gus sat there, pumping his fist, waiting for the medicine to work, the medicine that did not kill the pain so much as distance him from it (and from me).

"It was like it was personal," Gus said quietly. "Like he was mad at us for some reason. Van Houten, I mean." He drank the rest of his champagne in a quick series of gulps and soon fell asleep.

My dad was waiting for us in baggage claim, standing amid all the limo drivers in suits holding signs printed with the last names of their passengers: JOHNSON, BARRINGTON, CARMICHAEL. Dad had a sign of his own. MY BEAUTIFUL FAMILY, it read, and then underneath that (AND GUS).

I hugged him, and he started crying (of course). As we drove home, Gus and I told Dad stories of Amsterdam, but it wasn't until I was home and hooked up to Philip watching good ol' American television with Dad and eating American pizza off napkins on our laps that I told him about Gus.

"Gus had a recurrence," I said.

"I know," he said. He scooted over toward me, and then added, "His mom told us before the trip. I'm sorry he kept it from you. I'm . . . I'm sorry, Hazel." I didn't say anything for a long time. The show we were watching was about people who are trying to pick which house they are going to buy. "So I read *An Imperial Affliction* while you guys were gone," Dad said.

I turned my head up to him. "Oh, cool. What'd you think?"

"It was good. A little over my head. I was a biochemistry major, remember, not a literature guy. I do wish it had ended."

"Yeah," I said. "Common complaint."

"Also, it was a bit hopeless," he said. "A bit defeatist."

"If by defeatist you mean *honest*, then I agree."

"I don't think defeatism is honest," Dad answered. "I refuse to accept that."

"So everything happens for a reason and we'll all go live in the clouds and play harps and live in mansions?"

Dad smiled. He put a big arm around me and pulled

me to him, kissing the side of my head. "I don't know what I believe, Hazel. I thought being an adult meant knowing what you believe, but that has not been my experience."

"Yeah," I said. "Okay."

He told me again that he was sorry about Gus, and then we went back to watching the show, and the people picked a house, and Dad still had his arm around me, and I was kinda starting to fall asleep, but I didn't want to go to bed, and then Dad said, "You know what I believe? I remember in college I was taking this math class, this really great math class taught by this tiny old woman. She was talking about fast Fourier transforms and she stopped midsentence and said, 'Sometimes it seems the universe wants to be noticed.'

"That's what I believe. I believe the universe wants to be noticed. I think the universe is improbably biased toward consciousness, that it rewards intelligence in part because the universe enjoys its elegance being observed. And who am I, living in the middle of history, to tell the universe that it—or my observation of it—is temporary?"

"You are fairly smart," I said after a while.

"You are fairly good at compliments," he answered.

The next afternoon, I drove over to Gus's house and ate peanut-butter-and-jelly sandwiches with his parents and told them stories about Amsterdam while Gus napped on the living room couch, where we'd watched *V for Vendetta.*

I could just see him from the kitchen: He lay on his back, head turned away from me, a PICC line already in. They were attacking the cancer with a new cocktail: two chemo drugs and a protein receptor that they hoped would turn off the oncogene in Gus's cancer. He was lucky to get enrolled in the trial, they told me. Lucky. I knew one of the drugs. Hearing the sound of its name made me want to barf.

After a while, Isaac's mom brought him over.

"Isaac, hi, it's Hazel from Support Group, not your evil ex-girlfriend." His mom walked him to me, and I pulled myself out of the dining room chair and hugged him, his body taking a moment to find me before he hugged me back, hard.

"How was Amsterdam?" he asked.

"Awesome," I said.

"Waters," he said. "Where are ya, bro?"

"He's napping," I said, and my voice caught. Isaac shook his head, everyone quiet.

"Sucks," Isaac said after a second. His mom walked him to a chair she'd pulled out. He sat.

"I can still dominate your blind ass at Counterinsurgence," Augustus said without turning toward us. The medicine slowed his speech a bit, but only to the speed of regular people.

"I'm pretty sure all asses are blind," Isaac answered, reaching his hands into the air vaguely, looking for his mom. She grabbed him, pulled him up, and they walked over to the couch, where Gus and Isaac hugged awkwardly. "How are you feeling?" Isaac asked.

"Everything tastes like pennies. Aside from that, I'm on a roller coaster that only goes up, kid," Gus answered. Isaac laughed. "How are the eyes?"

"Oh, excellent," he said. "I mean, they're not in my head is the only problem."

"Awesome, yeah," Gus said. "Not to one-up you or anything, but my body is made out of cancer."

"So I heard," Isaac said, trying not to let it get to him. He fumbled toward Gus's hand and found only his thigh.

"I'm taken," Gus said.

Isaac's mom brought over two dining room chairs, and Isaac and I sat down next to Gus. I took Gus's hand, stroking circles around the space between his thumb and forefinger.

The adults headed down to the basement to commiserate or whatever, leaving the three of us alone in the living room. After a while, Augustus turned his head to us, the waking up slow. "How's Monica?" he asked.

"Haven't heard from her once," Isaac said. "No cards; no emails. I got this machine that reads me my emails. It's awesome. I can change the voice's gender or accent or whatever."

"So I can like send you a porn story and you can have an old German man read it to you?"

"Exactly," Isaac said. "Although Mom still has to help

me with it, so maybe hold off on the German porno for a week or two."

"She hasn't even, like, texted you to ask how you're doing?" I asked. This struck me as an unfathomable injustice.

"Total radio silence," Isaac said.

"Ridiculous," I said.

"I've stopped thinking about it. I don't have time to have a girlfriend. I have like a full-time job Learning How to Be Blind."

Gus turned his head back away from us, staring out the window at the patio in his backyard. His eyes closed.

Isaac asked how I was doing, and I said I was good, and he told me there was a new girl in Support Group with a really hot voice and he needed me to go to tell him if she was actually hot. Then out of nowhere Augustus said, "You can't just not contact your former boyfriend after his eyes get cut out of his freaking head."

"Just one of—" Isaac started.

"Hazel Grace, do you have four dollars?" asked Gus.

"Um," I said. "Yes?"

"Excellent. You'll find my leg under the coffee table," he said. Gus pushed himself upright and scooted down to the edge of the couch. I handed him the prosthetic; he fastened it in slow motion.

I helped him to stand and then offered my arm to Isaac, guiding him past furniture that suddenly seemed intrusive, realizing that, for the first time in years, I was the healthiest person in the room.

I drove. Augustus rode shotgun. Isaac sat in the back. We stopped at a grocery store, where, per Augustus's instruction, I bought a dozen eggs while he and Isaac waited in the car. And then Isaac guided us by his memory to Monica's house, an aggressively sterile, two-story house near the JCC. Monica's bright green 1990s Pontiac Firebird sat fat-wheeled in the driveway.

"Is it there?" Isaac asked when he felt me coming to a stop.

"Oh, it's there," Augustus said. "You know what it looks like, Isaac? It looks like all the hopes we were foolish to hope."

"So she's inside?"

Gus turned his head around slowly to look at Isaac. "Who cares where she is? This is not about her. This is about *you*." Gus gripped the egg carton in his lap, then opened the door and pulled his legs out onto the street. He opened the door for Isaac, and I watched through the mirror as Gus helped Isaac out of the car, the two of them leaning on each other at the shoulder then tapering away, like praying hands that don't quite meet at the palms.

I rolled down the windows and watched from the car, because vandalism made me nervous. They took a few steps toward the car, then Gus flipped open the egg carton and handed Isaac an egg. Isaac tossed it, missing the car by a solid forty feet.

"A little to the left," Gus said.

"My throw was a little to the left or I need to aim a little to the left?"

"Aim left." Isaac swiveled his shoulders. "Lefter," Gus said. Isaac swiveled again. "Yes. Excellent. And throw hard." Gus handed him another egg, and Isaac hurled it, the egg arcing over the car and smashing against the slow-sloping roof of the house. "Bull's-eye!" Gus said.

"Really?" Isaac asked excitedly.

"No, you threw it like twenty feet over the car. Just, throw hard, but keep it low. And a little right of where you were last time." Isaac reached over and found an egg himself from the carton Gus cradled. He tossed it, hitting a taillight. "Yes!" Gus said. "Yes! TAILLIGHT!"

Isaac reached for another egg, missed wide right, then another, missing low, then another, hitting the back windshield. He then nailed three in a row against the trunk. "Hazel Grace," Gus shouted back to me. "Take a picture of this so Isaac can see it when they invent robot eyes." I pulled myself up so I was sitting in the rolled-down window, my elbows on the roof of the car, and snapped a picture with my phone: Augustus, an unlit cigarette in his mouth, his smile deliciously crooked, holds the mostly empty pink egg carton above his head. His other hand is draped around Isaac's shoulder, whose sunglasses are turned not quite toward the camera. Behind them, egg yolks drip down the windshield and bumper of the green Firebird. And behind that, a door is opening.

"What," asked the middle-aged woman a moment after I'd snapped the picture, "in God's name—" and then she stopped talking.

"Ma'am," Augustus said, nodding toward her, "your daughter's car has just been deservedly egged by a blind man. Please close the door and go back inside or we'll be forced to call the police." After wavering for a moment, Monica's mom closed the door and disappeared. Isaac threw the last three eggs in quick succession and Gus then guided him back toward the car. "See, Isaac, if you just take—we're coming to the curb now—the feeling of legitimacy away from them, if you turn it around so they feel like *they* are committing a crime by watching—a few more steps—their cars get egged, they'll be confused and scared and worried and they'll just return to their—you'll find the door handle directly in front of you—quietly desperate lives." Gus hurried around the front of the car and installed himself in the shotgun seat. The doors closed, and I roared off, driving for several hundred feet before I realized I was headed down a dead-end street. I circled the cul-de-sac and raced back past Monica's house.

I never took another picture of him.

CHAPTER FIFTEEN

A few days later, at Gus's house, his parents and my parents and Gus and me all squeezed around the dining room table, eating stuffed peppers on a tablecloth that had, according to Gus's dad, last seen use in the previous century.

My dad: "Emily, this risotto . . ."

My mom: "It's just delicious."

Gus's mom: "Oh, thanks. I'd be happy to give you the recipe."

Gus, swallowing a bite: "You know, the primary taste I'm getting is not-Oranjee."

Me: "Good observation, Gus. This food, while delicious, does not taste like Oranjee."

My mom: "Hazel."

Gus: "It tastes like . . ."

Me: "Food."

Gus: "Yes, precisely. It tastes like food, excellently prepared. But it does not taste, how do I put this delicately . . . ?"

Me: "It does not taste like God Himself cooked heaven into a series of five dishes which were then served to you accompanied by several luminous balls of fermented, bubbly plasma while actual and literal flower petals floated down all around your canal-side dinner table."

Gus: "Nicely phrased."

Gus's father: "Our children are weird."

My dad: "Nicely phrased."

A week after our dinner, Gus ended up in the ER with chest pain, and they admitted him overnight, so I drove over to Memorial the next morning and visited him on the fourth floor. I hadn't been to Memorial since visiting Isaac. It didn't have any of the cloyingly bright primary color–painted walls or the framed paintings of dogs driving cars that one found at Children's, but the absolute sterility of the place made me nostalgic for the happy-kid bullshit at Children's. Memorial was so *functional*. It was a storage facility. A prematorium.

When the elevator doors opened on the fourth floor, I saw Gus's mom pacing in the waiting room, talking on a cell phone. She hung up quickly, then hugged me and offered to take my cart.

"I'm okay," I said. "How's Gus?"

"He had a tough night, Hazel," she said. "His heart is working too hard. He needs to scale back on activity. Wheelchairs from here on out. They're putting him on some new medicine that should be better for the pain. His sisters just drove in."

"Okay," I said. "Can I see him?"

She put her arm around me and squeezed my shoulder. It felt weird. "You know we love you, Hazel, but right now we just need to be a family. Gus agrees with that. Okay?"

"Okay," I said.

"I'll tell him you visited."

"Okay," I said. "I'm just gonna read here for a while, I think."

She went down the hall, back to where he was. I understood, but I still missed him, still thought maybe I was missing my last chance to see him, to say good-bye or whatever. The waiting room was all brown carpet and brown overstuffed cloth chairs. I sat in a love seat for a while, my oxygen cart tucked by my feet. I'd worn my Chuck Taylors and my *Ceci n'est pas une pipe* shirt, the exact outfit I'd been wearing two weeks before on the Late Afternoon of the Venn Diagram, and he wouldn't see it. I started scrolling through the pictures on my phone, a backward flip-book of the last few months, beginning with him and Isaac outside of Monica's house and ending with the first picture I'd taken of him, on the drive to *Funky Bones*. It seemed like forever ago, like we'd had this brief but still infinite forever. Some infinities are bigger than other infinities.

Two weeks later, I wheeled Gus across the art park toward *Funky Bones* with one entire bottle of very expensive champagne and my oxygen tank in his lap. The champagne had been donated by one of Gus's doctors—Gus being the kind of person who inspires doctors to give their best bottles of champagne to children. We sat, Gus in his chair and me on the damp grass, as near to *Funky Bones* as we could get him in the chair. I pointed at the little kids goading each other to jump from rib cage to shoulder and Gus answered just loud enough for me to hear over the din, "Last time, I imagined myself as the kid. This time, the skeleton."

We drank from paper Winnie-the-Pooh cups.

CHAPTER SIXTEEN

A typical day with late-stage Gus:

I went over to his house about noon, after he had eaten and puked up breakfast. He met me at the door in his wheelchair, no longer the muscular, gorgeous boy who stared at me at Support Group, but still half smiling, still smoking his unlit cigarette, his blue eyes bright and alive.

We ate lunch with his parents at the dining room table. Peanut-butter-and-jelly sandwiches and last night's asparagus. Gus didn't eat. I asked how he was feeling.

"Grand," he said. "And you?"

"Good. What'd you do last night?"

"I slept quite a lot. I want to write you a sequel, Hazel Grace, but I'm just so damned tired all the time."

"You can just tell it to me," I said.

"Well, I stand by my pre–Van Houten analysis of the Dutch Tulip Man. Not a con man, but not as rich as he was letting on."

"And what about Anna's mom?"

"Haven't settled on an opinion there. Patience, Grasshopper." Augustus smiled. His parents were quiet, watching him, never looking away, like they just wanted to enjoy The Gus Waters Show while it was still in town. "Sometimes I dream that I'm writing a memoir. A memoir would be just the thing to keep me in the hearts and memories of my adoring public."

"Why do you need an adoring public when you've got me?" I asked.

"Hazel Grace, when you're as charming and physically attractive as myself, it's easy enough to win over people you meet. But getting strangers to love you . . . now, *that's* the trick."

I rolled my eyes.

After lunch, we went outside to the backyard. He was still well enough to push his own wheelchair, pulling miniature wheelies to get the front wheels over the bump in the doorway. Still athletic, in spite of it all, blessed with balance and quick reflexes that even the abundant narcotics could not fully mask.

His parents stayed inside, but when I glanced back into the dining room, they were always watching us.

We sat out there in silence for a minute and then Gus said, "I wish we had that swing set sometimes."

"The one from my backyard?"

"Yeah. My nostalgia is so extreme that I am capable of missing a swing my butt never actually touched."

"Nostalgia is a side effect of cancer," I told him.

"Nah, nostalgia is a side effect of dying," he answered. Above us, the wind blew and the branching shadows rearranged themselves on our skin. Gus squeezed my hand. "It is a good life, Hazel Grace."

We went inside when he needed meds, which were pressed into him along with liquid nutrition through his G-tube, a bit of plastic that disappeared into his belly. He was quiet for a while, zoned out. His mom wanted him to take a nap, but he kept shaking his head no when she suggested it, so we just let him sit there half asleep in the chair for a while.

His parents watched an old video of Gus with his sisters—they were probably my age and Gus was about five. They were playing basketball in the driveway of a different house, and even though Gus was tiny, he could dribble like he'd been born doing it, running circles around his sisters as they laughed. It was the first time I'd even seen him play basketball. "He was good," I said.

"Should've seen him in high school," his dad said. "Started varsity as a freshman."

Gus mumbled, "Can I go downstairs?"

His mom and dad wheeled the chair downstairs with Gus still in it, bouncing down crazily in a way that would have been dangerous if danger retained its relevance, and then they left us alone. He got into bed and we lay there together under the covers, me on my side and Gus on his back, my head on his bony shoulder, his heat radiating through his polo shirt and into my skin, my feet tangled with his real foot, my hand on his cheek.

When I got his face nose-touchingly close so that I could only see his eyes, I couldn't tell he was sick. We kissed for a while and then lay together listening to The Hectic Glow's eponymous album, and eventually we fell asleep like that, a quantum entanglement of tubes and bodies.

We woke up later and arranged an armada of pillows so that we could sit comfortably against the edge of the bed and played Counterinsurgence 2: The Price of Dawn. I sucked at it, of course, but my sucking was useful to him: It made it easier for him to die beautifully, to jump in front of a sniper's bullet and sacrifice himself for me, or else to kill a sentry who was just about to shoot me. How he reveled in saving me. He shouted, "You will *not* kill my girlfriend today, International Terrorist of Ambiguous Nationality!"

It crossed my mind to fake a choking incident or something so that he might give me the Heimlich. Maybe then he could rid himself of this fear that his life had been lived and lost for no greater good. But then I imagined him being physically unable to Heimlich, and me having to reveal that it was all a ruse, and the ensuing mutual humiliation.

It's hard as hell to hold on to your dignity when the risen sun is too bright in your losing eyes, and that's what I was thinking about as we hunted for bad guys through the ruins of a city that didn't exist.

Finally, his dad came down and dragged Gus back upstairs, and in the entryway, beneath an Encouragement telling me that Friends Are Forever, I knelt to kiss him good night. I went home and ate dinner with my parents, leaving Gus to eat (and puke up) his own dinner.

After some TV, I went to sleep.

I woke up.

Around noon, I went over there again.

CHAPTER SEVENTEEN

One morning, a month after returning home from Amsterdam, I drove over to his house. His parents told me he was still sleeping downstairs, so I knocked loudly on the basement door before entering, then asked, "Gus?"

I found him mumbling in a language of his own creation. He'd pissed the bed. It was awful. I couldn't even look, really. I just shouted for his parents and they came down, and I went upstairs while they cleaned him up.

When I came back down, he was slowly waking up out of the narcotics to the excruciating day. I arranged his pillows so we could play Counterinsurgence on the bare sheetless mattress, but he was so tired and out of it that he sucked almost as bad as I did, and we couldn't go five minutes without both getting dead. Not fancy heroic deaths either, just careless ones.

I didn't really say anything to him. I almost wanted him to forget I was there, I guess, and I was hoping he didn't remember that I'd found the boy I love deranged in a wide pool of his own piss. I kept kind of hoping that he'd look over at me and say, "Oh, Hazel Grace. How'd you get here?"

But unfortunately, he remembered. "With each passing minute, I'm developing a deeper appreciation of the word *mortified*," he said finally.

"I've pissed the bed, Gus, believe me. It's no big deal."

"You used," he said, and then took a sharp breath, "to call me Augustus."

"You know," he said after a while, "it's kids' stuff, but I always thought my obituary would be in all the newspapers, that I'd have a story worth telling. I always had this secret suspicion that I was special."

"You are," I said.

"You know what I mean, though," he said.

I did know what he meant. I just didn't agree. "I don't care if the *New York Times* writes an obituary for me. I just want you to write one," I told him. "You say you're not special because the world doesn't know about you, but that's an insult to me. *I* know about you."

"I don't think I'm gonna make it to write your obituary," he said, instead of apologizing.

I was so frustrated with him. "I just want to be enough for you, but I never can be. This can never be enough for you. But this is all you get. You get me, and your family, and this world. This is your life. I'm sorry if it sucks. But you're not going to be the first man on Mars, and you're not going to be an NBA star, and you're not going to hunt Nazis. I mean, look at yourself, Gus." He didn't respond. "I don't mean—" I started.

"Oh, you meant it," he interrupted. I started to apologize and he said, "No, I'm sorry. You're right. Let's just play."

So we just played.

CHAPTER EIGHTEEN

I woke up to my phone singing a song by The Hectic Glow. Gus's favorite. That meant he was calling—or someone was calling from his phone. I glanced at the alarm clock: 2:35 A.M. *He's gone,* I thought as everything inside of me collapsed into a singularity.

I could barely creak out a *"Hello?"*

I waited for the sound of a parent's annihilated voice.

"Hazel Grace," Augustus said weakly.

"Oh, thank God it's you. Hi. Hi, I love you."

"Hazel Grace, I'm at the gas station. Something's wrong. You gotta help me."

"What? Where are you?"

"The Speedway at Eighty-sixth and Ditch. I did something wrong with the G-tube and I can't figure it out and—"

"I'm calling nine-one-one," I said.

"No no no no no, they'll take me to a hospital. Hazel, listen to me. Do not call nine-one-one or my parents I will never forgive you don't please just come please just come and fix my goddamned G-tube. I'm just, God, this is the stupidest thing. I don't want my parents to know I'm gone. Please. I have the medicine with me; I just can't get it in. Please." He was crying. I'd never heard him sob like this except from outside his house before Amsterdam.

"Okay," I said. "I'm leaving now."

I took the BiPAP off and connected myself to an oxygen tank, lifted the tank into my cart, and put on sneakers to go with my pink cotton pajama pants and a Butler basketball T-shirt, which had originally been Gus's. I grabbed the keys from the kitchen drawer where Mom kept them and wrote a note in case they woke up while I was gone.

Went to check on Gus. It's important. Sorry.
Love, H

As I drove the couple miles to the gas station, I woke up enough to wonder why Gus had left the house in the middle of the night. Maybe he'd been hallucinating, or his martyrdom fantasies had gotten the better of him.

I sped up Ditch Road past flashing yellow lights, going too fast partly to reach him and partly in the hopes a cop would pull me over and give me an excuse to tell someone that my dying boyfriend was stuck outside of a gas station with a malfunctioning G-tube. But no cop showed up to make my decision for me.

There were only two cars in the lot. I pulled up next to his. I opened the door. The interior lights came on. Augustus sat in the driver's seat, covered in his own vomit, his hands pressed to his belly where the G-tube went in. "Hi," he mumbled.

"Oh, God, Augustus, we have to get you to a hospital."

"Please just look at it." I gagged from the smell but bent forward to inspect the place above his belly button where they'd surgically installed the tube. The skin of his abdomen was warm and bright red.

"Gus, I think something's infected. I can't fix this. Why are you here? Why aren't you at home?" He puked, without even the energy to turn his mouth away from his lap. "Oh, sweetie," I said.

"I wanted to buy a pack of cigarettes," he mumbled. "I lost my pack. Or they took it away from me. I don't know. They said they'd get me another one, but I wanted . . . to do it myself. Do one little thing myself."

He was staring straight ahead. Quietly, I pulled out my phone and glanced down to dial 911.

"I'm sorry," I told him. *Nine-one-one, what is your*

emergency? "Hi, I'm at the Speedway at Eighty-sixth and Ditch, and I need an ambulance. The great love of my life has a malfunctioning G-tube."

He looked up at me. It was horrible. I could hardly look at him. The Augustus Waters of the crooked smiles and unsmoked cigarettes was gone, replaced by this desperate humiliated creature sitting there beneath me.

"This is it. I can't even not smoke anymore."

"Gus, I love you."

"Where is my chance to be somebody's Peter Van Houten?" He hit the steering wheel weakly, the car honking as he cried. He leaned his head back, looking up. "I hate myself I hate myself I hate this I hate this I disgust myself I hate it I hate it I hate it just let me fucking die."

According to the conventions of the genre, Augustus Waters kept his sense of humor till the end, did not for a moment waiver in his courage, and his spirit soared like an indomitable eagle until the world itself could not contain his joyous soul.

But this was the truth, a pitiful boy who desperately wanted not to be pitiful, screaming and crying, poisoned by an infected G-tube that kept him alive, but not alive enough.

I wiped his chin and grabbed his face in my hands and knelt down close to him so that I could see his eyes, which still lived. "I'm sorry. I wish it was like that movie, with the Persians and the Spartans."

"Me too," he said.

"But it isn't," I said.

"I know," he said.

"There are no bad guys."

"Yeah."

"Even cancer isn't a bad guy really: Cancer just wants to be alive."

"Yeah."

"You're okay," I told him. I could hear the sirens.

"Okay," he said. He was losing consciousness.

"Gus, you have to promise not to try this again. I'll get you cigarettes, okay?" He looked at me. His eyes swam in their sockets. "You have to promise."

He nodded a little and then his eyes closed, his head swiveling on his neck.

"Gus," I said. "Stay with me."

"Read me something," he said as the goddamned ambulance roared right past us. So while I waited for them to turn around and find us, I recited the only poem I could bring to mind, "The Red Wheelbarrow" by William Carlos Williams.

so much depends
upon

a red wheel
barrow

glazed with rain
water

beside the white
chickens.

Williams was a doctor. It seemed to me like a doctor's poem. The poem was over, but the ambulance was still driving away from us, so I kept writing it.

And so much depends, I told Augustus, upon a blue sky cut open by the branches of the trees above. So much depends upon the transparent G-tube erupting from the gut of the blue-lipped boy. So much depends upon this observer of the universe.

Half conscious, he glanced over at me and mumbled, "And you say you don't write poetry."

CHAPTER NINETEEN

He came home from the hospital a few days later, finally and irrevocably robbed of his ambitions. It took more medication to remove him from the pain. He moved upstairs permanently, into a hospital bed near the living room window.

These were days of pajamas and beard scruff, of mumblings and requests and him endlessly thanking everyone for all they were doing on his behalf. One afternoon, he pointed vaguely toward a laundry basket in a corner of the room and asked me, "What's that?"

"That laundry basket?"

"No, next to it."

"I don't see anything next to it."

"It's my last shred of dignity. It's very small."

. . .

The next day, I let myself in. They didn't like me to ring the doorbell anymore because it might wake him up. His sisters were there with their banker husbands and three kids, all boys, who ran up to me and chanted *who are you who are you who are you*, running circles around the entryway like lung capacity was a renewable resource. I'd met the sisters before, but never the kids or their dads.

"I'm Hazel," I said.

"Gus has a *girlfriend*," one of the kids said.

"I am aware that Gus has a girlfriend," I said.

"She's got boobies," another said.

"Is that so?"

"Why do you have that?" the first one asked, pointing at my oxygen cart.

"It helps me breathe," I said. "Is Gus awake?"

"No, he's sleeping."

"He's dying," said another.

"He's dying," the third one confirmed, suddenly serious. It was quiet for a moment, and I wondered what I was supposed to say, but then one of them kicked another and they were off to the races again, falling all over each other in a scrum that migrated toward the kitchen.

I made my way to Gus's parents in the living room and met his brothers-in-law, Chris and Dave.

I hadn't gotten to know his half sisters, really, but they

both hugged me anyway. Julie was sitting on the edge of the bed, talking to a sleeping Gus in precisely the same voice that one would use to tell an infant he was adorable, saying, "Oh, Gussy Gussy, our little Gussy Gussy." Our Gussy? Had they acquired him?

"What's up, Augustus?" I said, trying to model appropriate behavior.

"Our beautiful Gussy," Martha said, leaning in toward him. I began to wonder if he was actually asleep or if he'd just laid a heavy finger on the pain pump to avoid the Attack of the Well-Meaning Sisters.

He woke up after a while and the first thing he said was, "Hazel," which I have to admit made me kind of happy, like maybe I was part of his family, too. "Outside," he said quietly. "Can we go?"

We went, his mom pushing the wheelchair, sisters and brothers-in-law and dad and nephews and me trailing. It was a cloudy day, still and hot as summer settled in. He wore a long-sleeve navy T-shirt and fleece sweatpants. He was cold all the time for some reason. He wanted some water, so his dad went and got some for him.

Martha tried to engage Gus in conversation, kneeling down next to him and saying, "You've always had such beautiful eyes." He nodded a little.

One of the husbands put an arm on Gus's shoulder and said, "How's that fresh air feel?" Gus shrugged.

"Do you want meds?" his mom asked, joining the circle kneeling around him. I took a step back, watching as the nephews tore through a flower bed on their way to the little patch of grass in Gus's backyard. They immediately commenced to play a game that involved throwing one another to the ground.

"Kids!" Julie shouted vaguely.

"I can only hope," Julie said, turning back to Gus, "they grow into the kind of thoughtful, intelligent young men you've become."

I resisted the urge to audibly gag. "He's not that smart," I said to Julie.

"She's right. It's just that most really good-looking people are stupid, so I exceed expectations."

"Right, it's primarily his hotness," I said.

"It can be sort of blinding," he said.

"It actually did blind our friend Isaac," I said.

"Terrible tragedy, that. But can I help my own deadly beauty?"

"You cannot."

"It is my burden, this beautiful face."

"Not to mention your body."

"Seriously, don't even get me started on my hot bod. You don't want to see me naked, Dave. Seeing me naked actually took Hazel Grace's breath away," he said, nodding toward the oxygen tank.

"Okay, enough," Gus's dad said, and then out of

nowhere, his dad put an arm around me and kissed the side of my head and whispered, "I thank God for you every day, kid."

Anyway, that was the last good day I had with Gus until the Last Good Day.

CHAPTER TWENTY

One of the less bullshitty conventions of the cancer kid genre is the Last Good Day convention, wherein the victim of cancer finds herself with some unexpected hours when it seems like the inexorable decline has suddenly plateaued, when the pain is for a moment bearable. The problem, of course, is that there's no way of knowing that your last good day is your Last Good Day. At the time, it is just another good day.

I'd taken a day off from visiting Augustus because I was feeling a bit unwell myself: nothing specific, just tired. It had been a lazy day, and when Augustus called just after five P.M., I was already attached to the BiPAP, which we'd dragged out to the living room so I could watch TV with Mom and Dad.

"Hi, Augustus," I said.

He answered in the voice I'd fallen for. "Good evening, Hazel Grace. Do you suppose you could find your way to the Literal Heart of Jesus around eight P.M.?"

"Um, yes?"

"Excellent. Also, if it's not too much trouble, please prepare a eulogy."

"Um," I said.

"I love you," he said.

"And I you," I answered. Then the phone clicked off.

"Um," I said. "I have to go to Support Group at eight tonight. Emergency session."

My mom muted the TV. "Is everything okay?"

I looked at her for a second, my eyebrows raised. "I assume that's a rhetorical question."

"But why would there—"

"Because Gus needs me for some reason. It's fine. I can drive." I fiddled with the BiPAP so Mom would help me take it off, but she didn't. "Hazel," she said, "your dad and I feel like we hardly even *see* you anymore."

"Particularly those of us who work all week," Dad said.

"He needs me," I said, finally unfastening the BiPAP myself.

"We need you, too, kiddo," my dad said. He took hold

of my wrist, like I was a two-year-old about to dart out into the street, and gripped it.

"Well, get a terminal disease, Dad, and then I'll stay home more."

"Hazel," my mom said.

"You were the one who didn't want me to be a homebody," I said to her. Dad was still clutching my arm. "And now you want him to go ahead and die so I'll be back here chained to this place, letting you take care of me like I always used to. But I don't need it, Mom. I don't need you like I used to. *You're* the one who needs to get a life."

"Hazel!" Dad said, squeezing harder. "Apologize to your mother."

I was tugging at my arm but he wouldn't let go, and I couldn't get my cannula on with only one hand. It was infuriating. All I wanted was an old-fashioned Teenager Walkout, wherein I stomp out of the room and slam the door to my bedroom and turn up The Hectic Glow and furiously write a eulogy. But I couldn't because I couldn't freaking breathe. "The cannula," I whined. "I need it."

My dad immediately let go and rushed to connect me to the oxygen. I could see the guilt in his eyes, but he was still angry. "Hazel, apologize to your mother."

"Fine, I'm sorry, just please let me do this."

They didn't say anything. Mom just sat there with her arms folded, not even looking at me. After a while, I got up and went to my room to write about Augustus.

Both Mom and Dad tried a few times to knock on the door or whatever, but I just told them I was doing something important. It took me forever to figure out what I wanted to say, and even then I wasn't very happy with it. Before I'd technically finished, I noticed it was 7:40, which meant that I would be late even if I *didn't* change, so in the end I wore baby blue cotton pajama pants, flip-flops, and Gus's Butler shirt.

I walked out of the room and tried to go right past them, but my dad said, "You can't leave the house without permission."

"Oh, my God, Dad. He wanted me to write him a *eulogy*, okay? I'll be home every. Freaking. Night. Starting any day now, okay?" That finally shut them up.

It took the entire drive to calm down about my parents. I pulled up around the back of the church and parked in the semicircular driveway behind Augustus's car. The back door to the church was held open by a fist-size rock. Inside, I contemplated taking the stairs but decided to wait for the ancient creaking elevator.

When the elevator doors unscrolled, I was in the Support Group room, the chairs arranged in the same circle. But now I saw only Gus in a wheelchair, ghoulishly thin. He was facing me from the center of the circle. He'd been waiting for the elevator doors to open.

"Hazel Grace," he said, "you look ravishing."

"I know, right?"

I heard a shuffling in a dark corner of the room. Isaac stood behind a little wooden lectern, clinging to it. "You want to sit?" I asked him.

"No, I'm about to eulogize. You're late."

"You're . . . I'm . . . what?"

Gus gestured for me to sit. I pulled a chair into the center of the circle with him as he spun the chair to face Isaac. "I want to attend my funeral," Gus said. "By the way, will you speak at my funeral?"

"Um, of course, yeah," I said, letting my head fall onto his shoulder. I reached across his back and hugged both him and the wheelchair. He winced. I let go.

"Awesome," he said. "I'm hopeful I'll get to attend as a ghost, but just to make sure, I thought I'd—well, not to put you on the spot, but I just this afternoon thought I could arrange a prefuneral, and I figured since I'm in reasonably good spirits, there's no time like the present."

"How did you even get in here?" I asked him.

"Would you believe they leave the door open all night?" Gus asked.

"Um, no," I said.

"As well you shouldn't." Gus smiled. "Anyway, I know it's a bit self-aggrandizing."

"Hey, you're stealing my eulogy," Isaac said. "My first bit is about how you were a self-aggrandizing bastard."

I laughed.

"Okay, okay," Gus said. "At your leisure."

Isaac cleared his throat. "Augustus Waters was a self-aggrandizing bastard. But we forgive him. We forgive him not because he had a heart as figuratively good as his literal one sucked, or because he knew more about how to hold a cigarette than any nonsmoker in history, or because he got eighteen years when he should have gotten more."

"Seventeen," Gus corrected.

"I'm assuming you've got some time, you interrupting bastard.

"I'm telling you," Isaac continued, "Augustus Waters talked so much that he'd interrupt you at his own funeral. And he was pretentious: Sweet Jesus Christ, that kid never took a piss without pondering the abundant metaphorical resonances of human waste production. And he was vain: I do not believe I have ever met a more physically attractive person who was more acutely aware of his own physical attractiveness.

"But I will say this: When the scientists of the future show up at my house with robot eyes and they tell me to try them on, I will tell the scientists to screw off, because I do not want to see a world without him."

I was kind of crying by then.

"And then, having made my rhetorical point, I will put my robot eyes on, because I mean, with robot eyes you can probably see through girls' shirts and stuff. Augustus, my friend, Godspeed."

Augustus nodded for a while, his lips pursed, and then gave Isaac a thumbs-up. After he'd recovered his composure, he added, "I would cut the bit about seeing through girls' shirts."

Isaac was still clinging to the lectern. He started to cry. He pressed his forehead down to the podium and I watched his shoulders shake, and then finally, he said, "Goddamn it, Augustus, editing your own eulogy."

"Don't swear in the Literal Heart of Jesus," Gus said.

"Goddamn it," Isaac said again. He raised his head and swallowed. "Hazel, can I get a hand here?"

I'd forgotten he couldn't make his own way back to the circle. I got up, placed his hand on my arm, and walked him slowly back to the chair next to Gus where I'd been sitting. Then I walked up to the podium and unfolded the piece of paper on which I'd printed my eulogy.

"My name is Hazel. Augustus Waters was the great star-crossed love of my life. Ours was an epic love story, and I won't be able to get more than a sentence into it without disappearing into a puddle of tears. Gus knew. Gus knows. I will not tell you our love story, because—like all real love stories—it will die with us, as it should. I'd hoped that he'd be eulogizing me, because there's no one I'd rather have . . ." I started crying. "Okay, how not to cry. How am I—okay. Okay."

I took a few breaths and went back to the page. "I can't talk about our love story, so I will talk about math. I am not a mathematician, but I know this: There are infinite numbers between 0 and 1. There's .1 and .12 and .112 and an infinite collection of others. Of course, there is a *bigger* infinite set of numbers between 0 and 2, or between 0 and a million. Some infinities are bigger than other infinities. A writer we used to like taught us that. There are days, many of them, when I resent the size of my unbounded set. I want more numbers than I'm likely to get, and God, I want more numbers for Augustus Waters than he got. But, Gus, my love, I cannot tell you how thankful I am for our little infinity. I wouldn't trade it for the world. You gave me a forever within the numbered days, and I'm grateful."

CHAPTER TWENTY-ONE

Augustus Waters died eight days after his prefuneral, at Memorial, in the ICU, when the cancer, which was made of him, finally stopped his heart, which was also made of him.

He was with his mom and dad and sisters. His mom called me at three thirty in the morning. I'd known, of course, that he was going. I'd talked to his dad before going to bed, and he told me, "It could be tonight," but still, when I grabbed the phone from the bedside table and saw *Gus's Mom* on the caller ID, everything inside of me collapsed. She was just crying on the other end of the line, and she told me she was sorry, and I said I was sorry, too, and she told me that he was unconscious for a couple hours before he died.

My parents came in then, looking expectant, and I just nodded and they fell into each other, feeling, I'm sure, the harmonic terror that would in time come for them directly.

I called Isaac, who cursed life and the universe and God Himself and who said where are the goddamned trophies to break when you need them, and then I realized there was no one else to call, which was the saddest thing. The only person I really wanted to talk to about Augustus Waters's death was Augustus Waters.

My parents stayed in my room forever until it was morning and finally Dad said, "Do you want to be alone?" and I nodded and Mom said, "We'll be right outside the door," me thinking, *I don't doubt it.*

It was unbearable. The whole thing. Every second worse than the last. I just kept thinking about calling him, wondering what would happen, if anyone would answer. In the last weeks, we'd been reduced to spending our time together in recollection, but that was not nothing: The pleasure of remembering had been taken from me, because there was no longer anyone to remember with. It felt like losing your co-rememberer meant losing the memory itself, as if the things we'd done were less real and important than they had been hours before.

When you go into the ER, one of the first things they ask you to do is to rate your pain on a scale of one to ten, and from there they decide which drugs to use and how quickly to use them. I'd been asked this question hundreds of times over the years, and I remember once early on when I couldn't get my breath and it felt like my chest was on fire, flames licking the inside of my ribs fighting for a way to burn out of my body, my parents took me to the ER. A nurse asked me about the pain, and I couldn't even speak, so I held up nine fingers.

Later, after they'd given me something, the nurse came in and she was kind of stroking my hand while she took my blood pressure and she said, "You know how I know you're a fighter? You called a ten a nine."

But that wasn't quite right. I called it a nine because I was saving my ten. And here it was, the great and terrible ten, slamming me again and again as I lay still and alone in my bed staring at the ceiling, the waves tossing me against the rocks then pulling me back out to sea so they could launch me again into the jagged face of the cliff, leaving me floating faceup on the water, undrowned.

Finally I did call him. His phone rang five times and then went to voice mail. "You've reached the voice mail of Augustus Waters," he said, the clarion voice I'd fallen for. "Leave a message." It beeped. The dead air on the line was so eerie. I just wanted to go back to that secret post-terrestrial third space with him that we visited when we talked on the phone. I waited for that feeling, but it never came: The dead air on the line was no comfort, and finally I hung up.

I got my laptop out from under the bed and fired it up and went onto his wall page, where already the condolences were flooding in. The most recent one said:

I love you, bro. See you on the other side.

. . . Written by someone I'd never heard of. In fact, almost all the wall posts, which arrived nearly as fast as I could read them, were written by people I'd never met and whom he'd never spoken about, people who were extolling his various virtues now that he was dead, even though I knew for a fact they hadn't seen him in months and had made no effort to visit him. I wondered if my wall would look like this if I died, or if I'd been out of school and life long enough to escape widespread memorialization.

I kept reading.

I miss you already, bro.

I love you, Augustus. God bless and keep you.

You'll live forever in our hearts, big man.

(That particularly galled me, because it implied the immortality of those left behind: You will live forever in my memory, because I will live forever! I AM YOUR GOD

NOW, DEAD BOY! I OWN YOU! Thinking you won't die is yet another side effect of dying.)

> You were always such a great friend I'm sorry I didn't see more of you after you left school, bro. I bet you're already playing ball in heaven.

I imagined the Augustus Waters analysis of that comment: If I am playing basketball in heaven, does that imply a physical location of a heaven containing physical basketballs? Who makes the basketballs in question? Are there less fortunate souls in heaven who work in a celestial basketball factory so that I can play? Or did an omnipotent God create the basketballs out of the vacuum of space? Is this heaven in some kind of unobservable universe where the laws of physics don't apply, and if so, why in the hell would I be playing basketball when I could be flying or reading or looking at beautiful people or something else I actually enjoy? It's almost as if the way you imagine my dead self says more about you than it says about either the person I was or the whatever I am now.

His parents called around noon to say the funeral would be in five days, on Saturday. I pictured a church packed with people who thought he liked basketball, and I wanted to puke, but I knew I had to go, since I was speaking and everything. When I hung up, I went back to reading his wall:

> Just heard that Gus Waters died after a lengthy battle with cancer. Rest in peace, buddy.

I knew these people were genuinely sad, and that I wasn't really mad at them. I was mad at the universe. Even so, it infuriated me: You get all these friends just when you don't need friends anymore. I wrote a reply to his comment:

> We live in a universe devoted to the creation, and eradication, of awareness. Augustus Waters did not die after a lengthy battle with cancer. He died after a lengthy battle with human consciousness, a victim—as you will be—of the universe's need to make and unmake all that is possible.

I posted it and waited for someone to reply, refreshing over and over again. Nothing. My comment got lost in the blizzard of new posts. Everyone was going to miss him so much. Everyone was praying for his family. I remembered Van Houten's letter: Writing does not resurrect. It buries.

After a while, I went out into the living room to sit with my parents and watch TV. I couldn't tell you what the show was, but at some point, my mom said, "Hazel, what can we do for you?"

And I just shook my head. I started crying again.

"What can we do?" Mom asked again.

I shrugged.

But she kept asking, as if there were something she could do, until finally I just kind of crawled across the couch into her lap and my dad came over and held my legs really tight and I wrapped my arms all the way around my mom's middle and they held on to me for hours while the tide rolled in.

CHAPTER TWENTY-TWO

When we first got there, I sat in the back of the visitation room, a little room of exposed stone walls off to the side of the sanctuary in the Literal Heart of Jesus church. There were maybe eighty chairs set up in the room, and it was two-thirds full but felt one-third empty.

For a while, I just watched people walk up to the coffin, which was on some kind of cart covered in a purple tablecloth. All these people I'd never seen before would kneel down next to him or stand over him and look at him for a while, maybe crying, maybe saying something, and then all of them would touch the coffin instead of touching him, because no one wants to touch the dead.

Gus's mom and dad were standing next to the coffin, hugging everybody as they passed by, but when they noticed me, they smiled and shuffled over. I got up and hugged first his dad and then his mom, who held on to me too tight, like Gus used to, squeezing my shoulder blades. They both looked so old—their eye sockets hollowed, the skin sagging from their exhausted faces. They had reached the end of a hurdling sprint, too.

"He loved you so much," Gus's mom said. "He really did. It wasn't—it wasn't puppy love or anything," she added, as if I didn't know that.

"He loved you so much, too," I said quietly. It's hard to explain, but talking to them felt like stabbing and being stabbed. "I'm sorry," I said. And then his parents were talking to my parents—the conversation all nodding and tight lips. I looked up at the casket and saw it unattended, so I decided to walk up there. I pulled the oxygen tube from my nostrils and raised the tube up over my head, handing it to Dad. I wanted it to be just me and just him. I grabbed my little clutch and walked up the makeshift aisle between the rows of chairs.

The walk felt long, but I kept telling my lungs to shut up, that they were strong, that they could do this. I could see him as I approached: His hair was parted neatly on the left side in a way that he would have found absolutely horrifying, and his face was plasticized. But he was still Gus. My lanky, beautiful Gus.

I wanted to wear the little black dress I'd bought for my fifteenth birthday party, my death dress, but I didn't fit into it anymore, so I wore a plain black dress, knee-length. Augustus wore the same thin-lapeled suit he'd worn to Oranjee.

As I knelt, I realized they'd closed his eyes—of course they had—and that I would never again see his blue eyes. "I love you present tense," I whispered, and then put my hand on the middle of his chest and said, "It's okay, Gus. It's okay. It is. It's okay, you hear me?" I had—and have—absolutely no confidence that he could hear me. I leaned forward and kissed his cheek. "Okay," I said. "Okay."

I suddenly felt conscious that there were all these people watching us, that the last time so many people saw us kiss we were in the Anne Frank House. But there was, properly speaking, no us left to watch. Only a me.

I snapped open the clutch, reached in, and pulled out a hard pack of Camel Lights. In a quick motion I hoped no one behind would notice, I snuck them into the space between his side and the coffin's plush silver lining. "You can light these," I whispered to him. "I won't mind."

While I was talking to him, Mom and Dad had moved up to the second row with my tank, so I didn't have a long walk back. Dad handed me a tissue as I sat down. I blew my nose, threaded the tubes around my ears, and put the nubbins back in.

I thought we'd go into the proper sanctuary for the

real funeral, but it all happened in that little side room—the Literal Hand of Jesus, I guess, the part of the cross he'd been nailed to. A minister walked up and stood behind the coffin, almost like the coffin was a pulpit or something, and talked a little bit about how Augustus had a courageous battle and how his heroism in the face of illness was an inspiration to us all, and I was already starting to get pissed off at the minister when he said, "In heaven, Augustus will finally be healed and whole," implying that he had been less whole than other people due to his leglessness, and I kind of could not repress my sigh of disgust. My dad grabbed me just above the knee and cut me a disapproving look, but from the row behind me, someone muttered almost inaudibly near my ear, "What a load of horse crap, eh, kid?"

I spun around.

Peter Van Houten wore a white linen suit, tailored to account for his rotundity, a powder-blue dress shirt, and a green tie. He looked like he was dressed for a colonial occupation of Panama, not a funeral. The minister said, "Let us pray," but as everyone else bowed their head, I could only stare slack-jawed at the sight of Peter Van Houten. After a moment, he whispered, "We gotta fake pray," and bowed his head.

I tried to forget about him and just pray for Augustus. I made a point of listening to the minister and not looking back.

The minister called up Isaac, who was much more serious than he'd been at the prefuneral. "Augustus Waters was the Mayor of the Secret City of Cancervania, and he is not replaceable," Isaac began. "Other people will be able to tell you funny stories about Gus, because he was a funny guy, but let me tell you a serious one: A day after I got my eye cut out, Gus showed up at the hospital. I was blind and heartbroken and didn't want to do anything and Gus burst into my room and shouted, 'I have wonderful news!' And I was like, 'I don't really want to hear wonderful news right now,' and Gus said, 'This is wonderful news you want to hear,' and I asked him, 'Fine, what is it?' and he said, 'You are going to live a good and long life filled with great and terrible moments that you cannot even imagine yet!'"

Isaac couldn't go on, or maybe that was all he had written.

After a high school friend told some stories about Gus's considerable basketball talents and his many qualities as a teammate, the minister said, "We'll now hear a few words from Augustus's special friend, Hazel." *Special friend?* There were some titters in the audience, so I figured it was safe for me to start out by saying to the minister, "I was his girlfriend." That got a laugh. Then I began reading from the eulogy I'd written.

"There's a great quote in Gus's house, one that both he and I found very comforting: *Without pain, we couldn't know joy.*"

I went on spouting bullshit Encouragements as Gus's parents, arm in arm, hugged each other and nodded at every word. Funerals, I had decided, are for the living.

After his sister Julie spoke, the service ended with a prayer about Gus's union with God, and I thought back to what he'd told me at Oranjee, that he didn't believe in mansions and harps, but did believe in capital-*S* Something, and so I tried to imagine him capital-*S* Somewhere as we prayed, but even then I could not quite convince myself that he and I would be together again. I already knew too many dead people. I knew that time would now pass for me differently than it would for him—that I, like everyone in that room, would go on accumulating loves and losses while he would not. And for me, that was the final and truly unbearable tragedy: Like all the innumerable dead, he'd once and for all been demoted from haunted to haunter.

And then one of Gus's brothers-in-law brought up a boom box and they played this song Gus had picked out—a sad and quiet song by The Hectic Glow called "The New Partner." I just wanted to go home, honestly. I didn't know hardly any of these people, and I felt Peter Van Houten's little eyes boring into my exposed shoulder blades, but after the song was over, everyone had to come up to me and tell me that I'd spoken beautifully, and that it was a lovely service, which was a lie: It was a funeral. It looked like any other funeral.

His pallbearers—cousins, his dad, an uncle, friends I'd never seen—came and got him, and they all started walking toward the hearse.

When Mom and Dad and I got in the car, I said, "I don't want to go. I'm tired."

"Hazel," Mom said.

"Mom, there won't be a place to sit and it'll last forever and I'm exhausted."

"Hazel, we have to go for Mr. and Mrs. Waters," Mom said.

"Just . . ." I said. I felt so little in the backseat for some reason. I kind of wanted to *be* little. I wanted to be like six years old or something. "Fine," I said.

I just stared out the window awhile. I really didn't want to go. I didn't want to see them lower him into the ground in the spot he'd picked out with his dad, and I didn't want to see his parents sink to their knees in the dew-wet grass and moan in pain, and I didn't want to see Peter Van Houten's alcoholic belly stretched against his linen jacket, and I didn't want to cry in front of a bunch of people, and I didn't want to toss a handful of dirt onto his grave, and I didn't want my parents to have to stand there beneath the clear blue sky with its certain slant of afternoon light, thinking about their day and their kid and my plot and my casket and my dirt.

But I did these things. I did all of them and worse, because Mom and Dad felt we should.

. . .

After it was over, Van Houten walked up to me and put a fat hand on my shoulder and said, "Could I hitch a ride? Left my rental at the bottom of the hill." I shrugged, and he opened the door to the backseat right as my dad unlocked the car.

Inside, he leaned between the front seats and said, "Peter Van Houten: Novelist Emeritus and Semiprofessional Disappointer."

My parents introduced themselves. He shook their hands. I was pretty surprised that Peter Van Houten had flown halfway across the world to attend a funeral. "How did you even—" I started, but he cut me off.

"I used the infernal Internet of yours to follow the Indianapolis obituary notices." He reached into his linen suit and produced a fifth of whiskey.

"And you just like bought a ticket and—"

He interrupted again while unscrewing the cap. "It was fifteen thousand for a first-class ticket, but I'm sufficiently capitalized to indulge such whims. And the drinks are free on the flight. If you're ambitious, you can almost break even."

Van Houten took a swig of the whiskey and then leaned forward to offer it to my dad, who said, "Um, no thanks." Then Van Houten nodded the bottle toward me. I grabbed it.

"Hazel," my mom said, but I unscrewed the cap and sipped. It made my stomach feel like my lungs. I handed the bottle back to Van Houten, who took a long slug from it and then said, "So. *Omnis cellula e cellula.*"

"Huh?"

"Your boy Waters and I corresponded a bit, and in his last—"

"Wait, you read your fan mail now?"

"No, he sent it to my house, not through my publisher. And I'd hardly call him a fan. He despised me. But at any rate he was quite insistent that I'd be absolved for my misbehavior if I attended his funeral and told you what became of Anna's mother. So here I am, and there's your answer: *Omnis cellula e cellula.*"

"What?" I asked again.

"Omnis cellula e cellula," he said again. "All cells come from cells. Every cell is born of a previous cell, which was born of a previous cell. Life comes from life. Life begets life begets life begets life begets life."

We reached the bottom of the hill. "Okay, yeah," I said. I was in no mood for this. Peter Van Houten would not hijack Gus's funeral. I wouldn't allow it. "Thanks," I said. "Well, I guess we're at the bottom of the hill."

"You don't want an explanation?" he asked.

"No," I said. "I'm good. I think you're a pathetic alcoholic who says fancy things to get attention like a really precocious eleven-year-old and I feel super bad for you. But yeah, no, you're not the guy who wrote *An Imperial Affliction* anymore, so you couldn't sequel it even if you wanted to. Thanks, though. Have an excellent life."

"But—"

"Thanks for the booze," I said. "Now get out of the car." He looked scolded. Dad had stopped the car and we just idled there below Gus's grave for a minute until Van Houten opened the door and, finally silent, left.

As we drove away, I watched through the back window as he took a drink and raised the bottle in my direction, as if toasting me. His eyes looked so sad. I felt kinda bad for him, to be honest.

We finally got home around six, and I was exhausted. I just wanted to sleep, but Mom made me eat some cheesy pasta, although she at least allowed me to eat in bed. I slept with the BiPAP for a couple hours. Waking up was horrible, because for a disoriented moment I felt like everything was fine, and then it crushed me anew. Mom took me off the BiPAP, I tethered myself to a portable tank, and stumbled into my bathroom to brush my teeth.

Appraising myself in the mirror as I brushed my teeth, I kept thinking there were two kinds of adults: There were Peter Van Houtens—miserable creatures who scoured the earth in search of something to hurt. And then there were people like my parents, who walked around zombically, doing whatever they had to do to keep walking around.

Neither of these futures struck me as particularly desirable. It seemed to me that I had already seen everything pure and good in the world, and I was beginning to suspect that even if death didn't get in the way, the kind of love that Augustus and I share could never last. *So dawn goes down to day*, the poet wrote. *Nothing gold can stay*.

Someone knocked on the bathroom door.

"Occupada," I said.

"Hazel," my dad said. "Can I come in?" I didn't answer, but after a while I unlocked the door. I sat down on the closed toilet seat. Why did breathing have to be such work? Dad knelt down next to me. He grabbed my head and pulled it into his collarbone, and he said, "I'm sorry Gus died." I felt kind of suffocated by his T-shirt, but it felt good to be held so hard, pressed into the comfortable smell of my dad. It was almost like he was angry or something, and I liked that, because I was angry, too. "It's total bullshit," he said. "The whole thing. Eighty percent survival rate and he's in the twenty percent? Bullshit. He was such a bright kid. It's bullshit. I hate it. But it was sure a privilege to love him, huh?"

I nodded into his shirt.

"Gives you an idea how I feel about you," he said.

My old man. He always knew just what to say.

CHAPTER TWENTY-THREE

A couple days later, I got up around noon and drove over to Isaac's house. He answered the door himself. "My mom took Graham to a movie," he said.

"We should go do something," I said.

"Can the something be play blind-guy video games while sitting on the couch?"

"Yeah, that's just the kind of something I had in mind."

So we sat there for a couple hours talking to the screen together, navigating this invisible labyrinthine cave without a single lumen of light. The most entertaining part of the game by far was trying to get the computer to engage us in humorous conversation:

Me: "Touch the cave wall."

Computer: "You touch the cave wall. It is moist."

Isaac: "Lick the cave wall."

Computer: "I do not understand. Repeat?"

Me: "Hump the moist cave wall."

Computer: "You attempt to jump. You hit your head."

Isaac: "Not *jump. HUMP.*"

Computer: "I don't understand."

Isaac: "Dude, I've been alone in the dark in this cave for weeks and I need some relief. HUMP THE CAVE WALL."

Computer: "You attempt to ju–"

Me: "Thrust pelvis against the cave wall."

Computer: "I do not–"

Isaac: "Make sweet love to the cave."

Computer: "I do not–"

Me: "*FINE.* Follow left branch."

Computer: "You follow the left branch. The passage narrows."

Me: "Crawl."

Computer: "You crawl for one hundred yards. The passage narrows."

Me: "Snake crawl."

Computer: "You snake crawl for thirty yards. A trickle of water runs down your body. You reach a mound of small rocks blocking the passageway."

Me: "Can I hump the cave now?"

Computer: "You cannot jump without standing."

Isaac: "I dislike living in a world without Augustus Waters."

Computer: "I don't understand—"

Isaac: "Me neither. Pause."

He dropped the remote onto the couch between us and asked, "Do you know if it hurt or whatever?"

"He was really fighting for breath, I guess," I said. "He eventually went unconscious, but it sounds like, yeah, it wasn't great or anything. Dying sucks."

"Yeah," Isaac said. And then after a long time, "It just seems so impossible."

"Happens all the time," I said.

"You seem angry," he said.

"Yeah," I said. We just sat there quiet for a long time, which was fine, and I was thinking about way back in the very beginning in the Literal Heart of Jesus when Gus told us that he feared oblivion, and I told him that he was fearing something universal and inevitable, and how really, the problem is not suffering itself or oblivion itself but the depraved meaninglessness of these things, the absolutely inhuman nihilism of suffering. I thought of my dad telling me that the universe wants to be noticed. But what we want is to be noticed by the universe, to have the universe give a shit what happens to us—not the collective idea of sentient life but each of us, as individuals.

"Gus really loved you, you know," he said.

"I know."

"He wouldn't shut up about it."

"I know," I said.

"It was annoying."

"I didn't find it that annoying," I said.

"Did he ever give you that thing he was writing?"

"What thing?"

"That sequel or whatever to that book you liked."

I turned to Isaac. "What?"

"He said he was working on something for you but he wasn't that good of a writer."

"When did he say this?"

"I don't know. Like, after he got back from Amsterdam at some point."

"At which point?" I pressed. Had he not had a chance to finish it? Had he finished it and left it on his computer or something?

"Um," Isaac sighed. "Um, I don't know. We talked about it over here once. He was over here, like—uh, we played with my email machine and I'd just gotten an email from my grandmother. I can check on the machine if you—"

"Yeah, yeah, where is it?"

He'd mentioned it a month before. A month. Not a good month, admittedly, but still—a month. That was enough time for him to have written *something*, at least. There was still something of him, or by him at least, floating around out there. I needed it.

"I'm gonna go to his house," I told Isaac.

I hurried out to the minivan and hauled the oxygen cart up and into the passenger seat. I started the car. A hip-hop beat blared from the stereo, and as I reached to change the radio station, someone started rapping. In Swedish.

I swiveled around and screamed when I saw Peter Van Houten sitting in the backseat.

"I apologize for alarming you," Peter Van Houten said over the rapping. He was still wearing the funeral suit, almost a week later. He smelled like he was sweating alcohol. "You're welcome to keep the CD," he said. "It's Snook, one of the major Swedish—"

"Ah ah ah ah GET OUT OF MY CAR." I turned off the stereo.

"It's your mother's car, as I understand it," he said. "Also, it wasn't locked."

"Oh, my God! Get out of the car or I'll call nine-one-one. Dude, what is your *problem*?"

"If only there were just one," he mused. "I am here simply to apologize. You were correct in noting earlier that I am a pathetic little man, dependent upon alcohol. I had one acquaintance who only spent time with me because I paid her to do so—worse, still, she has since quit, leaving me the rare soul who cannot acquire companionship even through bribery. It is all true, Hazel. All that and more."

"Okay," I said. It would have been a more moving speech had he not slurred his words.

"You remind me of Anna."

"I remind a lot of people of a lot of people," I answered. "I really have to go."

"So drive," he said.

"Get out."

"No. You remind me of Anna," he said again. After a second, I put the car in reverse and backed out. I couldn't make him leave, and I didn't have to. I'd drive to Gus's house, and Gus's parents would make him leave.

"You are, of course, familiar," Van Houten said, "with Antonietta Meo."

"Yeah, no," I said. I turned on the stereo, and the Swedish hip-hop blared, but Van Houten yelled over it.

"She may soon be the youngest nonmartyr saint ever beatified by the Catholic Church. She had the same cancer that Mr. Waters had, osteosarcoma. They removed her right leg. The pain was excruciating. As Antonietta Meo lay dying at the ripened age of six from this agonizing cancer, she told her father, 'Pain is like fabric: The stronger it is, the more it's worth.' Is that true, Hazel?"

I wasn't looking at him directly but at his reflection in the mirror. "No," I shouted over the music. "That's bullshit."

"But don't you wish it were true!" he cried back. I cut the music. "I'm sorry I ruined your trip. You were too young. You were—" He broke down. As if he had a right to cry over Gus. Van Houten was just another of the endless mourners who did not know him, another too-late lamentation on his wall.

"You didn't ruin our trip, you self-important bastard. We had an awesome trip."

"I am trying," he said. *"I am trying, I swear."* It was around then that I realized Peter Van Houten had a dead person in his family. I considered the honesty with which he had written about cancer kids; the fact that he couldn't speak to me in Amsterdam except to ask if I'd dressed like her on purpose; his shittiness around me and Augustus; his aching question about the relationship between pain's extremity and its value. He sat back there drinking, an old man who'd been drunk for years. I thought of a statistic I wish I didn't know: Half of marriages end in the year after a child's death. I looked back at Van Houten. I was driving down College and I pulled over behind a line of parked cars and asked, "You had a kid who died?"

"My daughter," he said. "She was eight. Suffered beautifully. Will never be beatified."

"She had leukemia?" I asked. He nodded. "Like Anna," I said.

"Very much like her, yes."

"You were married?"

"No. Well, not at the time of her death. I was insufferable long before we lost her. Grief does not change you, Hazel. It reveals you."

"Did you live with her?"

"No, not primarily, although at the end, we brought her to New York, where I was living, for a series of experimental tortures that increased the misery of her days without increasing the number of them."

After a second, I said, "So it's like you gave her this second life where she got to be a teenager."

"I suppose that would be a fair assessment," he said, and then quickly added, "I assume you are familiar with Philippa Foot's Trolley Problem thought experiment?"

"And then I show up at your house and I'm dressed like the girl you hoped she would live to become and you're, like, all taken aback by it."

"There's a trolley running out of control down a track," he said.

"I don't care about your stupid thought experiment," I said.

"It's Philippa Foot's, actually."

"Well, hers either," I said.

"She didn't understand why it was happening," he said. "I had to tell her she would die. Her social worker said I had to tell her. I had to tell her she would die, so I told her she was going to heaven. She asked if I would be there, and

I said that I would not, not yet. But eventually, she said, and I promised that yes, of course, very soon. And I told her that in the meantime we had great family up there that would take care of her. And she asked me when I would be there, and I told her soon. Twenty-two years ago."

"I'm sorry."

"So am I."

After a while, I asked, "What happened to her mom?"

He smiled. "You're still looking for your sequel, you little rat."

I smiled back. "You should go home," I told him. "Sober up. Write another novel. Do the thing you're good at. Not many people are lucky enough to be so good at something."

He stared at me through the mirror for a long time. "Okay," he said. "Yeah. You're right. You're right." But even as he said it, he pulled out his mostly empty fifth of whiskey. He drank, recapped the bottle, and opened the door. "Good-bye, Hazel."

"Take it easy, Van Houten."

He sat down on the curb behind the car. As I watched him shrink in the rearview mirror, he pulled out the bottle and for a second it looked like he would leave it on the curb. And then he took a swig.

It was a hot afternoon in Indianapolis, the air thick and still like we were inside a cloud. It was the worst kind of air for me, and I told myself it was just the air when the walk from his driveway to his front door felt infinite. I rang the doorbell, and Gus's mom answered.

"Oh, Hazel," she said, and kind of enveloped me, crying.

She made me eat some eggplant lasagna—I guess a lot of people had brought them food or whatever—with her and Gus's dad. "How are you?"

"I miss him."

"Yeah."

I didn't really know what to say. I just wanted to go downstairs and find whatever he'd written for me. Plus, the silence in the room really bothered me. I wanted them to be talking to each other, comforting or holding hands or whatever. But they just sat there eating very small amounts of lasagna, not even looking at each other. "Heaven needed an angel," his dad said after a while.

"I know," I said. Then his sisters and their mess of kids showed up and piled into the kitchen. I got up and hugged both his sisters and then watched the kids run around the kitchen with their sorely needed surplus of noise and movement, excited molecules bouncing against each other and shouting, "You're it no you're it no I was it but then I tagged you you didn't tag me you missed me well I'm tagging you now no dumb butt it's a time-out DANIEL DO NOT CALL YOUR BROTHER A DUMB BUTT Mom if I'm not allowed to use that word how come you just used it dumb butt dumb butt," and then, chorally, *dumb butt dumb butt dumb butt dumb butt*, and at the table Gus's parents were now holding hands, which made me feel better.

"Isaac told me Gus was writing something, something for me," I said. The kids were still singing their dumb-butt song.

"We can check his computer," his mom said.

"He wasn't on it much the last few weeks," I said.

"That's true. I'm not even sure we brought it upstairs. Is it still in the basement, Mark?"

"No idea."

"Well," I said, "can I . . ." I nodded toward the basement door.

"We're not ready," his dad said. "But of course, *yes*, Hazel. Of course you can."

I walked downstairs, past his unmade bed, past the gaming chairs beneath the TV. His computer was still on. I tapped the mouse to wake it up and then searched for his most recently edited files. Nothing in the last month. The most recent thing was a response paper to Toni Morrison's *The Bluest Eye*.

Maybe he'd written something by hand. I walked over to his bookshelves, looking for a journal or a notebook. Nothing. I flipped through his copy of *An Imperial Affliction*. He hadn't left a single mark in it.

I walked to his bedside table next. *Infinite Mayhem*, the ninth sequel to *The Price of Dawn*, lay atop the table next to his reading lamp, the corner of page 138 turned down. He'd never made it to the end of the book. "Spoiler alert: Mayhem survives," I said out loud to him, just in case he could hear me.

And then I crawled into his unmade bed, wrapping myself in his comforter like a cocoon, surrounding myself with his smell. I took out my cannula so I could smell better, breathing him in and breathing him out, the scent fading even as I lay there, my chest burning until I couldn't distinguish among the pains.

I sat up in the bed after a while and reinserted my cannula and breathed for a while before going up the stairs. I just shook my head no in response to his parents' expectant looks. The kids raced past me. One of Gus's sisters—I could not tell them apart—said, "Mom, do you want me to take them to the park or something?"

"No, no, they're fine."

"Is there anywhere he might have put a notebook? Like by his hospital bed or something?" The bed was already gone, reclaimed by hospice.

"Hazel," his dad said, "you were there every day with us. You— he wasn't alone much, sweetie. He wouldn't have had time to write anything. I know you want . . . I want that, too. But the messages he leaves for us now are coming from above, Hazel." He pointed toward the ceiling, as if Gus were hovering just above the house. Maybe he was. I don't know. I didn't feel his presence, though.

"Yeah," I said. I promised to visit them again in a few days.

I never quite caught his scent again.

CHAPTER TWENTY-FOUR

Three days later, on the eleventh day AG, Gus's father called me in the morning. I was still hooked to the BiPAP, so I didn't answer, but I listened to his message the moment it beeped through to my phone. "Hazel, hi, it's Gus's dad. I found a, uh, black Moleskine notebook in the magazine rack that was near his hospital bed, I think near enough that he could have reached it. Unfortunately there's no writing in the notebook. All the pages are blank. But the first—I think three or four—the first few pages are torn out of the notebook. We looked through the house but couldn't find the pages. So I don't know what to make of that. But maybe those pages are what Isaac was referring to? Anyway,

I hope that you are doing okay. You're in our prayers every day, Hazel. Okay, bye."

Three or four pages ripped from a Moleskine notebook no longer in Augustus Waters's house. Where would he leave them for me? Taped to *Funky Bones*? No, he wasn't well enough to get there.

The Literal Heart of Jesus. Maybe he'd left it there for me on his Last Good Day.

So I left twenty minutes early for Support Group the next day. I drove over to Isaac's house, picked him up, and then we drove down to the Literal Heart of Jesus with the windows of the minivan down, listening to The Hectic Glow's leaked new album, which Gus would never hear.

We took the elevator. I walked Isaac to a seat in the Circle of Trust then slowly worked my way around the Literal Heart. I checked everywhere: under the chairs, around the lectern I'd stood behind while delivering my eulogy, under the treat table, on the bulletin board packed with Sunday school kids' drawings of God's love. Nothing. It was the only place we'd been together in those last days besides his house, and it either wasn't here or I was missing something. Perhaps he'd left it for me in the hospital, but if so, it had almost certainly been thrown away after his death.

I was really out of breath by the time I settled into a chair next to Isaac, and I devoted the entirety of Patrick's nutless testimonial to telling my lungs they were okay, that they could breathe, that there was enough oxygen. They'd been drained only a week before Gus died—I watched the amber cancer water dribble out of me through the tube—and yet already they felt full again. I was so focused on telling myself to breathe that I didn't notice Patrick saying my name at first.

I snapped to attention. "Yeah?" I asked.

"How are you?"

"I'm okay, Patrick. I'm a little out of breath."

"Would you like to share a memory of Augustus with the group?"

"I wish I would just die, Patrick. Do you ever wish you would just die?"

"Yes," Patrick said, without his usual pause. "Yes, of course. So why don't you?"

I thought about it. My old stock answer was that I wanted to stay alive for my parents, because they would be all gutted and childless in the wake of me, and that was still true kind of, but that wasn't it, exactly. "I don't know."

"In the hopes that you'll get better?"

"No," I said. "No, it's not that. I really don't know. Isaac?" I asked. I was tired of talking.

Isaac started talking about true love. I couldn't tell them what I was thinking because it seemed cheesy to me, but I was thinking about the universe wanting to be noticed, and how I had to notice it as best I could. I felt that

I owed a debt to the universe that only my attention could repay, and also that I owed a debt to everybody who didn't get to be a person anymore and everyone who hadn't gotten to be a person yet. What my dad had told me, basically.

I stayed quiet for the rest of Support Group, and Patrick said a special prayer for me, and Gus's name was tacked onto the long list of the dead—fourteen of them for every one of us—and we promised to live our best life today, and then I took Isaac to the car.

When I got home, Mom and Dad were at the dining room table on their separate laptops, and the moment I walked in the door, Mom slammed her laptop shut. "What's on the computer?"

"Just some antioxidant recipes. Ready for BiPAP and *America's Next Top Model*?" she asked.

"I'm just going to lie down for a minute."

"Are you okay?"

"Yeah, just tired."

"Well, you've gotta eat before you—"

"Mom, I am aggressively unhungry." I took a step toward the door but she cut me off.

"Hazel, you have to eat. Just some ch—"

"No. I'm going to bed."

"No," Mom said. "You're not." I glanced at my dad, who shrugged.

"It's my life," I said.

"You're not going to starve yourself to death just because Augustus died. You're going to eat dinner."

I was really pissed off for some reason. "I can't eat, Mom. I can't. Okay?"

I tried to push past her but she grabbed both my shoulders and said, "Hazel, you're eating dinner. You need to stay healthy."

"NO!" I shouted. "I'm not eating dinner, and I can't stay healthy, because I'm not healthy. I am dying, Mom. I am going to die and leave you here alone and you won't have a me to hover around and you won't be a mother anymore, and I'm sorry, but I can't do anything about it, okay?!"

I regretted it as soon as I said it.

"You heard me."

"What?"

"Did you hear me say that to your father?" Her eyes welled up. "Did you?" I nodded. "Oh, God, Hazel. I'm sorry. I was wrong, sweetie. That wasn't true. I said that in a desperate moment. It's not something I believe." She sat down, and I sat down with her. I was thinking that I should have just puked up some pasta for her instead of getting pissed off.

"What do you believe, then?" I asked.

"As long as either of us is alive, I will be your mother," she said. "Even if you die, I—"

"When," I said.

She nodded. "Even when you die, I will still be your mom, Hazel. I won't stop being your mom. Have you stopped loving Gus?" I shook my head. "Well, then how could I stop loving you?"

"Okay," I said. My dad was crying now.

"I want you guys to have a life," I said. "I worry that you won't have a life, that you'll sit around here all day with no me to look after and stare at the walls and want to off yourselves."

After a minute, Mom said, "I'm taking some classes. Online, through IU. To get my master's in social work. In fact, I wasn't looking at antioxidant recipes; I was writing a paper."

"Seriously?"

"I don't want you to think I'm imagining a world without you. But if I get my MSW, I can counsel families in crisis or lead groups dealing with illness in their families or—"

"Wait, you're going to become a Patrick?"

"Well, not exactly. There are all kinds of social work jobs."

Dad said, "We've both been worried that you'll feel abandoned. It's important for you to know that we will *always* be here for you, Hazel. Your mom isn't going anywhere."

"No, this is great. This is fantastic!" I was really smiling.

"Mom is going to become a Patrick. She'll be a great Patrick! She'll be so much better at it than Patrick is."

"Thank you, Hazel. That means everything to me."

I nodded. I was crying. I couldn't get over how happy I was, crying genuine tears of actual happiness for the first time in maybe forever, imagining my mom as a Patrick. It made me think of Anna's mom. She would've been a good social worker, too.

After a while we turned on the TV and watched *ANTM*. But I paused it after five seconds because I had all these questions for Mom. "So how close are you to finishing?"

"If I go up to Bloomington for a week this summer, I should be able to finish by December."

"How long have you been keeping this from me, exactly?"

"A year."

"Mom."

"I didn't want to hurt you, Hazel."

Amazing. "So when you're waiting for me outside of MCC or Support Group or whatever, you're always—"

"Yes, working or reading."

"This is so great. If I'm dead, I want you to know I will be sighing at you from heaven every time you ask someone to share their feelings."

My dad laughed. "I'll be right there with ya, kiddo," he assured me.

Finally, we watched *ANTM*. Dad tried really hard not to die of boredom, and he kept messing up which girl was which, saying, "We like her?"

"No, no. We *revile* Anastasia. We like *Antonia*, the other blonde," Mom explained.

"They're all tall and horrible," Dad responded. "Forgive me for failing to tell the difference." Dad reached across me for Mom's hand.

"Do you think you guys will stay together if I die?" I asked.

"Hazel, what? Sweetie." She fumbled for the remote control and paused the TV again. "What's wrong?"

"Just, do you think you would?"

"Yes, of course. Of course," Dad said. "Your mom and I love each other, and if we lose you, we'll go through it together."

"Swear to God," I said.

"I swear to God," he said.

I looked back at Mom. "Swear to God," she agreed. "Why are you even worrying about this?"

"I just don't want to ruin your life or anything."

Mom leaned forward and pressed her face into my messy puff of hair and kissed me at the very top of my head. I said to Dad, "I don't want you to become like a miserable unemployed alcoholic or whatever."

My mom smiled. "Your father isn't Peter Van Houten,

Hazel. You of all people know it is possible to live with pain."

"Yeah, okay," I said. Mom hugged me and I let her even though I didn't really want to be hugged. "Okay, you can unpause it," I said. Anastasia got kicked off. She threw a fit. It was awesome.

I ate a few bites of dinner—bow-tie pasta with pesto—and managed to keep it down.

CHAPTER TWENTY-FIVE

I woke up the next morning panicked because I'd dreamed of being alone and boatless in a huge lake. I bolted up, straining against the BiPAP, and felt Mom's arm on me.

"Hi, you okay?"

My heart raced, but I nodded. Mom said, "Kaitlyn's on the phone for you." I pointed at my BiPAP. She helped me get it off and hooked me up to Philip and then finally I took my cell from Mom and said, "Hey, Kaitlyn."

"Just calling to check in," she said. "See how you're doing."

"Yeah, thanks," I said. "I'm doing okay."

"You've just had the worst luck, darling. It's *unconscionable.*"

"I guess," I said. I didn't think much about my luck anymore one way or the other. Honestly, I didn't really want to talk with Kaitlyn about anything, but she kept dragging the conversation along.

"So what was it like?" she asked.

"Having your boyfriend die? Um, it sucks."

"No," she said. "Being in love."

"Oh," I said. "Oh. It was . . . it was nice to spend time with someone so interesting. We were very different, and we disagreed about a lot of things, but he was always so interesting, you know?"

"Alas, I do not. The boys I'm acquainted with are vastly uninteresting."

"He wasn't perfect or anything. He wasn't your fairy-tale Prince Charming or whatever. He tried to be like that sometimes, but I liked him best when that stuff fell away."

"Do you have like a scrapbook of pictures and letters he wrote?"

"I have some pictures, but he never really wrote me letters. Except, well there are some missing pages from his notebook that might have been something for me, but I guess he threw them away or they got lost or something."

"Maybe he mailed them to you," she said.

"Nah, they'd've gotten here."

"Then maybe they weren't written for you," she said. "Maybe . . . I mean, not to depress you or anything, but maybe he wrote them for someone else and mailed them—"

"VAN HOUTEN!" I shouted.

"Are you okay? Was that a cough?"

"Kaitlyn, I love you. You are a genius. I have to go."

I hung up, rolled over, reached for my laptop, turned it on, and emailed lidewij.vliegenthart.

Lidewij,

I believe Augustus Waters sent a few pages from a notebook to Peter Van Houten shortly before he (Augustus) died. It is very important to me that someone reads these pages. I want to read them, of course, but maybe they weren't written for me. Regardless, they must be read. They must be.

Can you help?

Your friend,
Hazel Grace Lancaster

She responded late that afternoon.

Dear Hazel,

I did not know that Augustus had died. I am very sad to hear this news. He was such a very charismatic young man. I am so sorry, and so sad.

I have not spoken to Peter since I resigned that day we met. It is very late at night here, but I am going

> over to his house first thing in the morning to find this letter and force him to read it. Mornings were his best time, usually.

Your friend,
Lidewij Vliegenthart

> p.s. I am bringing my boyfriend in case we have to physically restrain Peter.

I wondered why he'd written Van Houten in those last days instead of me, telling Van Houten that he'd be redeemed if only he gave me my sequel. Maybe the notebook pages had just repeated his request to Van Houten. It made sense, Gus leveraging his terminality to make my dream come true: The sequel was a tiny thing to die for, but it was the biggest thing left at his disposal.

I refreshed my email continually that night, slept for a few hours, and then commenced to refreshing around five in the morning. But nothing arrived. I tried to watch TV to distract myself, but my thoughts kept drifting back to Amsterdam, imagining Lidewij Vliegenthart and her boyfriend bicycling around town on this crazy mission to find a dead kid's last correspondence. How fun it would be to bounce on the back of Lidewij Vliegenthart's bike down the brick streets, her curly red hair blowing into my face, the smell of the canals and cigarette smoke, all the people sitting outside the cafés drinking beer, saying their *r*'s and *g*'s in a way I'd never learn.

I missed the future. Obviously I knew even before his recurrence that I'd never grow old with Augustus Waters. But thinking about Lidewij and her boyfriend, I felt robbed. I would probably never again see the ocean from thirty thousand feet above, so far up that you can't make out the waves or any boats, so that the ocean is a great and endless monolith. I could imagine it. I could remember it. But I couldn't see it again, and it occurred to me that the voracious ambition of humans is never sated by dreams coming true, because there is always the thought that everything might be done better and again.

That is probably true even if you live to be ninety—although I'm jealous of the people who get to find out for sure. Then again, I'd already lived twice as long as Van Houten's daughter. What he wouldn't have given to have a kid die at sixteen.

Suddenly Mom was standing between the TV and me, her hands folded behind her back. "Hazel," she said. Her voice was so serious I thought something might be wrong.

"Yes?"

"Do you know what today is?"

"It's not my birthday, is it?"

She laughed. "Not just yet. It's July fourteenth, Hazel."

"Is it *your* birthday?"

"No . . ."

"Is it Harry Houdini's birthday?"

"No . . ."

"I am really tired of guessing."

"IT IS BASTILLE DAY!" She pulled her arms from behind her back, producing two small plastic French flags and waving them enthusiastically.

"That sounds like a fake thing. Like Cholera Awareness Day."

"I assure you, Hazel, that there is nothing fake about Bastille Day. Did you know that two hundred and twenty-three years ago today, the people of France stormed the Bastille prison to arm themselves to fight for their freedom?"

"Wow," I said. "We should celebrate this momentous anniversary."

"It so happens that I have just now scheduled a picnic with your father in Holliday Park."

She never stopped trying, my mom. I pushed against the couch and stood up. Together, we cobbled together some sandwich makings and found a dusty picnic basket in the hallway utility closet.

It was kind of a beautiful day, finally real summer in Indianapolis, warm and humid—the kind of weather that reminds you after a long winter that while the world wasn't built for humans, we were built for the world. Dad was waiting for us, wearing a tan suit, standing in a handicapped parking spot typing away on his handheld. He waved as we parked and then hugged me. "What a day," he said. "If we lived in California, they'd all be like this."

"Yeah, but then you wouldn't enjoy them," my mom said. She was wrong, but I didn't correct her.

We ended up putting our blanket down by the Ruins, this weird rectangle of Roman ruins plopped down in the middle of a field in Indianapolis. But they aren't real ruins: They're like a sculptural re-creation of ruins built eighty years ago, but the fake Ruins have been neglected pretty badly, so they have kind of become actual ruins by accident. Van Houten would like the Ruins. Gus, too.

So we sat in the shadow of the Ruins and ate a little lunch. "Do you need sunscreen?" Mom asked.

"I'm okay," I said.

You could hear the wind in the leaves, and on that wind traveled the screams of the kids on the playground in the distance, the little kids figuring out how to be alive, how to navigate a world that was not built for them by navigating a playground that was. Dad saw me watching the kids and said, "You miss running around like that?"

"Sometimes, I guess." But that wasn't what I was thinking. I was just trying to notice everything: the light on the ruined Ruins, this little kid who could barely walk discovering a stick at the corner of the playground, my indefatigable mother zigzagging mustard across her turkey sandwich, my dad patting his handheld in his pocket and resisting the urge to check it, a guy throwing a Frisbee that his dog kept running under and catching and returning to him.

Who am I to say that these things might not be forever? Who is Peter Van Houten to assert as fact the conjecture that our labor is temporary? All I know of heaven and all I know of death is in this park: an elegant universe in ceaseless motion, teeming with ruined ruins and screaming children.

My dad was waving his hand in front of my face. "Tune in, Hazel. Are you there?"

"Sorry, yeah, what?"

"Mom suggested we go see Gus?"

"Oh. Yeah," I said.

So after lunch, we drove down to Crown Hill Cemetery, the last and final resting place of three vice presidents, one president, and Augustus Waters. We drove up the hill and parked. Cars roared by behind us on Thirty-eighth Street. It was easy to find his grave: It was the newest. The earth was still mounded above his coffin. No headstone yet.

I didn't feel like he was there or anything, but I still took one of Mom's dumb little French flags and stuck it in the ground at the foot of his grave. Maybe passersby would think he was a member of the French Foreign Legion or some heroic mercenary.

• • •

Lidewij finally wrote back just after six P.M. while I was on the couch watching both TV and videos on my laptop. I saw immediately there were four attachments to the email and I wanted to open them first, but I resisted temptation and read the email.

Dear Hazel,

> Peter was very intoxicated when we arrived at his house this morning, but this made our job somewhat easier. Bas (my boyfriend) distracted him while I searched through the garbage bag Peter keeps with the fan mail in it, but then I realized that Augustus knew Peter's address. There was a large pile of mail on his dining room table, where I found the letter very quickly. I opened it and saw that it was addressed to Peter, so I asked him to read it.
>
> He refused.
>
> At this point, I became very angry, Hazel, but I did not yell at him. Instead, I told him that he owed it to his dead daughter to read this letter from a dead boy, and I gave him the letter and he read the entire thing and said—I quote him directly—"Send it to the girl and tell her I have nothing to add."
>
> I have not read the letter, although my eyes did fall on some phrases while scanning the pages. I have attached them here and then will mail them to you at

your home; your address is the same?

May God bless and keep you, Hazel.

Your friend,
Lidewij Vliegenthart

I clicked open the four attachments. His handwriting was messy, slanting across the page, the size of the letters varying, the color of the pen changing. He'd written it over many days in varying degrees of consciousness.

Van Houten,

I'm a good person but a shitty writer. You're a shitty person but a good writer. We'd make a good team. I don't want to ask you any favors, but if you have time—and from what I saw, you have plenty—I was wondering if you could write a eulogy for Hazel. I've got notes and everything, but if you could just make it into a coherent whole or whatever? Or even just tell me what I should say differently.

Here's the thing about Hazel: Almost everyone is obsessed with leaving a mark upon the world. Bequeathing a legacy. Outlasting death. We all want to be remembered. I do, too. That's what bothers me most, is being another unremembered casualty in the ancient and inglorious war against disease.

I want to leave a mark.

But Van Houten: The marks humans leave are too often scars. You build a hideous minimall or start a coup or try to become a rock star and you think, "They'll remember me now," but (a) they don't remember you, and (b) all you leave behind are more scars. Your coup becomes a dictatorship. Your minimall becomes a lesion.

(Okay, maybe I'm not such a shitty writer. But I can't pull my ideas together, Van Houten. My thoughts are stars I can't fathom into constellations.)

We are like a bunch of dogs squirting on fire hydrants. We poison the groundwater with our toxic piss, marking everything MINE in a ridiculous attempt to survive our deaths. I can't stop pissing on fire hydrants. I know it's silly and useless—epically useless in my current state—but I am an animal like any other.

Hazel is different. She walks lightly, old man. She

walks lightly upon the earth. Hazel knows the truth: We're as likely to hurt the universe as we are to help it, and we're not likely to do either.

People will say it's sad that she leaves a lesser scar, that fewer remember her, that she was loved deeply but not widely. But it's not sad, Van Houten. It's triumphant. It's heroic. Isn't that the real heroism? Like the doctors say: First, do no harm.

The real heroes anyway aren't the people doing things; the real heroes are the people NOTICING things, paying attention. The guy who invented the smallpox vaccine didn't actually invent anything. He just noticed that people with cowpox didn't get smallpox.

After my PET scan lit up, I snuck into the ICU and saw her while she was unconscious. I just walked in behind a nurse with a badge and I got to sit next to her for like ten minutes before I got caught. I really thought she was going to die before I could tell her that I was going to die, too. It was brutal: the incessant mechanized haranguing of intensive care. She had this dark cancer water dripping out of her chest. Eyes closed. Intubated. But her hand was still her hand, still warm and the nails painted this almost black dark blue and I just held her hand and tried to imagine the world without us and for about one second I was a good enough person to hope she died so she would never know that I was going, too. But then I wanted more time so we could fall in love. I got my wish, I suppose. I left my scar.

A nurse guy came in and told me I had to leave, that visitors weren't allowed, and I asked if she was doing okay, and the guy said, "She's still taking on water." A desert blessing, an ocean curse.

What else? She is so beautiful. You don't get tired of looking at her. You never worry if she is smarter than you: You know she is. She is funny without ever being mean. I love her. I am so lucky to love her, Van Houten. You don't get to choose if you get hurt in this world, old man, but you do have some say in who hurts you. I like my choices. I hope she likes hers.

I do, Augustus.
I do.

ACKNOWLEDGMENTS

The author would like to acknowledge:

That disease and its treatment are treated fictitiously in this novel. For example, there is no such thing as Phalanxifor. I made it up, because I would like for it to exist. Anyone seeking an actual history of cancer ought to read *The Emperor of All Maladies* by Siddhartha Mukherjee. I am also indebted to *The Biology of Cancer* by Robert A. Weinberg, and to Josh Sundquist, Marshall Urist, and Jonneke Hollanders, who shared their time and expertise with me on medical matters, which I cheerfully ignored when it suited my whims.

Esther Earl, whose life was a gift to me and to many. I am grateful also to the Earl family—Lori, Wayne, Abby, Angie, Graham, and Abe—for their generosity and friendship. Inspired by Esther, the Earls have founded a nonprofit, This Star Won't Go Out, in her memory. You can learn more at tswgo.org.

The Dutch Literature Foundation, for giving me two months in Amsterdam to write. I'm particularly grateful to Fleur van Koppen, Jean Cristophe Boele van Hensbroek, Janetta de With, Carlijn van Ravenstein, Margje Scheepsma, and the Dutch nerdfighter community.

My editor and publisher, Julie Strauss-Gabel, who stuck with this story through many years of twists and turns, as did an extraordinary team at Penguin. Particular thanks to Rosanne Lauer, Deborah Kaplan, Liza Kaplan, Elyse Marshall, Steve Meltzer, Nova Ren Suma, and Irene Vandervoort.

Ilene Cooper, my mentor and fairy godmother.

My agent, Jodi Reamer, whose sage counsel has saved me from countless disasters.

Nerdfighters, for being awesome.

Catitude, for wanting nothing more than to make the world suck less.

My brother, Hank, who is my best friend and closest collaborator.

My wife, Sarah, who is not only the great love of my life but also my first and most trusted reader. Also, the baby, Henry, to whom she gave birth. Furthermore, my own parents, Mike and Sydney Green, and parents-in-law, Connie and Marshall Urist.

My friends Chris and Marina Waters, who helped with this story at vital moments, as did Joellen Hosler, Shannon James, Vi Hart, the Venn diagramatically brilliant Karen Kavett, Valerie Barr, Rosianna Halse Rojas, and John Darnielle.

Turn the page to read an excerpt from JOHN GREEN's #1 *New York Times* bestselling novel.

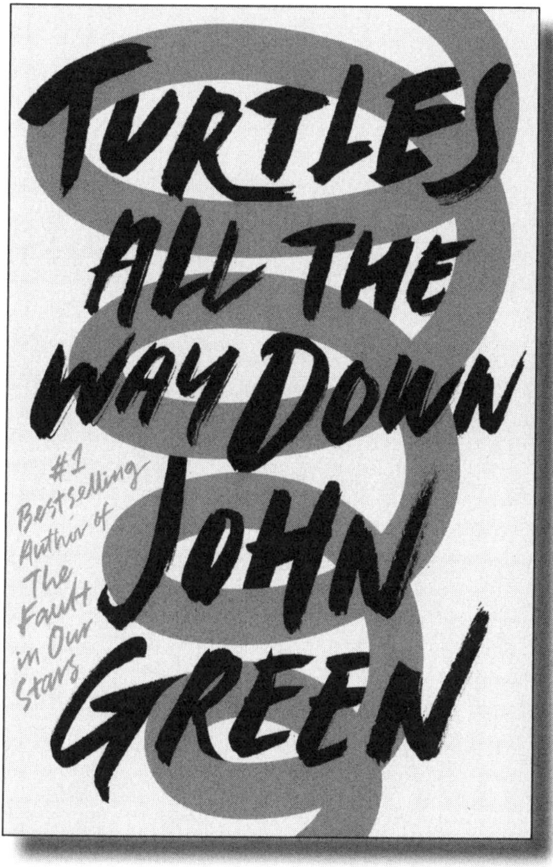

"So surprising and moving and true that I became completely unstrung . . . One needn't be suffering like Aza to identify with it. One need only be human."

—*The New York Times*

ONE

AT THE TIME I FIRST REALIZED I might be fictional, my weekdays were spent at a publicly funded institution on the north side of Indianapolis called White River High School, where I was required to eat lunch at a particular time—between 12:37 P.M. and 1:14 P.M.—by forces so much larger than myself that I couldn't even begin to identify them. If those forces had given me a different lunch period, or if the tablemates who helped author my fate had chosen a different topic of conversation that September day, I would've met a different end—or at least a different middle. But I was beginning to learn that your life is a story told about you, not one that you tell.

Of course, you pretend to be the author. You have to. You

think, *I now choose to go to lunch*, when that monotone beep rings from on high at 12:37. But really, the bell decides. You think you're the painter, but you're the canvas.

Hundreds of voices were shouting over one another in the cafeteria, so that the conversation became mere sound, the rushing of a river over rocks. And as I sat beneath fluorescent cylinders spewing aggressively artificial light, I thought about how we all believed ourselves to be the hero of some personal epic, when in fact we were basically identical organisms colonizing a vast and windowless room that smelled of Lysol and lard.

I was eating a peanut butter and honey sandwich and drinking a Dr Pepper. To be honest, I find the whole process of masticating plants and animals and then shoving them down my esophagus kind of disgusting, so I was trying not to think about the fact that I was eating, which is a form of thinking about it.

Across the table from me, Mychal Turner was scribbling in a yellow-paper notebook. Our lunch table was like a long-running play on Broadway: The cast changed over the years, but the roles never did. Mychal was The Artsy One. He was talking with Daisy Ramirez, who'd played the role of my Best and Most Fearless Friend since elementary school, but I couldn't follow their conversation over the noise of all the others.

What was my part in this play? The Sidekick. I was

Daisy's Friend, or Ms. Holmes's Daughter. I was somebody's something.

I felt my stomach begin to work on the sandwich, and even over everybody's talking, I could *hear* it digesting, all the bacteria chewing the slime of peanut butter—the students inside of me eating at my internal cafeteria. A shiver convulsed through me.

"Didn't you go to camp with him?" Daisy asked me.

"With who?"

"Davis Pickett," she said.

"Yeah," I said. "Why?"

"Aren't you listening?" Daisy asked. *I am listening*, I thought, *to the cacophony of my digestive tract*. Of course I'd long known that I was playing host to a massive collection of parasitic organisms, but I didn't much like being reminded of it. By cell count, humans are approximately 50 percent microbial, meaning that about half of the cells that make you up are not yours at all. There are something like a thousand times more microbes living in my particular biome than there are human beings on earth, and it often seems like I can *feel* them living and breeding and dying in and on me. I wiped my sweaty palms on my jeans and tried to control my breathing. Admittedly, I have some anxiety problems, but I would argue it isn't irrational to be concerned about the fact that you are a skin-encased bacterial colony.

Mychal said, "His dad was about to be arrested for bribery

or something, but the night before the raid he disappeared. There's a hundred-thousand-dollar reward out for him."

"And you know his kid," Daisy said.

"*Knew* him," I answered.

I watched Daisy attack her school-provided rectangular pizza and green beans with a fork. She kept glancing up at me, her eyes widening as if to say, *Well?* I could tell she wanted me to ask her about something, but I couldn't tell what, because my stomach wouldn't shut up, which was forcing me deep inside a worry that I'd somehow contracted a parasitic infection.

I could half hear Mychal telling Daisy about his new art project, in which he was using Photoshop to average the faces of a hundred people named Mychal, and the average of their faces would be this new, one-hundred-and-first Mychal, which was an interesting idea, and I wanted to listen, but the cafeteria was so loud, and I couldn't stop wondering whether there was something wrong with the microbial balance of power inside me.

Excessive abdominal noise is an uncommon, but not unprecedented, presenting symptom of infection with the bacteria *Clostridium difficile*, which can be fatal. I pulled out my phone and searched "human microbiome" to reread Wikipedia's introduction to the trillions of microorganisms currently inside me. I clicked over to the article about *C. diff*, scrolling to the part about how most *C. diff* infections occur in hospitals. I scrolled down farther to a list of symptoms, none of which I had, except for the excessive abdominal noises, although I knew from previous searches that the Cleveland Clinic had reported the case of one person who'd died of *C. diff* after presenting at the hospital with only abdominal pain and fever. I reminded myself that I didn't have a fever, and my self replied: *You don't have a fever YET.*

At the cafeteria, where a shrinking slice of my consciousness still resided, Daisy was telling Mychal that his averaging project shouldn't be about people named Mychal but about imprisoned men who'd later been exonerated. "It'll be easier, anyway," she said, "because they all have mug shots taken from the same angle, and then it's not just about names but about race and class and mass incarceration," and Mychal was like, "You're a genius, Daisy," and she said, "You sound surprised," and meanwhile I was thinking that if half the cells inside of you are not you, doesn't that challenge the whole notion of *me* as a singular pronoun, let alone as the author of my fate? And I fell pretty far down that recursive wormhole until it transported me completely out of the White River High School cafeteria into some non-sensorial place only properly crazy people get to visit.

Ever since I was little, I've pressed my right thumbnail into the finger pad of my middle finger, and so now there's this weird callus over my fingerprint. After so many years of doing this, I can open up a crack in the skin really easily, so I cover it up with a Band-Aid to try to prevent infection. But sometimes I get worried that there already is an infection, and so I need to drain it, and the only way to do that is to reopen the wound and press out any blood that will come. Once I start thinking about splitting the skin apart, I literally cannot not do it. I apologize for the double negative, but it's a real double negative of a situation, a bind from which negating the negation is truly the only escape. So anyway, I started to want to feel my thumbnail biting into the skin of my finger pad, and I knew that resistance was more or less futile, so beneath the cafeteria table, I slipped the Band-Aid off my finger and dug my thumbnail into the callused skin until I felt the crack open.

"Holmesy," Daisy said. I looked up at her. "We're almost through lunch and you haven't even mentioned my hair." She shook out her hair, with so-red-they-were-pink highlights. Right. She'd dyed her hair.

I swum up out of the depths and said, "It's bold."

"I know, right? It says, 'Ladies and gentlemen and also people who do not identify as ladies or gentlemen, Daisy Ramirez won't break her promises, but she will break your heart.'" Daisy's self-proclaimed life motto was "Break Hearts, Not Promises." She kept threatening to get it tattooed on her ankle when she turned eighteen. Daisy turned back to Mychal, and I to my thoughts. The stomach grumbling had grown, if anything, louder. I felt like I might vomit. For someone who actively dislikes bodily fluids, I throw up quite a lot.

"Holmesy, you okay?" Daisy asked. I nodded. Sometimes I wondered why she liked me, or at least tolerated me. Why any of them did. Even I found myself annoying.

I could feel sweat sprouting from my forehead, and once I begin to sweat, it's impossible to stop. I'll keep sweating for hours, and not just my face or my armpits. My neck sweats. My boobs sweat. My calves sweat. Maybe I did have a fever.

Beneath the table, I slid the old Band-Aid into my pocket and, without looking, pulled out a new one, unwrapped it, and then glanced down to apply it to my finger. All the while, I was breathing in through my nose and out through my mouth, in the manner advised by Dr. Karen Singh, exhaling at a pace "that would make a candle flicker but not go out. Imagine that candle, Aza, flickering from your breath but still there, always there." So I tried that, but the thought spiral kept tightening anyway. I could hear Dr. Singh saying I shouldn't get out my phone, that I mustn't look up the same questions over and over, but I got it out anyway, and reread the "Human Microbiota" Wikipedia article.

The thing about a spiral is, if you follow it inward, it never actually ends. It just keeps tightening, infinitely.

I sealed the Ziploc bag around the last quarter of my sandwich, got up, and tossed it into an overfilled trash can. I heard a voice from behind me. "How concerned should I be that you haven't said more than two words in a row all day?"

"Thought spiral," I mumbled in reply. Daisy had known me since we were six, long enough to get it.

"I figured. Sorry, man. Let's hang out today."

This girl Molly walked up to us, smiling, and said, "Uh, Daisy, just FYI, your Kool-Aid dye job is staining your shirt."

Daisy looked down at her shoulders, and indeed, her striped top had turned pink in spots. She flinched for a second, then straightened her spine. "Yeah, it's part of the look, Molly. Stained shirts are huge in Paris right now." She turned away from Molly and said, "Right, so we'll go to your house and watch *Star Wars: Rebels*." Daisy was really into Star Wars—and not just the movies, but also the books and the animated shows and the kids' show where they're all made out of Lego. Like, she wrote fan fiction about Chewbacca's love life. "And we will improve your mood until you are able to say three or even four words in a row; sound good?"

"Sounds good."

"And then you can take me to work. Sorry, but I need a ride."

"Okay." I wanted to say more, but the thoughts kept coming, unbidden and unwanted. If I'd been the author, I would've stopped thinking about my microbiome. I would've told Daisy how much I liked her idea for Mychal's art project, and I would've told her that I did remember Davis Pickett, that I remembered being eleven and carrying a vague but constant fear. I would've told her that I remembered once at camp lying next to Davis on the edge of a dock, our legs dangling over, our backs against the rough-hewn planks of wood, staring together up at a cloudless summer sky. I would've told her that Davis and I never talked much, or even looked at each other, but it didn't matter, because we were looking at the same sky together, which is maybe more intimate than eye contact anyway. Anybody can look at you. It's quite rare to find someone who sees the same world you see.

Paper Towns

PB: 978-0-14-241493-4

HC: 978-0-525-47818-8

QUENTIN JACOBSEN has spent a lifetime loving the magnificently adventurous Margo Roth Spiegelman from afar. So when she cracks open a window and climbs back into his life—dressed like a ninja and summoning him for an ingenious campaign of revenge—he follows. After their all-nighter ends, and a new day breaks, Q arrives at school to discover that Margo, always an enigma, has now become a mystery for him to solve. Urged down a disconnected path, the closer he gets, the less Q sees the girl he thought he knew.

A *New York Times* Bestseller

Winner of the Edgar Award for Best Young Adult Mystery

★ "Green is not only clever and wonderfully witty but also deeply thoughtful and insightful. In addition, he's a superb stylist, with a voice perfectly matched to his amusing, illuminating material."

—***Booklist*, starred review**

★ "Profoundly moving." —***SLJ*, starred review**